Of Slippers and Secrets

A.B. Twichell

DEDICATION

To my mother, Andrea Miller, who encouraged my writing from the first

ACKNOWLEDGMENTS

This book would not have been possible without the love and support of my family, and especially without the numerous individual contributions that were made. Therefore, I would like to thank them accordingly. First, I would like to thank my husband, Jason Twichell, for listening to each chapter as it was written. Your patience and feedback is, as always, immensely appreciated. Second, I would like to thank my aunt, Penny Jordan, for being the first to officially read this book and enthusiastically demand the next one. Third, I would like to thank the brave friends and family members who test-read the book—Andrea Miller, Hannah Peterson, Caroline Miller, Mary Anne Miller, Megan Jordan, and Stephanie Kristl. Your enthusiasm and demand for the book encouraged me to finally publish it. Finally, I would like to thank my uncle, Jonathan Miller, for answering my questions about self-publishing and guiding me through the process. Without you all, this book would still be but a dream in my head.

Chapter One

The Invitation

THERE was something strange on the wind that day; the day that Ellie Kate Marchand found the invitation to the ball. As she walked home from the market, her basket weighing heavily on her arm, she could sense an odd change in the winds. They were blowing in several different directions all at once, seeming to signal the shifting of an allegiance. She couldn't say why exactly, but she felt that it was tugging at her skin, pulling her hair loose from her cap. A foul smell drifted off the river, like the stench of old, dead fish. The winds still scurried this way and that, tangling her hair and rattling her nerves. But Ellie took a deep breath, opened the iron gates, and then lifted the lid on their post box, pulling out the envelopes that were within.

She flipped through them with a careless, casual manner until she saw a thick stiff envelope with gold embossing on the front: *Lady Frances Hardwick Marchand, and all the ladies of the household.* Ellie knew that this wasn't an ordinary invitation. Her stepmother, Frances, had received plenty of those throughout the years, but they were never as nice as this. The paper was silky and smooth, and the lettering had been done in a neat and practiced hand. The insignia on the top gave it away—this was a royal invitation.

Ellie tried not to rip the paper as she pulled out the card within. In shining gold letters, she read as her mind flooded with excitement.

Ladies of Maplecroft Manor,
You are cordially invited to a formal Ball
Held in honor of His Royal Highness,
Prince Fillip Westenra of Trenway
Eight 'o' clock until dawn
The night of the seventh of June
at
The Palace of Penchester
Please present your invitation at the gates

Ellie read it through several times again as the impossible began to register in her mind. A ball. A royal ball held in honor of Prince Fillip. All the ladies of the household were invited. Ellie frowned as she thought of this line. Her stepmother would never interpret that to include her. *You're not a lady anymore, are you,* she could hear the sneering reply even now. And so she decided to do something terrible. Something dangerous and risky.

Shoving the invitation deep in her dress pocket, she decided to keep it a secret from her stepmother. She would attend the ball herself, as the only lady of Maplecroft Manor.

As she walked through the iron gates and down the long and cobbled driveway to her house, the secret invitation seemed to burn through her pockets, and Ellie hoped that the flush in her cheeks wouldn't give her secret away. She couldn't wait to run inside the kitchen, pull Mrs. Tuttle to the side, and tell her all about the ball and her plan. Mrs. Tuttle would find a way to help her. She always had, ever since her father's death. Like a mother goose, she had taken Ellie in under her wing, and tried to be like a grandmother to her.

Naturally, Mrs. Tuttle was appalled that a lady of the house, such as Ellie, had been forced to wash the windows and scrub the floors. But in the days following Cornelius Marchand's death, his widow's power became absolute, and was only solidified during the reading of the will. Because Ellie was only thirteen years old at the time, she was not permitted to have any control over her own assets. She had been left a considerable sum, but it was to be under the governance of her stepmother, who had promptly spent it all within a fortnight, outfitting her own daughters in new gowns and bedecking herself in jewels.

In that one horrible moment of realization, the truth had come crashing down upon Ellie. Frances had spent her entire inheritance. There had been no legal recourse—as appointed guardian, it had been up to Frances' discretion to use the funds as she saw fit. And she saw fit to reduce Ellie's state to that of a pauper. Furthermore, she saw fit to make Ellie a servant of the house. Any thoughts of an independent future Ellie might have had went rushing down the drain, emptied out with the dirty water into the River Morrow.

Ellie shook those thoughts from her head. She didn't want to dwell on the unpleasantness of it. She had accepted the hard truth a long time ago. Her only solace came from the simple joys of life: the first bite of a crisp apple in the autumn, the smell of baking in the afternoon, and the warm sunshine after a long, cold winter. This was how the common people lived, and Ellie had not been born to snobbery. For now, her greatest joy was in contemplating an enchanted evening; a night off and a chance to wear a fancy dress and dance till dawn.

She crept into the kitchen and laid her basket on the wooden counter. Sneaking around, she finally found Mrs. Tuttle in the drawing room, dusting the draperies. Standing on a tall ladder, she had been quite frightened by Ellie's sudden appearance and exclaimed aloud, inhaling a great bit of dust and then sneezing.

"Ellie Kate!" she admonished. "I wish you wouldn't sneak up on people like that!"

"Come quickly! I want to show you something."

Ellie led Mrs. Tuttle back into the kitchen, and then grabbed her arm, pulling her into the pantry and closing the door.

"What are we doing in here?" Mrs. Tuttle asked shrilly. "It's hot and cramped."

"*This* came in the post today!" Ellie whispered excitedly, handing Mrs. Tuttle the invitation.

"Oh, Ellie, you know good and well that I can't read," she snapped.

"Yes, you can! Have my lessons been for nothing, then?"

"No, but these words are far too big for what you've taught me!"

"It doesn't matter about the words," Ellie insisted. "You know the letters, and once you've learnt that, you can sound any word out."

Mrs. Tuttle frowned, but then furrowed her eyebrows and squinted at the envelope, slowly sounding out the words. When she had finished, she looked up at Ellie with an unmistakable gleam in her eyes.

"Has the mistress seen this yet?"

"No, of course not! And hush, I don't want her finding out about it."

"Oh, Ellie, that's risky," Mrs. Tuttle pointed out. "There's bound to be word about this around town, and once she hears of it…"

"She might hear of it, but without the invitation, what can she do?" Ellie asked. "She doesn't have to know that the ladies of Maplecroft Manor were issued an invitation. She'll think she and her precious daughters were excluded."

Mrs. Tuttle frowned. "But what are you going to do? You can't burn it; it says right here you'll need it to get in. And if she finds this…"

"She won't find it," Ellie reassured her. "Trust me. Now, let's move on to the more important questions like: what shall I wear?"

Despite her misgivings, Mrs. Tuttle couldn't help but smile broadly and clutch Ellie's hands in excitement.

"Oh, Ellie, this will be *wonderful* for you, I just know it! And if I'm not mistaken, I think I remember where I stored some of your mother's old dresses. I'm sure we can find something of hers that will fit the bill."

She eyed Ellie's frame and pinched the skin around her waist.

"Of course, you're a bit thinner than your mother was at your age," she remarked. "But then again, your mother wasn't forced to eat servants' rations in a house of dwindling means."

Ellie laughed. "I'm sure we can take it in a bit," she said.

Mrs. Tuttle smiled at her again, a small tear forming at the edge of her eye.

"I'm sure we can," she agreed. "Now, you go and hide that letter so that even the hungriest rat wouldn't find it!"

"Why, Mrs. Tuttle, that's the best description of Frances you've come up with yet!"

The old housekeeper laughed and then shooed Ellie away with another admonishing tut. Mrs. Tuttle had been taught to never speak ill of her employers, but Ellie knew that Frances Hardwick had pushed the infinitely patient housekeeper to her wit's end, and that several years ago, the floodgates had opened and Mrs. Tuttle had spilled all her nastiest thoughts and observations to an astounded and amused Ellie over a bottle of nicked wine.

That night had ended with Mrs. Tuttle brushing Ellie's hair and telling her stories about her mother, the one she had never known. When Leonora Marchand had died, her father had been so disconsolate in his grief that he couldn't bear anyone to mention his wife at all. Therefore, Ellie had grown up in a complete vacuum of the woman who had been her mother, and had been forced to think of her merely as some benevolent ghost. Growing up without a mother had been hard, but not nearly as hard as gaining one in pre-adolescence after having gone so long without.

The transition had been made less smooth by her father's frequent absence and her new stepmother's mercurial and unpleasant disposition. Frances Hardwick, the widow of a baronet, was insistent upon high standards of cleanliness and absolute obedience. Precociousness, which might as well have been Ellie's middle name, was viewed as a sin of the worst kind. *Cheek,* as her stepmother called it, was not going to be tolerated under any circumstance.

Under her stepmother's harsh, draconian rule, Ellie's conception of a mother figure became blackened and tarred. Therefore, she was grateful when Mrs. Tuttle told her about her real mother, Leonora Marchand. She had been a gentle and kind woman, who had loved Ellie with all her heart, and who had also possessed a streak of precociousness, one for which she was unapologetic. After learning that her own mother had loved to read, Ellie became a devoted reader, spending as much free time as she could ensconced in the library, devouring tome after tome. She endeavored to learn as much as she could, to be as much like her educated mother as possible.

"You're already her spitting image," Mrs. Tuttle would always say. "It's like Mr. Marchand had very little to do with it. You've got her golden hair, that fair complexion, and those striking eyes, like violets."

In a matter of months, Ellie had gone from thinking of her mother as nothing more than a name on a headstone to thinking of her like an icon, like a guiding figure that was always with her and that she strived to emulate in all ways.

Ellie ran up the stairs and climbed the ladder to her cramped bedroom in the attic, thinking of her mother as she popped up a loose floorboard, and placed the envelope there, under a box of memorabilia she had salvaged from her old bedroom downstairs. Putting the floorboard back in place, she pulled a rug over it and smoothed down her dress and apron. Now for the real test of the evening: keeping calm and not giving anything away in front of her imperious stepmother.

She would be home any minute, along with her horrible daughters, and Ellie would be expected to serve them dinner. She had to keep her face neutral even *if* the subject of the ball came up. But a life of secrecy and a forced habit of constraining her emotions had prepared her for this. If she could thank her stepmother for anything, it would be for teaching her the arts of deception and concealment.

Chapter Two

Loathsome Lentils

DINNER was prepared and Frances was home with her daughters, but they had not yet come down into the dining room. As a general rule, Ellie and Mrs. Tuttle had to wait and keep the food warm until they were ready, and there was never any telling when that would be. Dinner was usually served at seven, but occasionally Frances would be struck with a mood and her fit might last anywhere from half an hour to two hours. One time, dinner had been served as late as ten 'o' clock. By the time Ellie had crawled into bed, it had been nearly three in the morning, only a few hours shy of the time she was expected to wake up.

As they waited in the kitchen, Ellie could only hope that Frances' mood would end soon, and that she hadn't heard any talk about the royal ball. The minutes ticked by on the clock and Ellie began to think of things she'd rather not, those unpleasant facts she didn't like to dwell on. But the prospect of the ball, and her rightful standing as a lady of Maplecroft Manor had put them back in her head.

Ellie had been born to a wealthy merchant and his wife who had lived in the fashionable end of Hartmere, the capitol city of the country, only twelve miles from the palace. Cornelius Marchand had done well for himself in his youth, rising up from the gutters to working as a clerk in the merchant guild.

11

Eventually, with his opportunistic streak and connections from all classes in various parts of the city, he had bought a ship and gone into business for himself. He had married a woman only a few years younger than him, a famed beauty with a sizeable dowry, named Leonora Penwhistle.

Cornelius and Leonora were soon the 'it' couple of the day. With their youth, money, and joy for life, they soon became famous for their lavish parties and sincere generosity. Ellie would smile when Mrs. Tuttle would tell her stories of those days, and her face would light up thinking of all the music and happiness that must have filled the house. It was so different from what she had grown up with, and so different from what Frances had turned the house into.

Ellie had been born in April, in the tepid spring air that quickly gave way to a warm summer. Cornelius and Leonora had moved from wedded bliss to baby bliss. But Leonora fell ill suddenly, dying just after Ellie's third birthday to Cornelius Marchand's everlasting sorrow, and to the detriment of her only living daughter.

Cornelius had loved Leonora dearly, but he knew that his daughter would need a mother figure. He tried to fill both roles, and as a result, Ellie became very attached to him. And while Cornelius might have continued in this vein, it soon became clear that Ellie would need a woman's guidance.

"Ten years old and without a mother still!" he admonished himself. "What have I been doing all these years?"

Understandably, he felt guilty for not instantly remarrying and providing Ellie with a maternal figure. No one else in Ellie's

12

peer group had grown up in the way she had, with only a father. Of course, some of her friends' mothers had died, but their fathers had promptly remarried, refilling the coffers with another dowry and setting up a woman in charge of the household.

In Leonora's absence, and the absence of any commanding feminine presence, the household at Maplecroft Manor had deteriorated considerably. The furniture was old and creaky, the drapes were at least ten seasons out of fashion, there were never any fresh flowers in the house, and the windows were always in need of a good scrubbing. The rugs were filthy with dust, and the walls and ceilings were rarely scrubbed so that they were blackened with soot from the candles.

This had all come to a major head when Ellie was eleven, and Cornelius suddenly seemed to wake up from the decade-long stupor he had been in. The very next year, when Ellie was twelve, Cornelius had gone off one day and come back with a bride, much to everyone's surprise. Without any warning or correspondence at all, he had marched back from business abroad and opened the carriage door, holding his hand out for a very tall lady, dripping in furs and jewels.

Her name was Frances Hardwick, and she was a wealthy widowed baronetess with two children of her own, eleven and thirteen. She was to be Ellie's new stepmother, and as she fixed her with a slightly sinister look and a smirk pulling at the corners of her lips, Ellie felt a cold pit settle in her stomach. First impressions stick strongly and tend to determine the tenor of the relationship from the beginning. Ellie's first impression of

Frances was that she was some kind of predator, like a lynx, and she didn't trust her.

Her daughters, Anna and Emma, were not much better. They were like small, slightly diluted versions of their mother, but on the whole they were very catty and judgmental. They criticized Ellie's dresses, saying that they were all plain and ugly. Most of their insults were not things that Ellie would have taken offense at, but she knew that they meant unkindly by it.

They had a peculiar behavior that Ellie came to regard as very vapid and childish. Whenever they said something mean, they would cover their mouths and giggle into their hands, exchanging glances with their beady black eyes. Ellie quickly learned to ignore most of what they said, but every time she heard that sharp intake of breath, and the little tinkling of half-covered laughter, she knew that they had just said something horrible.

Almost from the moment Frances Hardwick had set foot on the threshold, she made it her singular mission in life to transform Maplecroft Manor into a house worthy of Cornelius Marchand's good name again. Cleanliness became her myopic obsession and if Ellie had thought she might embark on this mission alone, she was sorely mistaken. Anna and Emma were expected to help as well, but Ellie soon discovered that they found ways of getting out of it, and Frances would turn a blind eye to any laziness on their parts. Ellie, on the other hand, received no such lenience. And her father, for all his care and concern, could not see the favoritism at play. He thought it was good that Frances was putting her to work.

"Pay attention to the baronetess and learn from her," he had advised. "You'll be expected to run a household one day and sometimes it means you have to do things yourself. Even the baronetess isn't too proud to scrub a window!"

No, the baronetess wasn't too proud to scrub a window, but she would also rather Ellie do it. And as time wore on, she gradually started shifting all the work to Ellie whilst she merely 'supervised' over her shoulder. Day in and day out, it was constant nagging, endless criticism, and the unrelenting expectation of perfection. Frances would roll up her sleeves and dust the room in the early morning, before Cornelius left for the day, and as soon as he was gone, she would pull down her sleeves and her gray eyes would harden and fix Ellie with a mean stare that meant, *get to work.*

This grueling and terribly unfair domestic situation continued for around six months and then something completely unexpected happened. Cornelius Marchand died. It was as if someone had snuffed a candle. Relatively young and in good health, it was downright strange when he up and dropped dead one day.

In the weeks and months following her father's untimely death, Ellie struggled with conflicting feelings about it. On the one hand, she was angry that her father had abandoned her, seemingly on purpose. Or at least, he hadn't fought hard enough against it. She condemned him for being weak and not protecting her from the increasingly malignant influences of her stepmother.

On the other hand, Ellie had lost the only parent she'd ever known. And the bond between father and daughter had been unbreakable and stronger than most. Cornelius had been her guiding light: whatever was she to do without him? She knew that with her precociousness, she had been a difficult child, but her father had forgiven her everything, and she knew that she could always go to him to calm the raging tempest within.

This sort of unconditional love was not something that Frances was willing to offer. Not in the slightest. Almost as soon as Cornelius had died, she began to make new and permanent changes in the household. They had just come back from the funeral when she had pulled her black riding gloves off, pulling the tips of the fingers one by one.

"Girls, your attention please," she had prefaced. "Your father's tragic, *tragic* death necessitates some changes around here. No longer can we afford to languish in luxury. What with my pathetic pittance from the late baronet, and your father's lawyers doling my money out in drips and drabs, we will have to make some cutbacks to the hired help. They are a drain on our resources. We will have to do everything ourselves and be self-sufficient. And I don't want to hear any whining about it, is that understood?"

Of course, all three girls had solemnly nodded their heads and promised to do as she said. For Ellie, there wasn't another choice. Despite her mistrust of Frances, she had nowhere else to go. Her father had only married Frances six months ago, but he had entrusted Ellie's care to his wife in his newly made will. She was stuck; made a prisoner in her own home.

If Ellie had thought that she would be allowed a period of mourning for her dead father before these 'changes' took place,

16

she was to be again, sorely mistaken. Frances was not upset by the death of her husband at all. Why should she be? She had barely known the man, and Anna and Emma were hardly grieving either. So with the majority of the house in full spirits, they expected Ellie to simply do the same. They all demonstrated an obtuseness to her grief; one that Ellie felt was contrived and intentional. They constantly made fun of her for crying, berated her for sobbing, and Frances even went so far as to screech at her for *looking* sad.

"Stop that with your face!" she would snap. "Quit looking so *morose*. It's unbecoming, and worse…it's annoying."

With no support and no outlet for her emotions, Ellie soon learned to swallow them. She could cry quietly in the night, muffling the noises with her pillow. But if she didn't want to get chastised in the morning for having red eyes, then she would have to learn to do without that as well. She became an expert in the art of concealing her emotions, and biting her tongue.

For five long years, Ellie was forced to live under the thumb of her stepmother. With each year that passed, she was reduced: brought lower and lower, bit-by-bit, until she was no better than a maid. It had happened so slowly and so gradually, that Ellie hadn't paid much attention to it until she sat on a bare floor in the attic with the birds fluttering in the rafters above her. *Then* it had struck her like a blunt axe. Frances had wrought so many changes in the wake of her father's death that Maplecroft began to seem foreign and strange to her.

Fourteen, and relegated to a bare room in the attic, which was always dreadfully cold in the winter and swelteringly hot in

17

the summer, Ellie began to come to terms with her fate. The household staff had been reduced to just three: Ellie, Mrs. Tuttle, and her husband, Mr. Tuttle. The three of them were expected to serve the other three, Frances and her daughters. Ellie had one mattress, a few tattered books, and two linen shifts. All the rest of her belongings, her room and all its furniture, her dresses, books, instruments, and decorations had all been divided up between Anna and Emma.

By the autumn of Ellie's fifteenth year, Frances had decided that her own daughters were the hope of the household. After all, they were much better looking, according to her, and they had been brought up in a baronet's castle. Their formative upbringing had been much more proper than Ellie's provincial, merchant-class rearing. Therefore, Frances would put all of her efforts into finding them rich husbands while Ellie cleaned the house.

At seventeen, Ellie realized that she was probably everything her parents hoped she'd never be: dirty, common, and poor. These negative and self-destructive thoughts had never been far away, they'd always been dancing on the perimeter, skirting the border and occasionally slipping through. But for the first time, Ellie seemed to really comprehend that it had been five years of degradation. Five years of humiliation, disrespect, and manipulation. She had been browbeaten and controlled into the lowest caste of society, falling from one of its top echelons. Tears threatened to cloud her vision as she stood on the threshold of the dining room, looking around at the house of her birth, the house that should have been hers to run as its mistress.

Ellie sniffled and then wiped her nose on her sleeve, pushing the tears back down her throat and shaking her head, pinching her cheeks. No, she would not succumb to this. It was beneath her.

"Look lively!" Mrs. Tuttle whispered, going past her. "They're coming down for dinner now."

Frances Hardwick strode forcefully into the dining room, her chin tilted high, and her eyes cold and gray as always. Behind her, like puppets or dolls, came Ellie's stepsisters, Anna and Emma, each dressed in a garish shade of orange. Apparently it was the new fashionable color and Frances had insisted that her daughters have everything that was currently fashionable.

Unfortunately, both daughters shared their mother's olive complexion and the orange, no matter the shade, made them both look sallow and sickly.

"Lentils," Frances seethed, glaring at her bowl. *"Again. What is the meaning of this? You know I hate lentils."*

Before Ellie or Mrs. Tuttle could explain about the shortage in the larder, Frances had stood up, taken her bowl, and thrown the lentils into the sooty fireplace.

"Bring me something else," she commanded. "Potatoes, if you must. They're plain and dull, but anything is better than *lentils,"* she said shuddering for effect.

"I'll get you some potatoes, madam," Mrs. Tuttle said. "That was my oversight."

"Indeed, it was."

Ellie walked over to Mrs. Tuttle and touched her gently on the shoulder. "Never you mind, I'll get it," she offered in a hushed voice.

"No, Ellie, I want you to stay right here," Frances commanded. "Mrs. Tuttle will see to our needs tonight."

"Begging pardon, madam," Ellie said. "But it'll be easier if we can take turns doing the fetching and bringing out the courses, as we always do."

There was a long pause and Ellie instantly became nervous. It was never good when her stepmother paused like this. There was a sharp whistling noise that sounded like Frances was sucking air between the gaps of her front teeth. Only when Mrs. Tuttle had gone to fetch the potatoes did Frances speak.

"Ellie, come over to the rug," she said. "Stand behind that chair, so I can see you."

She did as she was told, placing her hands behind her back and forcing herself to look at the odious visage of her stepmother. Everything about the woman seemed repellent; her cold, marble face and those lifeless gray eyes. She did not seem real, this statue of a woman. She did not seem to be possessed of those usual qualities of humanity: love, forgiveness, patience, and compassion.

"It is not your place to correct me, Eleanor Katherine," she said imperiously. "When I say something, there is to be unquestioned obedience, every single time. Understood?"

Ellie bowed her head. "Yes, madam, of course."

"You know that I do not permit back talk in this house," she continued, eyeing her sharply. "You have a dreadful penchant for it, but I suppose that was your late mother's inheritance. Still, such things cannot be abided. I am the authority in this house, are we clear?"

"Yes, madam."

"Good. Now, go and pick out every single lentil from that fireplace."

Mrs. Tuttle returned with some berries for Frances to pick at while her potatoes cooked, and Ellie watched as her stepmother and stepsisters buttered their bread with fastidious, bird-like movements. Frances, whose waistline was permanently fixed at bulging, had altered her diet to no avail, but determined that her daughters would never run to fat.

The conversation eventually picked up amongst the three of them, as the daughters shared gossip with their mother. There wasn't much that Frances didn't already know, but she usually indulged them with a pronouncement or two about her opinion on the subject.

Ellie crouched uncomfortably on the rug, painstakingly picking out the lentils, listening as they ate while her stomach churned with hunger, and giving Mrs. Tuttle sympathetic looks as she marched in and out of the kitchen with platter after platter. Ellie knew that the older woman struggled with pain in her bones and joints. Frances knew it too. It was cruel of her to make Mrs. Tuttle serve them alone while she set Ellie to an impossible task. And what was the point? Did it matter if the lentils stayed in the fireplace? But those were usually the kinds of games that Frances liked to play with Ellie, and those she deemed beneath her.

For much of the dinner, Ellie let her mind wander until Anna said something that made her wake up and pay attention.

"Mama, I think the prince is looking for a wife...here in Hartmere."

"What makes you say that?" Frances demanded. "Tosh! What nonsense! A wife from Hartmere? The royals will want to make a foreign match, to win allies."

"Perhaps not," Anna replied, smirking. "The King and Queen are hosting a ball next week in the prince's honor."

"What of it? They always host balls in his honor."

"Yes, but not balls in which all the *ladies* of Hartmere are invited to," Emma countered. "Young men are excluded from the invitations. It says ladies only. And to what purpose could that be, except matchmaking?"

"What invitations?" Frances barked. "What are you talking about?"

Anna and Emma looked coy. "We only saw the invitation yesterday at Drusilla's house."

"Drusilla?" Frances snorted. "That sow? Well, *she* won't be asked back if it's a royal bride they're after. When did the Baltham's get their invitation?"

The girls shrugged. "She only said it came in the post. It couldn't have been long ago. She wouldn't have waited long to gloat over something like that."

"Well, where is *our* invitation?" she shouted. "Ellie! Did a royal invitation come for us in the post?"

"N-not that I'm aware of, madam," Ellie answered, shaken by her stepmother's sudden turn to anger.

22

"Not that you're aware of," she repeated in a mocking voice. "Are you an imbecile? There was either a royal invitation in our box or there wasn't. Even *you* would be able to recognize the royal crest."

"I didn't see any invitations in our box," Ellie clarified. "There hasn't been an invitation in the last few weeks."

Frances studied her for several long, uncomfortable minutes. Ellie tried to keep her gaze clear and calm. Averting her eyes would have been a sign of guilt.

"You're lying," she pronounced. "Here you stand in my house, clothed and fed by my generosity, and you lie to my face. How's that for gratitude?"

Ellie seethed and burned in rage. She had to keep it concealed and masked, however, no matter how righteous she was. But it was so hard to keep from screaming in response, to keep from losing her calm and shouting at the woman who had usurped her place and stolen her rightful money, then forced her to be a servant. No, gratitude did not come *close* to what Ellie felt for Frances Hardwick.

"Where is the invitation, Ellie?" Frances asked in a low, even tone.

Ellie stiffened her spine and stared right back at her.

"There is no invitation, madam," she said, as respectfully as she could.

For another moment of pause, Frances sat still in her chair, a strange serene smile on her face that smacked of insincerity. And then, in a flash, she had stood up, strode across the room and taken Ellie's chin hard, in a forceful grip.

"You think you can fool me," she said. "You think you can get away with your little covert operation? Do you even know what that means? Covert? It means secretive and stealthy. But you're neither of those things, my dear. You are as transparent as the window glass should be, if you had cleaned it properly. Now, *produce* that invitation, or you will pay for it with your flesh."

Once, many years ago, Ellie might have been bullied by such tactics. She might have felt uncontrollable anger and fear well up in the pit of her belly. It might have spilled over in the form of tears and inchoate pain. But years and years of the same, predictable behavior had hardened Ellie to the rough patterns of her stepmother. And she was no longer cowed or intimidated by the woman's malicious misuse of authority.

"How can I produce it when I don't have it?" she asked, gritting her teeth.

The rage built up within Frances, but unlike Ellie, she did not have the proper discipline to withhold it. She knew that Ellie was lying, could probably see it in her eyes. But she had never learned to control herself. She released Ellie's chin, but her hand went flying backward and then swung down, missing its target by inches. Ellie, anticipating the blow, had stepped back and watched as the momentum sent her stepmother stumbling in the other direction.

Even further enraged, Frances lunged forward, grabbing at Ellie, but the latter moved quickly, like lightning as she ran up the stairs. Ellie ran until she reached the ladder to her attic, and she climbed it with a rapid pace. Pulling the ladder up behind her, she knew that this was only a stalling tactic. It would only buy her some time, and more intense punishment.

She paced around the room, her veins flooding with excitement and also dread. Her stepmother's threat had not been idle. She would pay for it with her flesh. But even as the thought of torture disturbed her, the thought of her stepsisters attending the ball in their garish orange dresses while she was forced to stay behind tormented her further. It was a matter of pride and principle at this point. Ellie was the true mistress of Maplecroft Manor, and the only real lady of the house. The others were masked pretenders.

It wasn't long before she heard banging and shouting below. Frances was screaming at her daughters for the prong that would open the attic ladder. Ellie steeled herself for what was to come. She couldn't physically strike back at her stepmother, no matter how much she wanted to. But she promised herself that she wouldn't surrender and tell them where the invitation was.

With a sudden whoosh, the ladder went down, and Frances soon came up, the fury in her eyes terrifying to behold. She immediately charged Ellie to the corner and slapped her across the face, this time making sure that her blow found its target. Anna and Emma came up next, and while Frances pinned Ellie to the wall, she ordered them to search the room.

"Look everywhere," she commanded. "Tear apart the whole room if you have to."

There was a frightful noise as they ransacked her room, but Anna and Emma had come up with nothing. Frances tightened her grip around Ellie's throat.

"Tell us where it is," she growled.

Ellie shrugged, rolling her eyes coyly. Frances squeezed again and Ellie wheezed trying to catch her breath.

"You will be punished for this," Frances warned her. "It is insolence of the highest order. You do know what insolence means, right? Disobedience."

"I know what it means," Ellie croaked. "I am not an illiterate fool. Do you know what illiterate means? It means unable to read."

She should have resisted the urge. It earned her another slap across the face. But in a given day, there was only so much goading she could take. And her intelligence had always been a point of pride.

"You must be some kind of fool," Frances countered. "To play these games with me. What possible outcome could you hope for? How do you imagine this playing out?"

She did manage to resist that trap. She kept her mouth closed as she peeked over Frances' shoulder, wondering where Anna and Emma were looking. Emma was walking on the rug stepping right on the loose floorboard. Frances must have caught the glimmer of fear in her eye and then turned over her shoulder, shouting at her daughters.

"Look under the rug!" she said. "Yes, pull it up."

"There's nothing here, Mama," Anna whined.

"Check under the floorboards! She's hiding it there! Her face gave it away!"

After some inexpert fumbling, Emma managed to find the corner of the loose floorboard and pull it up. Ellie's face fell as she slumped her shoulders in defeat. Frances' grin grew wider, like a wolf about to devour its prey.

"There's nothing here, Mama," Anna called out. "Nothing but some old box full of jewels and such. No invitation."

Immediately, Frances looked alarmed, letting go of Ellie.

"Are you sure?" she barked, striding over and looking for herself. She dumped the box of memorabilia out on the floor, picking through each piece. And then she practically squeezed herself in the hole on the floor, reaching and groping in the tight space, her fingers grasping at the dusty wood. But she came up empty, and Ellie couldn't help herself.

She started laughing. It was a hoarse, raspy kind of laugh, given that her throat was still sore from Frances' abuse. But she cried tears of laughter at the perplexed and utterly distraught expressions on her stepfamily's faces. They had been duped, and she had been the one to dupe them, moving the invitation hours earlier to an even more secretive spot that they would never think to look.

"And you all think *I'm* the fool?" she sputtered, laughing harder.

"This only proves your guilt," Frances shouted. "For the last time, tell me where that invitation is!"

"I don't see how it does, *madam*," she replied, with feigned respect. "You are so determined to find this invitation— none of you stopped to think that maybe you didn't receive one. Maybe the royal family doesn't want *any* of you coming."

"Nonsense!" Frances snapped. "All the ladies of Hartmere are invited. Why wouldn't they invite us?"

"Why not, indeed?" Ellie asked rhetorically. "Perhaps your reputation has done you a disservice. Perhaps it's gone well ahead of you."

"QUIET!" Frances roared. "You have no idea what you're talking about! And it's all bluster anyway to cover up your insolence. Now, tell us where that invitation is or I swear you will be whipped!"

The prospect of being whipped almost caused Ellie to falter a bit. Frances had whipped her only two times before. Five lashes apiece, and it was terrible. Her back had bled for days, and in some cases, Mrs. Tuttle had had to sew her skin back together. Ellie was not eager to repeat that experience, and obviously it was horrendous enough for Frances to think it could induce a confession.

"Never mind that, Mother," Emma said nastily, from the window. "I know what'll make her squeal."

In her hand, she held Ellie's tiny gray kitten by the nape of its neck. She was dangling it out the window, over the sharp spires of the house. If it wasn't impaled when it fell, it would surely die from impact.

"No!" Ellie screamed, rushing forward, but Frances caught her by her shoulders and Anna helped restrain her as well. She fought against them as best as she could, but Anna hit her hard in the stomach, and Frances' grip found its way round her throat again.

"Tell us where the invitation is, or she'll drop that kitten to its death," Frances said coldly.

"I'll do it," Emma promised, as the kitten mewled pathetically. "And you'd better hope we did get an invitation. If we didn't, I'll drop it anyway."

"What is wrong with you?" Ellie demanded, tears brimming in her eyes. "How can you be so evil?"

"Scruples are for those who can afford them," Frances replied. "And judgment is hardly for the likes of you. Now go on, tell us."

Ellie swallowed her anger and pointed to the curtains by the window.

"There's a false panel behind the drapes," she said. "It's hidden there."

"Anna, go check."

The kitten still meowed pitifully as it struggled to move, and Ellie worried that Emma's grip would slip from its movement, or purposefully.

"It's here!" Anna exclaimed. "Oh, Mother, you were right! She did have it."

Before even looking at it, Anna marched over and slapped Ellie while Frances laughed approvingly. Reluctantly, Emma pulled the kitten back in from the window and Frances released Ellie, who rushed over and took the kitten from her stepsister.

"You're a weak fool, Ellie," Frances proclaimed. "And you will pay for your deception."

"And you are an evil murderess," Ellie said darkly. "Training up her evil daughters to be murderesses as well."

"It's not murder to kill a stupid kitten," Frances said. "And besides, I had nothing to do with that. It was Emma's idea."

"I wasn't talking about the kitten," Ellie said, staring her stepmother directly in her coal gray eyes.

The amusement disappeared from Frances' face as she cleared her throat uncomfortably and turned away, wiping her hands on her dress. Ellie glared at her, imagining blood on those white palms. *If I ever have any proof,* she vowed in her head, *I swear I'll bring you down.*

"What is she talking about?" Anna asked dully.

"Nothing," Frances said dismissively. "Now, let's leave Ellie to her filthy kitten while we discuss the ball and what you will wear."

"But what are you going to do to her?" Emma asked, trailing behind them as they began to descend the ladder.

"All in good time, my dears," Frances said. "She'll have all night to contemplate her punishment and justice will come swift at dawn."

As soon as they had stepped off the ladder, Ellie pulled it up again with a forceful slam. She held the kitten close to her chest and curled up with it on her bed, crying as she rubbed its downy fur. The kitten, named Teacup, purred contentedly, perfectly oblivious to her brush with death.

Ellie didn't sleep a wink the whole night. While Teacup scurried around, intermittently chasing mice and napping to her heart's content, Ellie stayed on her bed, her heart filling with anger and despair. She was used to unfairness—it was the rule of her life. But this seemed to be beyond unfair—it was hideously wrong, in every single way, that her stepmother and stepsisters should be rewarded at every turn for their malice and wickedness.

Even as the impotence of her rage dawned upon her, Ellie became singularly determined that she wouldn't go down without a fight. Frances and her daughters may have won the battle, but they wouldn't win the war.

Chapter Three

Enter the Godmother

"THAT horrid, horrid woman," Mrs. Tuttle said, shaking her head. "I've never spoken ill of an employer before, but I've never really had a reason to. She is the *worst* sort of person I think there is."

"You're right about that," Ellie concurred, wincing in pain.

She was lying on her stomach, as Mrs. Tuttle cleaned her back with a cold, wet cloth.

"Although, it doesn't look like I'll have to do any stitching this time," she said. "Maybe the old witch held back a bit?"

"Not likely, not from my memory," Ellie answered, shuddering. "If anything, she seemed more vigorous than usual."

"Well," Mrs. Tuttle said, biting her lip. "I won't let her get away with it. I just won't."

Ellie grinned. "And just what do you plan on doing about it?"

"I don't know yet," Mrs. Tuttle said. "But I'm going to get you to that ball one way or another."

"Even if you managed to physically get me there, how would I get in?" Ellie asked. "I need an invitation."

She bit her lip, thinking. "We'll come up with something. Besides, you're absolutely beautiful, Ellie. There's no way the guards would refuse you, all dressed up like a princess."

"Well, that seems like a lot to pin my hopes on," Ellie said. "I won't hold my breath. But even with my back all torn up, it would be nice to get out. Just for a night."

Mrs. Tuttle's eyes twinkled with merriment.

"And who knows, Ellie? You might even catch the eye of the prince, and then who knows? He might pick you to be his bride!"

Ellie snorted. "Fat chance of that. There'll be no less than a hundred girls there, all vying for his attention. I don't plan on speaking to him at all, let alone catching a glance of him. I'll be there for the food, the wine, and the dancing. If I go at all..."

"Oh, you'll go," Mrs. Tuttle promised. "If it's the last thing I do, I will make sure you go. But you'll have to avoid your stepmother."

"That will be easy," Ellie said. "She wouldn't recognize me without cinder on my cheeks."

Mrs. Tuttle laughed, lightly pinching her cheeks.

"My Cinderella," she said proudly. "Now, don't you worry. I'll get you to that ball."

A week passed until suddenly it was the day of the ball. Frances and her daughters had been out all day spending money they didn't have. Frances called it an 'investment' in their future.

"I have two beautiful daughters," she proclaimed magnanimously. "And odds are, one of them is bound to catch the eye of the prince. And when he chooses one of them, we'll be paid back for what we spent a thousand-fold."

Mrs. Tuttle had snorted back in the kitchen, when she'd told Ellie about it.

"If she honestly thinks any man would find either of those girls attractive, she's blind," she muttered. "They may have young, slim figures, but they're plain and homely. And their attitudes don't do them any credit either. A man doesn't want a harpy for a wife, let alone a prince!"

"Let them carry on with their games," Ellie advised. "It'll all be over soon anyway."

"Yes, but then it'll be weeks of complaining and whining about whoever he did choose!" Mrs. Tuttle replied. "Imagine the torture. I would slip some senna in their food if I didn't have to clean up the mess."

It was Ellie's turn to snort. "Yes, and senna is so strong; they'd notice and complain and probably wouldn't eat a bite."

"Not if I mixed it in some honeyed tea," Mrs. Tuttle said, gleefully. "Yes, that's what I'll do! I'll put honey and ginger and cloves in a tea, add some senna, and let them purge it out all day!"

Ellie smiled. "But as you said, we'd have to clean it up, and that's worse…"

"How about some valerian, then?" she suggested. "In their nightcaps? Then they'll sleep all day and they won't bother us."

"Better," Ellie said. "But if it were me, I'd slip them hemlock and wait until the corpses were cold."

"Oh, you would not!" Mrs. Tuttle exclaimed, playfully smacking Ellie with a linen cloth.

"No, I wouldn't," Ellie said pensively. "But I bet that's how Frances did it to my father."

"Ellie...you don't really think she did that?"

"I don't know," she answered honestly. "Look at the facts. He died suddenly, without warning, a relatively young man in good health. And she is wicked and evil. She didn't love him, and she only married him for his money. With his death, she got to sink her claws into more of it and steal my inheritance as well."

"Well, the motive is certainly there," Mrs. Tuttle admitted. "I wouldn't put it past the old witch. But it's a troubling accusation, and without any proof, it'll just sit in your mind until it rots. Whether we like it or not, we're stuck here with *her*—do you really want that idea festering about in your head?"

"It's not that I want it," Ellie said. "It's that I can't help it. Once it slithered its way in, it won't go out."

"That's the problem with having ideas!" Mrs. Tuttle exclaimed. "It's why I don't think at all."

"Well, I know that's not true," Ellie said smiling. "But maybe you're right."

"Come then," Mrs. Tuttle said, holding out her arm. "Let's go see them off, and then we'll figure out what to do for our night off."

Ellie went with Mrs. Tuttle into the main entrance hall. Mr. Tuttle was outside, tending to the horses and the carriage. Frances had hired a coachman for the night, but they had taken so long getting ready that the horses had become restless, and Mr. Tuttle was feeding them carrots.

Eventually, all three of them sauntered down the staircase with preening pomp and circumstance. Frances was first, fanning herself with a peacock feather fan, a look of lazy indifference on her face. Anna and Emma trailed behind her, in hideously bright shades of scarlet and pink. Ellie was surprised they had foregone the garish orange, but the trade wasn't much better.

"We'll be back at dawn," Frances drawled. "Have breakfast ready for us as soon as we walk in. We'll be famished, I'm sure. Even though we'll probably sleep all day, I expect you to complete your chores as usual and attend to us when we call..." she paused as she pulled on her gloves, shooting each of them a nasty look. "That will be all."

"Yes, madam," Ellie and Mrs. Tuttle said in unison.

Frances and her daughters traipsed out of the main hall, down the front steps, and climbed into their carriage. Within moments, they were out of the main gates and into the city of Hartmere. Mrs. Tuttle put her arm around Ellie's shoulders as Mr. Tuttle came in.

"Now, what do you say to the three of us settling down for a nice supper in the dining room?"

Ellie grinned. "Frances would kill us."

"All the more fun," Mrs. Tuttle said. "And she'll never know!"

36

Mrs. Tuttle had gone above and beyond, serving fried potatoes, kale greens, poached eggs, chicken cutlets, and her famous yeast rolls. But Ellie had only tucked into half of it when there was an ominous knock on the door. Winking at them, Mrs. Tuttle immediately stood up and went to answer it.

Curious at the pleasant greeting that she heard, Ellie followed her and when she went into the entrance hall, she was surprised to see one of her mother's old friends, Lady Talbot. Penelope, as she liked to be called, used to come and visit the house often in the years following Leonora's death. She was also the most persistent in calling even after Frances had taken over and Ellie's father had died. But eventually, she had been scared away. Ellie was completely surprised to see her now—it had been nearly two years.

Penelope gasped when she saw Ellie, and then gave her a broad closed-lip smile, like a friendly mother might do. She held out her arms, coming to envelope her in a hug. Ellie stood a bit awkwardly, patting her back gently.

"You've grown so much, Ellie," Penelope said, tucking a stray hair behind Ellie's ear. "Oh, you look exactly like your mother! Well, I'm sure you've heard that before," she said, laughing. "But you do. She would be so proud of you, and your father would be too."

Still flummoxed, Ellie didn't know what to say but to agree half-heartedly. She wasn't sure that her parents would be proud that she was a servant with no prospects, but it wasn't worth arguing the point. They were both dead—no one could really know what they would've thought.

"Why are you here?" Ellie blurted. "I don't mean to be rude, but it's been years since I saw you."

"Isn't it obvious?" Mrs. Tuttle asked, her eyes twinkling.

"No."

"Ellie, Mrs. Tuttle came by to see me a few days ago," Penelope explained. "She told me of your situation. Of course, I knew that it couldn't be good, judging by my past experience with your stepmother. But I had *no idea* that she had gone so far, and that things had gotten so bad. You must believe me."

"I do," Ellie said, a bit impatiently. "Even if you did know, there's nothing you can do anyway."

"Oh, but there is something I can do," she countered. "When Mrs. Tuttle told me your situation, and that your stepmother would exclude you from the ball, I thought—well, I can take her myself! She can come along with my family. They just need the one invitation per carriage, and your stepmother need never know."

Ellie almost gasped; she was speechless. Mrs. Tuttle was nodding at her excitedly, and she couldn't help but catch the feeling as well. It did seem like a foolproof plan...almost.

"But...but I have nothing to wear!" Ellie sputtered, looking down at her tattered dress and apron. "I certainly can't go like this!"

"Of course not!" Mrs. Tuttle said. "That's why I took out one of your mother's dresses, remember?"

She darted away for a moment and returned with a stunning gown in her hands, the cloth so exquisite it nearly dripped through her fingers.

"I've altered it to fit your measurements," Mrs. Tuttle said. "And she had these jeweled slippers that I think will fit you nicely."

Drawn to the gown, Ellie ran her fingers over the fabric—it was a rich shade of purple, and the satin was decadent.

"B-but how will I get ready?" Ellie asked, looking at them both wonderingly.

"That's why there's no time to waste!" Mrs. Tuttle said. "I've already got a quick bath drawn in your old room. Penelope and her daughters will help with your hair and accessories."

Ellie felt that there was no use arguing with them, or trying to talk her way out of going. And truthfully, she did want to go. She had wanted to go since she saw the invitation. What she didn't like was all the fuss and ado, and the fact that so many people had had to go out of their way to help her. It made Ellie feel a bit uncomfortable, because she had no way of paying them back.

Swallowing her pride, Ellie allowed herself to be led by Mrs. Tuttle into the bath while Penelope fetched her girls from the carriage. She allowed herself that one moment of honesty with Mrs. Tuttle.

"This is too much," she told her. "How can I ever repay you, or Lady Talbot?"

"You can go out and have a good time," Mrs. Tuttle answered curtly. "That's what we wanted from the beginning, and that's what motivates us to do all this."

"But it's too much...the dress, the shoes, the jewels...the time..."

"If your mother were alive, this is exactly what she'd be doing for you," Mrs. Tuttle said. "And this is what she'd want us to do in her absence. You don't think Lady Talbot and I know that good and well? Now, there'll be no more objections. We want you to have a good time, and there'll be no more of this nonsense about paying us back!"

She clucked her tongue and shook her head as she took a brush to Ellie's head.

"Honestly, child, some of the tosh you say!" she said playfully.

Penelope Talbot entered the room with her two daughters, who were a bit younger than Ellie. They couldn't have been more than twelve or thirteen. But they helped their mother hang up Ellie's dress, and go through the box of jewels that had belonged to Leonora Marchand. Frances had pawned or sold everything she could get her hands on, but Mrs. Tuttle had taken these jewels immediately following Frances' arrival, and ordered Mr. Tuttle to bury them somewhere on the property.

Ellie's father had forgotten about them, and never told Frances that they even existed. How could she miss what she didn't know? But Ellie could remember her stepmother poking her nose around the house, sniffing out finery and jewels, like a pig rooting for scraps. She had certainly asked about the late Mrs. Marchand's jewelry collection, suspicious that there was more. But she had never found it. Whatever could be saved from the grasping greed of Frances Hardwick was precious indeed.

When Ellie had been bathed and dried, she put on her chemise behind a changing screen, and then allowed Penelope and her daughters to help her step into her dress, which was full of complicated layers and skirts. The gown had a plain lavender silk kirtle with a fitted bodice. The overskirt and sleeves were made of brocade and had an elaborate paisley pattern sewn with what looked like silver thread. It was definitely an expensive dress made by a master craftsman.

Ellie tried not to flinch too much when they tied the sleeves on, and when they had tied the back of the bodice. Penelope and her daughters had not seen her scars, thanks to the cover of the chemise, but the pain had been hard to conceal when they had tightened the laces.

For her hair, they had braided a long strand in the front, pulled the rest back into a jeweled net and then pulled the braid over top, pinning it into place in the back of her head. Then they had sprinkled little pearl clips in the braid, to match the pearls of the jeweled net.

When Ellie stepped into the heeled slippers her mother had once worn, she felt resplendent and transformed. In her mother's beautiful dress, Ellie felt herself a princess, even if the prince didn't notice her at all.

"Ah, one final touch!" Mrs. Tuttle said, running to the jewelry box. She pulled out a pair of amethyst earrings.

"And another!" Penelope said, as Ellie put the earrings in. "You'll have to have a brooch," she said. "That dress was made for a brooch!"

She pulled out a brooch from her own silk purse and affixed it to the top of the bodice. It, too, was an amethyst set in gold with three pear-shaped pearls that dangled from the bottom.

"This is too much," Ellie said again, feeling that this was her mantra for the evening.

"No, it's just enough," Penelope insisted. "You look beautiful. Absolutely gorgeous!"

Mrs. Tuttle and the Talbot girls echoed their agreement, as they ushered Ellie from the room and back into the main hall.

"Don't forget this, in case there's a chill," Mrs. Tuttle said, handing her a fur drape. "Take good care of my girl," she said to Lady Talbot.

"Oh, I will," she promised. "We'll have her home shortly after midnight."

"Or later," Mrs. Tuttle said, smiling. "I can take care of the housework tomorrow if Ellie wants to sleep."

"Thank you, Mrs. Tuttle," Ellie said, kissing her cheeks. "But I'll be home just after midnight. It'll be better that way…less chance of running into Frances."

With another parting hug and an expression of sincere gratitude, Ellie followed Lady Penelope Talbot and her daughters to the carriage that was waiting outside. And when she climbed in and took her seat, she could hardly believe that it was happening. Even *as* it was happening, she had the feeling that it was surreal, like a dream come true.

Chapter Four

The Ball

PENELOPE and her daughters were great company in the short carriage ride to the palace. Their ease and charm went a long way in making Ellie feel less nervous. But as they passed under the gates to the palace, a resurgence of nerves struck the pit of her belly as she wondered if she had somehow made a terrible mistake. If Frances saw her, and recognized her, she would make a public scene. Ellie imagined her dress being ripped, insults hurled at her...it would be awful.

But Penelope seemed to sense her unease and placed a kind hand on her knee.

"Don't worry, my dear," she said. "I'll protect you if your stepmother tries to do anything...untoward..."

Ellie nodded her head gratefully. Penelope might be able to protect her in the moment, to spare her the public humiliation. But what would happen at Maplecroft Manor, in the isolation and silence of her tomb-like home? No one could protect her from that...unless she managed to get away with it.

"Try not to think about it," one of the daughters, Helena, advised. "There will be so many people here...you'll blend in with the crowd."

"And I don't think your stepmother would recognize you like this anyway," the other one, Maria, said. "She's not used to seeing you dressed up...she'll just assume you're someone else. Someone who might vaguely resemble her stepdaughter."

"Yes, let's hope," Ellie said. "I know I'll recognize her, but if I see her first, she won't see me."

"Good attitude," Penelope said, as the carriage came to a stop. "Shall we?"

Swallowing another lump in her throat, Ellie exited the carriage after Penelope and her daughters, stepping into a candlelit courtyard that seemed to glow with enchantment. In the early summer, the bushes and flowers were bursting with vibrant pink and violet petals, their stems a healthy verdant green. Votive candles had been placed throughout the garden and on the cobbled courtyard stones as well. The air buzzed and hummed with the noise of crickets and katydids, and the faint sound of lutes and viols from within.

They stepped under an arched pathway that led down a series of stairs, still outside, as they walked through the most extensive and well-kept garden that Ellie had ever seen. As they descended onto the lower level, there was a large rectangular pool in the middle with a fountain emerging from the center. Swans swam peacefully in the water, while Ellie could see silver flashes of fish below.

"Aren't the swans beautiful?" Maria crooned. "Oh, I want one!"

"No, you don't," Ellie said, chuckling. "They look nice now, but they're mean, old birds. They're very territorial and

44

aggressive. And the mess they leave on the lawn...let's just say that dogs put out smaller turds."

Maria and Helena looked a bit shocked, while Penelope merely smiled. Ellie's cheeks flushed in embarrassment. The realization that she had grown up much differently than her peers was now showing in a whole new light.

"I'm sorry," she blurted. "I can't believe I said that. I can't believe I even used the word 'turds' on a night like this, in a place like this..."

"It's all right, Ellie," Penelope said. "You were perfectly right. I've heard the same about swans. And one time my mother had an idea that she would have a peacock, for the vanity of it. I must tell you girls that I had the same experience as Ellie...turds as large as stones and an awful temper!"

Maria and Helena giggled as Penelope winked at Ellie.

"Suffice it to say we never had any birds ever again," Penelope continued. "The large ones are too mean, and the little ones are too annoying, and they all make a surprising mess."

"Indeed," Ellie agreed, smiling.

They continued through the lower level of the garden until they passed through another gate. A queue was forming, and as they waited, Ellie's gaze traveled up the high hedges, but she couldn't see anything past. Turning her gaze further upward, she looked at the stars, so dazzling and achingly out of reach.

"It looks like they're ferrying us across in groups," Penelope said to the girls.

"Ferrying?" Ellie repeated.

"Oh yes," she said. "You'll see."

When they passed through the gate, Penelope told the guard at the front that they had four, and he told them to go and stand at the third dock. Ellie struggled to keep up with Penelope as they walked, but she was too busy staring at the view that had opened up before her. After passing through the hedged gate, a massive expanse of flat water had met her eyes. They were standing very close to the water's edge, and set not far back in the distance was a large and impressive castle that gave the illusion it was floating on the lake.

"Whoa…" Ellie swore, staring at it.

Lit up in all its glory, the castle looked like an incredible painting that had somehow come to life.

"Not many people get to see this," Penelope said to them. "This is Bellbroke Castle, the home of the royal family. They call it the 'Glass Castle' and I only imagine we'll find out why."

"You mean, you've never been here?" Ellie asked, incredulously. "But I thought you were a courtier!"

"Oh no," she said. "My father was deemed important enough that I was formally introduced at court, but only as an entrance into society. And that was held at Penchester Palace, the 'business' palace, so to speak. When King Richard dispenses judgment and hears petitions, he comes to Penchester. He'll be ferried across in the morning and ferried back at night. No, I don't know anybody who's been to Bellbroke before."

The enormity of tonight's festivities seemed to hit her all at once. What if Anna was right? What if the prince *was* looking for a bride? It seemed odd that he would invite hundreds of women to his personal home. What could be the purpose? A

46

spectacle? A charade of good will? No, there was something else to it, and the marriage game seemed to be the only gambit that fit.

Ellie heard drums beating from across the water and then she heard the swooshing of oars in the lake. The ferryboats were coming back, and soon she saw the black figures rippling through the water, a lamp hung on a hook at the top of each boat. With the ominous beating of the drums, Ellie and the other women at the third dock climbed carefully into their boat. With all the heavy jewels and fabrics, Ellie suffered a quick dread of watery doom. She imagined the boat heaving over, all of them drowning and sinking to the bottom of the lake.

Shaking her head, she willed herself to quit it. Sometimes her imagination carried her away with it, and she often suffered from wildly spiraling thoughts. Her fears were alleviated as the oarsmen started rowing them across. And as she gripped the side of the boat, she felt herself getting less anxious the closer they came to the other dock.

Ellie was curious as to how the castle was physically supported. As they came closer, it still gave the illusion that it was floating. There seemed to be no land underneath it. When they came to the dock, she noticed the water lapping at the stone foundation, but she didn't see anything that indicated soil, grass, or land. There must be stone pillars, she thought, very thick stone pillars that were affixed somehow in the mud at the bottom of the lake.

But it would have to be very sturdy indeed, to withstand the tug and pull of the water, as well as natural erosion. She wondered that the royal family wasn't in constant fear of the castle collapsing and sinking. Ellie knew that it was highly unlikely that she would get to meet any of the royal family. Just looking around she knew that there were hundreds of girls here, all eager to meet the prince, practically salivating at the prospect. But she thought that if she did meet the prince, she would ask him how it was structurally possible to live in a floating castle. Probably not what the other girls would ask.

Ellie stayed close to Penelope as they formed a throng trying to ascend the main stairs. There seemed to be two attendants on either side of the gate who were inspecting invitations again.

When it was their turn at the top, Penelope presented her invitation to the attendant.

"Four for the House of Talbot," she said. "I am Lady Penelope, with my daughters, Maria and Helena, and my ward and goddaughter, Eleanor."

The attendant took the invitation, counted them through, and that was the end of it. Ellie breathed a sigh of relief. She shouldn't have been so worried. It wasn't as if these attendants could know every single inhabitant of the houses they invited. These weren't all noble or royal houses, after all.

Past the gate, they ascended a much larger stone staircase that led to the entrance of the castle. Ellie could see the massive wooden doors that had been thrust open, light and music spilling through. A wave of excitement passed over her, and she suddenly felt that she could put all the nerves and panic aside. Looping arms with Penelope and Helena, Ellie felt that she was truly part of a family. In her mother's violet dress, with her slippers and jewels, she felt as if she did belong here. And it was the best feeling in the world.

WHEN they passed through the double doors, Ellie's breath caught in her chest, and she had to blink and look again. They had entered on a balcony into a massive room that stretched both high above them and far below. And to the right and left were spiraling staircases that led up and down. They all indulged in a quick look on the balcony before descending. Ellie looked up at a high domed ceiling that was covered in heavenly frescoes and scenes of clouds with angelic figures.

When they had glutted their eyes, they went down the staircase where they were greeted by waiters with trays of wine and little bites of food. Ellie grabbed a flute of sparkling white wine and nibbled on some cheese and fruit. Looking around her, she saw mostly women and girls in dresses. But she did notice that there were men present, escorting women on the ballroom floor for dancing. She wondered who these men were, and she figured they were probably courtiers, required to come. After all, the prince couldn't possibly entertain *all* these women. Ellie thought it unlikely that he would get to meet all of them, even if they stood in a single-file line and got thirty seconds apiece to introduce themselves.

Ellie turned to Penelope, but was surprised to see that she wasn't there. Maria and Helena smirked at her.

"She's already seen at least ten people she knows," Maria explained. "Mama is a social butterfly."

Ellie nodded her head.

"Have you seen the prince?" she asked. "Or the king and queen?"

"Not yet," Helena said. "But it's just a little past nine. Mama thinks they will come out at half past, to ensure that everyone is here and that's when the gates will close."

Ellie didn't know that. She didn't know that they would close the gates at a certain time. She wondered how Maria and Helena knew that. It certainly wasn't on the invitation—she had memorized every word. But she figured that it did make sense. They couldn't have people traipsing in all night, there would have to be a cut-off.

Just as Ellie was musing about this, she was approached by one of the gentleman courtiers. Ellie nearly choked on her wine, she was so surprised by his appearance.

"I am sorry to have startled you," he said smoothly, as she coughed.

"It's fine," she said. "It appears my nerves have gotten the best of me, after all."

He smiled and Ellie felt as though she would melt on the spot. He was strikingly handsome, with what Ellie would call boyish good looks. His eyes were a deep blue that seemed to capture and hold her in thrall. He had an even, clear complexion and light brown hair. Best of all, he had white teeth and when he smiled, his lips tugged up on the left side, resulting in a very attractive grin that seemed to put her at ease.

50

"Would you like to dance?" he asked, extending his hand.

"I don't even know your name," she said. "And you don't know mine."

"How silly of me!" he said, grinning again. "Well, my name is Sir Leopold Evander Wallingford. But I often go by my middle name, Evander."

"Quite a name," she said. "Evander. I like it."

"Well, only with your approval," he said, grinning again. "And may I have your name? Or do angels merely have beautiful faces?"

Ellie tried not to blush. The flirtation was so heavy-handed, but she had heard that this was the way of the court. However, she was not used to it, and as blunt and clumsy as it might be, the smallest amount of attention would have had her head spinning.

"My name is Ellie Kate," she said. "Not nearly as grand as yours, I'm afraid."

"Ellie Kate," he repeated. "Behold the fair name of an angel!"

He lifted his hands dramatically and bowed low before her. Helena and Maria, who had unfortunately witnessed the whole scene, giggled in amusement. When he stood up straight again, he held his arm out and with another nervous laugh she took his hand and followed him to the ballroom floor.

Many years ago, Ellie's father had taught her how to dance formally. When she was still young, before he had married Frances, he had cleared the sitting room and brought in friends that could play the harp or viol. And then he had taught Ellie the steps to several common dances.

Even though this had been years ago, Ellie was fairly confident she could remember the steps. And her father had told her that the man does all the leading.

"Dancing is easy when you're a woman," he had said. "As long as you have a good partner, you just follow his lead."

Fortunately, Evander turned out to be a very good dancer. The first dance was rather quick and fast-paced, and Ellie felt as though she was being whirled around the whole floor, becoming dizzy and light-headed with each spin. But Evander's steadying hand was always right there on her waist, to prevent her from falling or going out of step, and his other hand held hers firmly in his. More guiding still were his bright blue eyes that never seemed to leave hers.

The second dance was much slower in its pace, and Ellie had more of a chance to enjoy the moment and notice the attractive features of her partner. Evander was wearing a gold brocade jerkin with breeches to match, and Ellie knew with her purple gown that they were sure to look good together. The gold jerkin brought out the golden highlights in his hair. Ellie imagined him outdoors from sunup to sundown in the summer, the rays of the sun bringing out even more gold.

When the second dance had finished, the musicians announced a break, and Ellie's face dropped in disappointment. Evander had given her two dances, but with the shortage of men, that was bound to be it. He would have to spread his attentions elsewhere, and it made her a bit sad. She was exhilarated by his presence, and yet also strangely put at ease.

Evander had a very casual way about him, a vibe that exuded calm and comfort. Throughout the dances, he had leaned close and whispered little jokes in her ear, and made running commentary about some of the more outrageously dressed women and outlandish hairpieces. Ellie found it all very amusing, if not somewhat childish. But she imagined that Evander's life must have held very little but entertainment and happiness. No doubt he could afford to be so flippant. Like his boyish good looks, it held a boyish charm that Ellie found refreshing. And she doubted that she would find another courtier like it—the others looked so stiff and bored.

"You are a wonderful dancer," Evander said, leading her off the dance floor.

"No, *you* are a wonderful dancer," she said. "I merely followed your lead."

When he had escorted her back to her table, he lifted her hand and placed the slightest kiss upon her skin.

"I hope we meet again, Ellie Kate," he said, grinning at her with those incredibly blue eyes.

"I hope so too," she said faintly.

And then he was gone, disappearing into the crowd as suddenly as he had come.

"And just *who* was *that?*" Penelope asked, appearing at Ellie's side.

"A courtier named Evander," she answered.

"Well, he was *very* good looking," Penelope commented. "And he seemed *very* into you."

Ellie shrugged. "It was all a ploy, I'm sure," she said, sounding jaded. "A courtier's game, nothing more. But it was enjoyable while it lasted."

"Well, come, come," she said. "They're going to announce the royal family now!"

Ellie sat next to Penelope at their table, which had a few other ladies at it. The tables all faced the southern wall of the room, which wasn't so much a wall, but rather just large glass windows with the drapes pulled back to let in the moonlight and starlight. Ellie imagined that the room was simply stunning at daybreak.

At the far end of the room, a group of trumpeters stood and then lifted their instruments, blowing several loud musical blasts to signal the arrival of the royal family.

"Presenting His Majesty, King Richard III of Trenway!"

A man walked through the doors and onto the dais at the center of the room where he sat in a large throne chair. Ellie was shocked by the relatively small size of the man. He was tall, certainly, but no bigger than an average, ordinary man. And from this distance, he seemed to look ordinary as well. If he hadn't been wearing a crown on his head, he could have been mistaken for any sort of man, a merchant or a butcher.

"Presenting Her Majesty, Queen Adelaide!"

The queen followed in robes of burgundy with ermine-lined sleeves and what appeared to be a sour look on her face. Some of the other women at the table had noticed it as well, as

54

she walked briskly to the dais and sat down in a less than graceful huff.

"She's always like that," one of the women at the table muttered. "Sour, and she ought to go back to Kronstadt. That's why the prince is looking for a bride here. Some say he doesn't want to make his father's mistake and marry a sour, old foreign bride."

Ellie didn't put much stock in the idle talk of women and gossips. But she could see with her own eyes that Queen Adelaide did not look very happy. But perhaps it was just because her personal home was being opened up to the public for the first time, and she resented the intrusion. Ellie could understand that.

"Presenting His Royal Highness, Prince Fillip Westenra of Trenway!"

And finally: the figure they had all been waiting for. Prince Fillip emerged with a grin and a quick wave to the applauding crowd. From a distance, Ellie could only make out his light brown hair and what appeared to be marginally good looks. Nothing compared to Evander, though, and with the thought of him, her stomach turned flips.

She leaned over and whispered to Penelope,

"Are they going to explain why they invited us?"

"Probably not," she answered. "Could you imagine the pandemonium if they announced it tonight? Right now? Oh no, bad enough that most people already *think* it and they'll be doing every obnoxious thing they can to throw their daughters in his way, but if they *knew*...well, it would probably be too overwhelming. And it could get vicious. Think of all these mothers like swans."

Ellie laughed. "Now, there's a funny image for you. All these swans and geese and hens mulling about, clucking and preening."

Penelope laughed too. "Exactly!"

As it turned out, no one in the royal party made any sort of speech at all. Instead, an older man came out and made an announcement. Penelope explained that he was the Grand Duke of Talbany, a principal advisor to the royal family, Lord Robert Cecil. As he was talking, the gentlemen courtiers came to each table and passed a card with a number on it to each young lady. Ellie noticed that they specifically handed them only to the younger ladies at each table.

Despite no official word on the purpose of the night's festivities, it was becoming more and more obvious. Whether for marriage, pleasure, or some sort of game, the prince was interested in meeting young, single women of marriageable age.

Ellie was barely listening, but she understood that if the number on your card was announced, you were to report to the west end of the room and enter a curtained antechamber. Presumably there, you got to meet the prince face-to-face. It seemed very convoluted to Ellie and she looked at her card which had the number *'forty-seven'* embossed in gold.

"Look, I'm nothing more than a number!" she said to Penelope.

"Well, we're less than that," Helena said sulkily. "We didn't even get a number. We must be too young."

"You are too young," Penelope said. "But your time will come."

"Yes, when the prince is already married to someone else."

Their spirits dulled, Penelope decided to take them outside for some fresh air and a walk through the other gardens. Alone and unsure of what to do, Ellie wandered the room for a bit, keeping a lookout for her stepmother and stepsisters. She thought she saw them at one point, but it had just been some women who looked similar. Ellie eventually decided to ascend the staircase and stand on the balcony, overlooking everything. It might be interesting to observe all the obsequious people, bumping elbows and shoving through trying to get the ear of the Grand Duke.

The king and queen had already disappeared, and the prince was probably safely ensconced in the antechamber, meeting his first numbered girl. But just as Penelope had said, there were a number of pushy, insistent mothers clucking like hens at the Grand Duke and other courtiers, clamoring to push their daughters further up in the line.

When a figure suddenly appeared at her side, Ellie thought nothing of it until she saw that it was Evander.

"Oh!" she said, letting out a gasp of surprise.

"That's the second time I've startled you," he said. "I must be shockingly unwelcome."

"No, not at all!" she said. "I was just...caught up, in watching all the people."

"Extraordinary, isn't it?" he said. "All these women desperate to make *the* match for their daughters. The lengths they'll go to..."

"So that *is* what tonight is all about then?" she asked. "The prince is actually looking for a bride? In Hartmere?"

"Did I say that?" he asked coyly.

"You *implied* it," she said.

"Ah, yes, I see the implication now," he said. "But really, these women do think they're securing a match for their daughters, despite whether or not it's the truth."

"Just be straight with me: is the prince looking for a bride?"

Evander thought for a minute, his hands behind his back.

"Yes, of course he is. A young prince, poised to take his father's throne, he'll need a princess by his side to give him children. Naturally he's looking."

Ellie narrowed her eyes, realizing her mistake.

"But is he looking for a bride tonight?" she clarified. "At this ball?"

"Perhaps," he answered. "Perhaps not. Perhaps tonight he just wants a little diversion."

"I'd hardly call this a diversion," she said dryly. "Having to stand in that room and meet a succession of women."

"I daresay he'll choose one or two to dance with," Evander said. "He won't stay cooped up all night. Would you like me to let you in on a little secret?"

"Oh, would you?" she asked playfully. "You would dare to share a crumb with me?"

"Oh, if I had my choice I would share far more than a crumb with you..." he said, fixing her with another dazzling grin.

Ellie blushed at his innuendo. "Go on, then," she said. "Give me your crumb."

Evander stepped closer to her and leaned on the balcony.

"The prince will only meet about half the women here tonight, maybe even just a quarter."

"Really!" she exclaimed. "Then why give all of us these cards?"

"If I tell you, you must *promise* to keep it a secret," he insisted.

"Promise," she said.

"Let's shake on it?" he suggested. "I'm serious, we need to shake on it."

Ellie held out her hand and grasped Evander's. She loved that his grip was strong and solid, but not crushing, and that his palms were warm and dry, not clammy or oily.

"Fine, we've shaken on it, now what is it?" she said.

"The prince is only interested in *certain* types of ladies, and because there are so many, he can't meet all of them without losing his mind. They would start to blur and he wouldn't remember. So, he's asked all of us, his gentlemen courtiers, to circulate the room and talk to some of the ladies and report back to Cecil. Then Cecil will announce the numbers we tell him, and that's who goes and sees the prince. Every eligible lady received a card to give the illusion that it's an orderly process. They'll think the numbers are being drawn at random, or if they have a large number, that there just wasn't enough time. Cecil still expects

59

complaints, of course, but this scheme was devised to cut back on that, and to keep the purpose obscured."

"Well, it doesn't seem that obscured," Ellie remarked. "It seems obvious that the prince is looking for a romantic match. I don't know if he would marry a commoner from Hartmere, but he might just be looking for a mistress or a companion. Either way, it seems clear that a romantic match is the aim."

Evander shrugged his shoulders.

"All part of the mystery and majesty."

"So why aren't you down there, mingling amongst all those ladies, gathering information?" she asked.

"And who says I'm not 'gathering information'?"

Ellie's eyebrows rose. "Oh, so you're gathering information on me?"

"Perhaps."

She let out a little laugh. "And what would you say about me to the Grand Duke?"

He grinned. "That's for me to know."

"Well, don't leave me in suspense. Are you going to suggest my name?"

Evander fixed her with another of his peculiar stares.

"Do you want me to?"

Ellie bit her lip, thinking. "You can if you want," she granted. "I give you my permission."

"But do you *want* to meet the prince?"

"Sure," she answered, half-heartedly. "I don't know. I didn't really come here to meet the prince, to be honest with you."

His eyebrows rose in surprise. "You didn't?" he said. "Why else come?"

Ellie became a bit uncomfortable. "I don't have the greatest...domestic situation," she explained as best as she could. "I just wanted a night away from it all, full of music and laughter and fun. I wanted to put on a beautiful gown and come to a castle and meet new people, or even just watch people, I guess. But I never had any expectation of meeting the prince. And I'm not saying that to be coy or anything, it's true."

"I know," Evander said. "I can tell when people are putting on, and you're not."

Ellie smiled at him, appreciating that he had understood. His demeanor had changed from playfully flirtatious to serious and interested.

"Well, I can tell you this," he said finally. "I will put in my best word to Cecil, and we'll go from there. I won't make any promises, but I do think the prince ought to meet you."

"Ought?" Ellie repeated, laughing. "That's a good one."

"I mean it," he said. "A girl like you shouldn't be overlooked."

"Well, thank you," she said.

"Ellie Kate, I would love to stay and chat," he prefaced. "But unfortunately, the prince put me to a task, and I must go to it. As you said, I must go and 'gather my information' on the other lovely ladies here. But I hope you do get to meet the prince, and I hope I get the chance to dance with you again later."

"Me too," she said awkwardly. "Er—same here, oh..."

He had already flounced down the steps and out of her sight again. She felt stupid for what she had said, and wondered if her vague hint of a 'domestic situation' had triggered any alarms. She noticed that his demeanor had changed after that. Could he see through all the silks and jewels to the cinder soot beneath? She had washed, of course, but still—could he tell? Did he know that she was no different than the maid who cleaned his chamber pot at night and freshened his linens and changed the logs in the fireplace?

Worried that she had given herself away, Ellie walked out to the gardens to try and find Penelope. She did not know if it was midnight yet, but she knew that she wanted to leave.

Chapter Five

An Interview with the Prince

AS Ellie went outside and down the stone staircase, she was suddenly struck by the impossibility of having gardens on a floating castle. Surely Penelope had been mistaken when she said she was taking her daughters to the gardens. But almost as soon as she reached the bottom of the stairs, she saw tree branches swaying in the wind directly to her right, and she knew that she wasn't imagining them.

She followed a path that led her to a walled enclosure with a small iron gate, the door propped open. When she went inside, she realized that they were hanging gardens. It wasn't very large and not nearly as ostentatious as the garden they had passed through on land, in the courtyard, but it was still very impressive and lovely. The builders must have used stone to create tiers that were filled with soil and then cultivated.

The result was an arena of greenery and flowers that one could walk through on different levels. Ellie glanced around and saw some people milling about, but none of them that she recognized as Penelope. This garden had also been filled with votive candles, providing ample illumination. And like the other garden, this one's center was complete with a fountain.

An old man sat on the edge, poking a stick in the water. Feeling it would be rude and unladylike to shout, Ellie walked down to where the man was.

"Excuse me," she said. "Have you seen a rather tall woman with two young daughters?"

The man looked up at her with a befuddled expression, his wispy white hair sticking out in all directions.

"Why, the place is full of women!" he exclaimed. "Women and daughters! Women and daughters!"

His sudden movement with the stick, his unkempt appearance, and his exclamations took Ellie aback. Sensing that he was perhaps a bit senile, she politely tried to disengage.

"Wait!" he called, drawing her back. "You're the one! You're the one he'll choose."

"What?" Ellie said, a bit baffled.

"Yes, my dear, it's you," he said. "Ah, you've come back. Forgive me, will you? Forgive an old man. The sight is there, but the mind is weak. I forgot, Ellie, but you must forgive me."

Goosebumps rose on her arms as he said her name. She had not introduced herself to him. How could he have known who she was? And what was he talking about? But the more she stood there, the more troubled he seemed, as he reached out achingly for her arm, his blue eyes terribly upset. Ellie didn't want to distress him, and in a moment of pity, she reached out and held his hand. As soon as she did, he seemed relieved.

"I have to go now," she said, patting his hand with her other arm.

"Yes, yes," he said. "Go across the sea, Ellie, where it's safe. Ellie of the daisies! Ellie of the buttercups! The princess bride!"

The old man giggled nonsensically and she pulled her hand away, realizing that in addition to being old, he was probably also insane. But even as she walked back toward the wooden doors, she still couldn't shake the fact that he had known her name.

BACK inside the ballroom, Ellie still struggled to find Penelope and her daughters. She was beginning to worry that they had left without her. She couldn't think why they would do such a thing, unless there had been some sort of emergency, in which case Ellie would be stranded without a ride back to Maplecroft Manor, putting her in somewhat of an emergency of her own.

Trying not to worry about these things, Ellie drank four more glasses of wine and allowed herself to be dragged around the dance floor by two different courtiers. Her head was so dizzy with wine that she didn't even remember their names, but they were handsome enough. Not nearly as good looking as Evander, but she figured that that was too high a standard for just any man to live up to. And though her eyes scanned the room for signs of him as well as Penelope, she did not see him.

After the fifth consecutive dance, Ellie was starting to feel a bit unsteady on her feet, and so she declined another round with the nameless courtier and took a few wobbly steps towards the food table. A nice woman, who looked about the same age as Penelope, gave her some crackers and a stiff, bitter drink that Ellie didn't recognize. It wasn't alcohol, more like a tea of some kind.

"This will help get your head straight," she explained.

Nodding her head, Ellie drank the bitter concoction and continued to eat more crackers until her stomach at least started to feel better. And that was when she saw her stepmother, gliding pretentiously over to the food table; her hand fluttering back and forth as she rapidly fanned herself. Anna and Emma were trailing like ducklings in her wake, both wearing sour, morose faces. Ellie would have grinned at that, except that she remembered that she was supposed to be avoiding them.

Attempting to move stealthily, she darted very quickly to her right, but her head was still a bit too foggy and this resulted in her movements being more spastic than she would have wished. She knocked a silver platter off the table and ran straight into a woman, causing her to spill her wine all over the floor.

"Oh, I'm so sorry," she muttered.

The woman was clattering on about it, but Ellie hardly heard her, she was too busy looking to see if Frances had noticed. It would have been hard not to. Ellie picked up the silver platter, but there was still food everywhere. Thankfully, since this was the royal castle, there was an army of servants waiting on deck for some such accident. They came from the corner swiftly, allowing Ellie a chance to exit behind them as Frances became aware of the commotion.

Very nearby she noticed a red velvet curtain at the entrance of a crenellated antechamber. Sneaking through the gap in the middle, Ellie had precious little time to appreciate the quick getaway from her stepmother.

"Eh hem!"

Slowly, Ellie turned around and saw that she was in the presence of Prince Fillip, the Grand Duke, and a lady. All of them were staring at her, and the Grand Duke and the lady looked very put out indeed.

"What are you doing in here?" the Grand Duke barked. "You are to come here when summoned. If you think that sneaking in here will make a good impression on the prince, you are sorely mistaken."

"I...I'm s-sorry," she said. "I d-didn't mean to c-come in here, I swear."

"Sure, you didn't," the young lady snarled, her arms crossed.

"I didn't!" Ellie insisted. "You see, I saw someone I knew and I didn't want them to see me, so I came in here...I had no idea this is where...well...I apologize, Your Highness."

Dipping low into a bow, Ellie thought it would be best to appeal to the prince. He, at least, was the only one who didn't look irritated. Instead, he wore a bit of an amused expression on his face.

"I humbly beg pardon, Your Highness," Ellie said again, still bowing. "I promise it was an honest mistake."

The Grand Duke snorted, clearly still dubious of her claim to ignorance. The lady's face was as cold as ice, but the prince smiled benevolently, and raised his arm to indicate that she was to stand up.

"What is your name?" he asked.

"E-Ellie Kate," she said, still nervous.

"What?" the Grand Duke barked.

"Uh—Eleanor Katherine, I mean," she amended. "Eleanor Katherine Marchand."

The Grand Duke pushed his spectacles further up the bridge of his nose and bent down to a piece of parchment.

"Your number?" he asked.

"Forty-seven."

Grumbling, the Grand Duke shuffled through his papers and then whispered something in the prince's ear. Satisfied, the prince nodded and then addressed the lady whose pale white face now resembled curdled milk.

"Miss Scrimshaw, it was a pleasure meeting you. I do hope we get the chance to meet again."

Taken aback at her dismissal instead of Ellie's, the lady known as Miss Scrimshaw stumbled over her words a bit as she took her leave.

"Y-yes, Your Highness," she said. "Yes, it was v-very nice to meet you as well, and I trust that we shall meet again the future. It is the desire closest to my heart."

Bowing low, Miss Scrimshaw made an artful flourish with her delicate white hands and then snapped back up like a weed, and as she made a gliding exit, she glared at Ellie with a look that could have killed.

"Step forward, Miss Marchand," the prince said amiably.

Ellie did as she was told, stepping further into the egg-like oval room, trying not to panic over the fact that she was less than ten feet away from the prince.

"We have been informed that you are quite a remarkable lady," the prince said. "A lady worth meeting. Tell us about yourself."

Thinking that Evander must have described her as such, Ellie blushed and squirmed under the direct gaze of the prince. She had no idea how to describe herself, especially since most of what she said would have to be a lie.

"Well, sir, I do not know what you wish you hear, but I am your humble servant, born in Hartmere. My father was a merchant, but he is deceased now, and I live with my stepmother and stepsisters."

"My goodness," the prince exclaimed. "How tragic. Do you like living with your stepmother?"

"May I be honest?"

"Of course," he said, chuckling. "I wish you would."

"Then I must say that I do not," she answered. "My stepmother is a difficult woman. I am afraid I have not known much better in the way of mothers, though, for my own died when I was a baby."

"So much tragedy in your past," the prince remarked. "Tell me, what brings you joy?"

"Oh, many things," Ellie said. "For instance, tonight has brought me much joy. Dressing up and dancing and drinking...I cannot remember when I had such a wonderful time!"

"Good!" he said, smiling. "I am glad to hear it."

"I wouldn't want you to think that I am some moping, morose moron," she said, the effects of the wine still lingering and clouding her mind.

"I would never think that," he assured her, a faint trace of amusement in his eyes.

"I have a kitten!" she burst out. "Yes, I have a kitten that gives me great enjoyment. Her name is Teacup, and she's tiny and gray and furry and perfect!"

"A kitten?" the prince repeated. "How extraordinary. I have a cat as well, named Marlinspike. He's only a few years old, but he's enormous and mostly black. He's a ferocious hunter—all mice of the castle, beware!"

"Teacup is a decent mouser too," she said. "But she's not as fierce. I think it's because we've spoiled her. I can't help but bring her saucers of milk and meat scraps from the kitchen, so I don't think she has much motivation to catch mice."

The prince laughed. "Oh, yes, Marlinspike is very spoiled as well. You can imagine that the prince's cat is like a prince himself. We've a special bed for him, and he gets treats all the time. You know, there's this special herb you can give them and they go crazy!"

Ellie nodded her head. "Catnip is what we call it," she said. "Mrs. Tuttle, our housekeeper started growing it in the garden several years ago. We've had lots of cats come and go, but Teacup is the first I've kept indoors. I think she was the runt of her litter, and she was so cute, I was afraid she wouldn't make it!"

"You seem very tender-hearted," the prince observed. "Marlinspike doesn't like many people. He growls and hisses at nearly everyone except me, but I daresay he would like you."

"I hope he would," she said. "I love cats. Much more than dogs, I'm afraid."

"My mother keeps a fair share of dogs," he said. "And my father likes them for hunting, but I'm rather like you. I prefer a cat any day," he finished, winking at her.

"Eh hem," the Grand Duke interjected, flashing an impatient look at the prince. Ellie was afraid that her time had run out, and all they'd talked about was her tragic past and cats. Hardly enough to get to know someone.

"Do you have any other hobbies or favorite pastimes?" the prince asked, ignoring his advisor.

"Well, I love to read," she replied. "And I used to love riding horses."

"Used to?" he asked, curious.

"Uh, yes..." she said, realizing she had to quickly come up with a lie. "I was...uh, recently injured...falling from a horse. It was terribly traumatic, you know, and even though I've gotten better, I'm still a bit spooked."

The prince nodded his head sagely.

"Yes, I know the feeling," he said. "What kind of books do you like to read?"

"Oh, anything I can get my hands on," she answered. "But mostly I love history books and novels. Although, lately I've been fascinated with mythology and astronomy."

Perking up, the prince said, "You know, we have a fantastic tower here that we use for stargazing. And there's been this amazing invention we've installed at the top called a telescope. You can see stars and planets close up, almost as if you were looking at the moon!"

"Really?" Ellie exclaimed. "That would be incredible!"

"Oh, it is. Maybe I can show you some time," he offered. "You know…if we ever have another ball again."

Ellie's face fell, remembering that she was talking to the prince, and that there were hundreds of other girls there, all vying for his attention. She had been so caught up in conversation that she had forgotten he was focused on a specific task. And because he was the prince, and she a mere commoner, he couldn't just invite her to come stargaze with him.

"Yes, that would be lovely," she agreed.

"Before you leave, Miss Marchand, a couple questions," the Grand Duke said brusquely. "Are you currently married?"

"No," she said, almost laughing.

"Have you ever been married?"

"No."

"How old are you?"

"Seventeen."

"Are you currently, or have you ever been with child?"

"With child?" she repeated, shocked.

The Grand Duke looked up from his piece of paper, lowering his glasses further down the bridge of his nose. His eyes were a watery blue, his stare intensive.

"Yes, with child?" he prodded.

"N-no," she said. "I've never even...been with a man..."

"Good," he said. "That answered my next question."

Flushed with embarrassment at having to answer these questions in front of the prince, Ellie wondered why Miss Scrimshaw hadn't been subjected to these questions before she had left.

"Where do you currently reside?" the Grand Duke asked.

"Maplecroft Manor," she said. "That's on Harfleur Street, right along the River Morrow, in the Silk District. The house number is 2109."

The Grand Duke made a furious scribbling noise on the parchment while Ellie stood awkwardly.

"Your father was a merchant?" he prodded. "His name, please?"

"Cornelius Marchand."

"And your mother? What of her people?"

"My mother was Leonora Penwhistle, eldest daughter of the Baron Windermere. Her family was originally from the northern woodland, I believe, the county of La Fôret."

He scribbled his quill furiously again and Ellie had the odd feeling that perhaps not *all* of the girls invited to this stage were interrogated so thoroughly. She might not have answered so honestly if she weren't afraid of lying to the prince.

"Very good, then," he said. "That is all. You may go."

She bowed low to the prince first. "Thank you, Your Highness, for speaking to me."

"No, thank you, Miss Marchand," he corrected. "The pleasure was all mine, I assure you. And I do fervently hope that we meet again."

Had she not been slightly intoxicated, Ellie would have been more confident that she saw the prince wink at her just after he said this. But as it was, she couldn't be sure that it wasn't just a trick of the light. So she took five steps backward and then turned around, exiting through the red velvet curtain. Panicking a bit, she realized that she hadn't even checked to see if her stepmother was still at the food table. But she didn't have long to worry about it.

Out of nowhere, it seemed, Penelope appeared at her side, clutching her elbow and leading her quickly toward the grand staircase.

"Oh, there you are, Ellie," she said. "I've been looking for you all over!"

"Strange," Ellie said. "I've been looking for you too."

"We must have kept missing each other," she replied. "Well, anyway it's just past midnight and I promised Mrs. Tuttle I would have you home. Plus, Helena is not feeling well. I think she drank too much of the wine, even though I warned her not to...foolish girl!"

"That makes two of us," Ellie commented dryly. "I've sobered up a bit thanks to a nice woman with crackers and a surprise interview with the prince, but for a while I thought I would fall over!"

Penelope nearly came to a screeching halt.

"What?" she exclaimed. "You talked to the prince?"

"Yes, just now."

"Just now?" she repeated shrilly. "You actually did? You talked to him?"

"Yes," she answered, bewildered. "It was funny, really, I didn't mean to go in that room he was in, but I saw Frances and so I darted in there and interrupted his conversation with another woman. Well, I think I was on the list to see him thanks to Evander because they didn't kick me out, even though the Grand Duke was annoyed, and instead they asked the other woman to leave and I talked with the prince for about ten minutes."

"Ten minutes?" she said shrilly, again. "Ellie, that's incredible!"

"Incredible?" Ellie snorted. "Pretty pathetic if you ask me. I blathered on about my kitten, Teacup."

"Oh, you didn't bore him, though, did you?" she asked.

"No, I don't think so," she said. "He brightened up when I mentioned Teacup, and started talking about his own cat, Marlinspike."

"The prince has a cat?" she said, incredulously. "The prince has a cat named Marlinspike. Wait until I tell that to my friends tomorrow at luncheon. They won't believe me!"

"I don't see why not," Ellie said. "It's perfectly true, after all, and it isn't as though it's some intimate detail."

"Ellie, I don't think you understand," Penelope said, as they reached the top of the staircase. "By my estimation, there were nearly two hundred girls here tonight. About a hundred of them got cards, and of that hundred, less than half were called in to speak with the prince. Those girls spent anywhere from one to

75

five minutes with him. Perhaps there were some others in there for longer, but don't you see what this means? You have an excellent chance of being the one he selects."

Ellie shook her head. It was kind of Penelope to think so, but Ellie sincerely doubted that the prince would choose her for his bride—*if* that was even what he was looking for.

"Ten minutes isn't long enough to choose what dress you want to wear, let alone your partner in marriage," Ellie said. "No, and we didn't talk about anything important, really."

"But you got along, didn't you?" Penelope said. "You had a common interest in cats, and I'm sure some other things as well. The thing is, Ellie, this is unprecedented. We don't know what the prince is going to do, or how this will play out. He might not pick his bride based on tonight, but he could've narrowed down the selection. It's very possible, if that's true, that you would receive an invitation back."

Ellie took a moment to absorb what Penelope was saying. But as she remembered her brief conversation with the prince, she doubted that she had said anything special enough to worthy a second go-round. *Except the astronomy,* a sly voice in her head whispered, *the prince invited you up to his stargazing tower. And the Grand Duke asking all those questions that Miss Scrimshaw hadn't been asked...*

"Ellie, do you want to stay longer?" Penelope asked, gripping her shoulders, her eyes open wide and intense.

"What?"

"You can stay longer, if you want," Penelope said again. "With your chances being as good as they are, it might be wise to
76

stick around. I could get one of my friends to take Helena back, and I'll stay here with you."

"Oh no," Ellie said immediately, shaking her head. "I don't think that's necessary."

"Stay here and think about it for a minute," Penelope advised. "I'll go down and talk to my friend. We'll be by the boats, when you're ready."

Without another word, she dashed off down the stone stairs, leaving Ellie alone to think about her dilemma. But in truth, it really wasn't a dilemma. If Ellie was honest with herself, she didn't think she had a shot in the dark of capturing the prince's interest, and she was still feeling a bit woozy from the wine. In truth, what she wanted was to go home and sleep.

Unfortunately, that was not to be, as Evander appeared suddenly by her side for the third time that night.

"That was a bold move, you know," he said smoothly. "Crashing into the antechamber like that."

"I didn't mean to!" she sputtered. "I didn't know that was where the prince was and I was trying to get away from someone…unpleasant."

"Not me, I hope," he said, grinning. "I was nearby you know, and watched the whole thing. Brilliantly artless! Stumbling drunkenly by the food table, causing a commotion that distracted everyone, and then darting into the antechamber. As I said, very bold! Thankfully, my prince likes bold women…"

"I wasn't trying to be *bold*," she insisted. "It was an accident! And I didn't 'stumble drunkenly'," she added, huffily, although she knew it was true.

Evander let out a big-bellied laugh, leaning back into it with a *ho-ho-ho*.

"Oh, it was *very* entertaining," he said, still laughing. "And trust me, it was *very* drunken, or at least it appeared to be, which I believe is what you were going for."

"I wasn't *going for* anything!" she snapped. "I saw someone I disliked, and it triggered a gut reaction which caused me to stumble into someone, drunkenly, as you put it. And to further hide myself, I went behind the curtain, not realizing it was where the prince was conducting his interviews."

"Well, after the stunt you pulled, I can assure you that there's at least one other person you should dislike here tonight. What can be said for sure is that she certainly dislikes *you*."

"Who?"

"The lady you interrupted," Evander said. "Miss Cecelia Scrimshaw. She came storming out of that velvet curtain with a thunderous expression; smoke nearly coming out of her ears and nostrils. She's a real piece of work and not a good enemy to have. She comes from a family of notorious gold diggers and she's no different. They've been trying to get back in the court for years now. Cecelia's mother disgraced the family—I won't go into how, but Cecelia is determined to get her way. And now she thinks you spoiled it. But between you and me, she had no chance with the prince anyway."

"And how would you know that?" Ellie asked. "Were you magically in the room with us also?"

"No," he said, grinning again. "But I've had discussions with the prince about her before. He only invited her because her father paid two hundred marks to the king as a bribe."

Ellie's jaw nearly dropped.

"Two hundred marks?" she repeated. "Just for the chance to talk to him?"

"Yes," Evander confirmed. "As I said, a family of notorious gold diggers. Sometimes, to make money, you've got to spend it."

Ellie let out a little laugh, thinking of Frances and how that had been her exact philosophy.

"So, what are you doing out here?" Evander asked. "Enjoying the fresh air?"

"Not exactly," she answered. "I was actually just about to leave."

Almost immediately his face fell, and Ellie might have been flattered if she thought it was more than just a courtly game.

"What?" he said, crestfallen. "You can't leave! It's only midnight and the ball goes on till dawn."

"Well, I don't remember the invitation saying you had to stay until then," she said, smiling. "Besides, my...my cousin has taken ill and we had best see her home."

"Must you go?" Evander asked earnestly.

"I must," she said, though suddenly not at all certain that it was true. "Besides, I'm sure you'll find plenty of other girls to flirt with. It's not like there's a shortage here."

"Oh, but there is," he said quickly. "There's none nearly as fascinating as you."

His blue gaze held her captive for a long moment, but then he broke it, shaking his head.

"I don't mean to say it like that," he said. "Fascinating, like you're some sort of scientific instrument. I mean there's no one here quite like you. Certainly, none as beautiful or captivating or interesting."

"Well, that's certainly flattering," she said, swallowing a bubble of apprehension. "Or at least it would be if this wasn't a courtly game."

"A courtly game?" Evander said, seeming truly puzzled. He let out a small laugh. "Oh, Ellie, is that what you think this is?"

"Well, I assume so!" she blurted. "That's why you're here, isn't it? To gather information and then show us all a good time by flirting and making us feel good about ourselves?"

The expression on his face made her feel naïve and foolish, like an ingénue. Ironically, she had been trying *not* to be that way by distancing herself from Evander's compliments. She didn't want to be the kind of girl that lost her head when an attractive man spoke to her. Growing up isolated at Maplecroft Manor made that all too easy, and she had been trying to protect herself from it by realizing the reality of the world.

"Ellie Kate," he said seriously. "Does this seem like a courtly game to you?"

Before she knew what was happening, Evander leaned in and kissed her full on the mouth, his hand snaking around her waist. She was so taken aback that she hardly had time to register what was happening, so she didn't immediately pull away. But

80

when she had the presence of mind to do so, she saw Evander's beautiful blue eyes staring into hers with a look of such longing and intensity.

His arm was still around her waist sending tingling sensations all down her spine. And when his other hand came up to touch her face, his fingers lightly tracing the skin of her cheek, she became so overwhelmed she thought she might swoon on the spot. Suddenly her laces felt much too tight—she couldn't breathe. But the wine in her belly lent her courage she might not have otherwise had.

After that breathless moment, she leaned forward and kissed him back. Boldly, her hands reached up behind his neck, sliding into his head of thick, light brown hair.

"Ellie!"

The sound of someone calling her name sent her reeling back into the true context of the situation. For a moment, it had seemed as if she and Evander had drifted up into the clouds. Breaking away from the kiss, she remembered that they were standing just outside the castle doors, and Penelope was marching up the stone steps with a sharp, pinched look on her face. Evander pulled away from her, his hands sliding expertly behind his back as he regarded Penelope with a small bow of his head.

"Madam," he said politely. "Do I have the pleasure of meeting Mrs. Marchand?"

"I am her godmother," Penelope replied stiffly. "Lady Penelope Talbot. And you are?"

"D-don't you remember?" Ellie interjected. "This is the courtier I was dancing with earlier, Sir Leopold Evander Wallingford."

"Oh, yes," Penelope said, surveying him with a distasteful expression. "Well, unfortunately I cannot find anyone to take Helena home for me. I am afraid that we must leave now."

"Now?" Ellie repeated, suddenly wanting to stay forever, until dawn at least.

"This very minute, I'm afraid," Penelope insisted.

Ellie would have asked for a moment to say goodbye to Evander, but he seemed to take Penelope's hint. Turning to Ellie, he took her hand and gently kissed it.

"I sincerely hope we meet again, Ellie Kate," he said, and she knew by the way he said it that he was sincere, and that he had been truthful when he told her it was no courtly game.

"I do too," she said, a bit breathlessly, as Penelope looped her arm in hers and then escorted her down the stairs. When they were near the bottom, Penelope turned to look over her shoulder and then sharply hissed in Ellie's ear.

"Are you insane? Kissing that courtier in plain view of everyone? After I had *just* explained your good chances with the prince? Ellie, if word gets back to the prince that you were kissing that Evander fellow, then he won't consider you at all. You'll be crossed off the list. How could you be so reckless?"

Ellie's mouth gaped open but she had no suitable response to the question. Truthfully, she hadn't been thinking about the prince at all. In fact, as soon as Evander had come within her eyesight, all thoughts of the prince had disappeared completely.

"It's a good thing I came up when I did!" Penelope exclaimed. "I might very well have saved your prospects completely. And to think! I was going to let you stay longer...no question of that now. I'll tell my friend not to bother with Helena. It's best if you leave on a good note with the prince. Your absence might make him miss you more, who knows? But I shudder to think what would've happened if I'd let you stay longer. That boy might have dragged you off somewhere and..." she actually shuddered in the middle of her thought. "Well, your reputation might've been lost in an instant!" she said, snapping her fingers for effect.

On some level, Ellie appreciated the motherly chord Penelope was trying to strike. She was a mother, after all, and Ellie supposed that in some ways she couldn't help it. But the lecturing in and of itself was still unwelcome, and served as a reminder of Frances and her unbearable sermonizing.

When they reached the dock, Ellie saw that Helena and Maria were already in the boat with a few other guests who were leaving early. Penelope stepped into the boat smoothly and quickly, but Ellie hesitated on the edge. She looked back over her shoulder, and saw a figure darting down the stone steps. Her stomach did a flip as she wondered if it was Evander, coming down to dramatically kiss her again and carry her off.

"Ellie!" Penelope said sharply, holding out her hand. "Come on! Let's go!"

Knocked out of her reverie, Ellie sighed and resigned herself to leaving with Penelope. She suffered a sudden sobering moment of realization: at the end of the day, even a day such as this one, she was still a servant. Frances had brought her so low that she could not ever be brought back up again. If Evander knew who she really was, he wouldn't cast her a second glance.

Lifting her skirts, Ellie lowered her foot into the boat, but the heel of her other shoe caught in the wooden planks of the dock. Losing her balance, Ellie fell rather clumsily into the boat, where thankfully Penelope and another woman caught her. The oarsmen, oblivious or uncaring to her fall, had already started rowing, and by the time Penelope got her settled on the bench, she realized that her shoe was gone.

Panicking a bit, she looked around for it, her eyes trying to see in the dim light of the boat lamp, but it wasn't there. Her shoe had to have been on the dock still, stuck between those wooden planks, or fallen into the lake. She tried to remember, but didn't think she had heard a splash. And when Ellie peered out to see the dock by Bellbroke Castle, she thought she saw a figure standing there, holding something in his hand that glinted in the moonlight, like the little diamonds that had been sewn on her slipper.

Chapter Six

The Morning After

ELLIE managed to get a few hours of sleep that night before she heard the crow of the chanticleer. Mrs. Tuttle, who had greeted her when she got home, told her that she could sleep in all day, but Ellie wouldn't hear of it. Her mind was much too restless for all that sleep, and it was better for her to have something to do with her hands, to help her forget that magical kiss with Evander. Nothing could ever come of it. Better to try and forget it had ever happened.

Still in a sad mood, Ellie joined Mrs. Tuttle in the kitchen, too tired and weary for words, although she could tell that the older woman was dying for the details. Perhaps she would tell her later, when she had mustered up the courage to talk of it without crying. The injustice of her situation had come crashing down upon her with full force on the carriage ride back to Maplecroft Manor. She had managed to put it aside during the ball—the glittering spectacle of the castle had seemed to erase the lines of time, making it feel as if there was no need to worry about tomorrow.

But in the disenchanting dark streets of Hartmere, bumping along the cobbles of the road by the river, the horizon had not seemed so blurry and indefinite. Instead, she was forced to remember that her time was up. Her farce of pretending to be a lady was over, and the endless days of toil and servitude with no foreseeable chance of respite stretched ahead of her like a road that led to nowhere.

"I'll be in touch," Penelope promised her when she had gotten out of the carriage. "And send a messenger immediately if you get another invitation from the palace!"

The hope that had been in Lady Penelope's eyes only an hour earlier, when they were still in the castle, had already seemed to fade. It was as if she, too, realized that even if Ellie had spent ten minutes with the prince, in the cold light of the real world, it didn't mean a thing. Her chances had always been slim, but they seemed even slimmer now. She squeezed Lady Penelope's hand in goodbye, frowning at the sad look of disappointment in the woman's eyes.

Perhaps her change in demeanor had also been due to catching Ellie in an amorous embrace with Evander Wallingford. Disappointment, Ellie realized, felt far worse than anger, and Frances had only ever given her the latter.

Mrs. Tuttle clucked her tongue in annoyance.

"I don't suppose you're going to give me *one* little detail, are you?" she demanded. "After all I did for you, Ellie, don't I deserve at least that much?"

"I'm sorry, Mrs. Tuttle," she said, polishing the silverware. "I don't mean to be ungrateful. I had a wonderful time, I truly did."

"Well, then what's the matter with you?"

"It's just…it's just that it's over," she said sadly. "I had a wonderful time, too wonderful, and now it's gone from me forever."

Mrs. Tuttle frowned sympathetically and then came over wrapping Ellie in a hug. The gesture of kindness produced a lump in her throat and she tried not to cry as she held onto Mrs. Tuttle tightly.

"You'll always have your memories," Mrs. Tuttle said softly. "And that'll carry you through. It'll have to."

Ellie sniffled, swallowing back tears and then nodded her head. In her usual pragmatic way, Mrs. Tuttle was right. No one, not even Frances, could take her memories from her. Evander had kissed her like he would a lady of the court. It was better for her not to see him again, for him to never know who she really was. Better to leave it at that: an enchanting memory.

When they heard the front doors open, Ellie and Mrs. Tuttle scrambled into action, running into the hall to greet Frances and her daughters. Down on the drive below, Mr. Tuttle had paid the driver and gave the horses another carrot or two. Looking bedraggled and unkempt, Ellie's stepmother and stepsister came in the house, dragging their feet like creatures of the undead. In any other situation, Ellie and Mrs. Tuttle might have exchanged giggles at their theatrics. Frances let out a long, exhausted sigh as she dropped into her chair at the head of the table.

"What a night," she exclaimed. "What a long, and marvelous night!"

"It certainly was," Anna said, sauntering over to her chair.

Their hair was half unpinned, falling down in loose straggles, and their gowns were filthy with dirt at the bottom, as were their feet, which were bare as they had come in carrying their shoes like common strumpets. It was gross, seeing their bare feet like that, especially given that they were emitting a rather foul smell.

Both Ellie and Mrs. Tuttle went back and forth into the kitchen to serve their breakfast, but when all the food had been brought out, they were forced to stand in the dining room and listen to Frances regale them with tales of their experience at the ball. Ellie rarely had patience for this domestic routine, but on this morning especially, her nerves felt fractiously thin.

"Just *grand*," Frances drawled. "Every inch of the castle was nothing but grand. Glittering in gold with damask curtains of rich violet and scarlet...oh, you can tell that the queen has fine taste indeed. Quite like my taste, really, I think we would get along spectacularly! For instance, if the queen were to see how I have redecorated this house, the fabrics I have chosen and the rugs, I think she would be very impressed indeed."

Ellie rolled her eyes. If the queen were to ever set foot in Maplecroft Manor, which was unlikely, she would probably sneeze from all the dust and break her neck trying not to fall into all the idiotic ornaments and knick-knacks that Frances was so fond of.

"You know, it really does say something of the royal family," Frances continued. "That they felt so comfortable with

88

us to invite them in their personal home. You see, the ball wasn't at Penchester Palace, which was where I thought it would be. No, they brought us to Bellbroke Castle, their home on the lake, which was absolutely *stunning!* I mean, how to describe it? A floating castle just dripping with majesty and awe-inspiring architecture!"

Frances went on like this for some time, prefacing her story with endless descriptions of everything from the garden in the courtyard, to the boat ride across the lake, to the grand staircases inside the main ballroom. Ellie tried to block most of it out, but she noticed that Mrs. Tuttle was hanging onto every word, no doubt trying to imagine Ellie in her purple dress, at all the wondrous places that Frances described. Ellie also noticed that while Anna tucked into her breakfast with a patient attentiveness to her mother's story, Emma sat churlishly at the table, staring sourly into the distance, her plate untouched. She wanted to snort with laughter at the sight alone, wondering why Emma had obviously had such a miserable time.

Ellie's unspoken question was answered when Frances explained that while both her daughters had received a card to see the prince, only Anna had been summoned to speak with him.

"They must not have had time to interview my dear Emma," Frances said kindly, looking pityingly upon her youngest daughter. "There were probably several hundred girls there, all desperate to be chosen. And many of them probably had useful family connections, though I cannot be faulted for not trying, can I, Emma dear?"

Looking pointedly at Emma, Frances batted her eyelashes, prompting her daughter to reveal what she had done for her.

"No, you can't, Mother," Emma finally said, sighing. "You did try to speak to that Grand Duke."

"Yes, I did," Frances said, grinning. "I pushed my way through at least a dozen dumpy, fat women to get through to that Grand Duke. I pled my case as strongly as any mother would, with honeyed words and bribes of jewels, but the old sot wouldn't take it."

"But someone did," Anna said, giggling, as she took a sip of water.

"Yes, someone did," Frances agreed. "As it turns out, I made a friend of one of the courtiers last night. A very charming gentleman, wasn't he, Anna? In fact, Emma dear, I wouldn't be too discouraged if I were you. Once your sister is princess, she can arrange a match between you and our young courtier friend."

At the word 'courtier', Ellie perked up, hoping against hope that Frances hadn't met and befriended Evander. It would have been too low a blow, to think that someone she had liked so much had accepted a bribe from her stepmother.

"What was his name again?" Frances asked.

"Geoffrey," Anna supplied.

Ellie breathed a sigh of relief.

"Yes, Geoffrey," Frances repeated. "But he asked us to call him Geoff. Anyway, Geoff was kind enough to take my bribe and speak to the Grand Duke on Anna's behalf. He told us that he was only allowed to make one suggestion to the prince, otherwise he would have mentioned both my girls. As it was, he had to make a hard decision."

Emma snorted. "Hard?" she questioned. "How could it have been hard when Anna was the one kissing him all night?"

"Emma!" Frances said sharply.

"I was not!" Anna protested hotly, her cheeks turning the same color scarlet as her dress.

"Yes, you were!" Emma retorted. "You didn't want me to tell Mother, but now I have! And if you like Geoff so much, why don't you marry him and give me the prince?"

Anna's mouth gaped open in shock, and Frances' lips thinned so much they almost disappeared. She banged her fist on the table for order and then glared at both her daughters, shaming them into silence.

"Enough!" she hissed. "There will be no more fighting on this subject. Emma, your sister was picked, now get over it. If the prince extends an offer of marriage, she *certainly* won't reject it and suggest he pick *you* instead. How absurd! As I told you earlier, once your sister is princess, she can arrange a perfectly good match for you."

"Well, I won't be marrying Geoff!" Emma declared. "I'll not have a husband who goes after my own sister, and I won't hang around to see her dance between two men."

Frances banged her fist on the table again, shooting daggers at Emma.

"Shut up," she said slowly, through clenched teeth. "Did I not tell you, Emma, that I will not tolerate such insolent talk again? Answer me!"

"Yes, Mother," she said in a low voice.

It was so refreshingly wonderful to see Frances' anger directed toward someone else, especially Emma. Ellie would never forgive her for dangling Teacup out of the window. As far as she was concerned, Emma hadn't even had a fraction of her comeuppance yet, but she was certainly glad she had been snubbed last night, and yelled at this morning.

"Anna had a delightful chat with the prince," Frances continued. "It lasted nearly ten whole minutes, didn't it darling? I asked other the women about their daughters, and from what I gathered, that's one of the longest interviews he had the whole night!"

Ellie thought about what Penelope had said. But she suffered a moment of worry, perhaps even jealousy, when hearing that he had spoken to Anna for as long as he'd spoken to her. She didn't think she would be able to bear it if Anna was chosen.

"Yes, I'd say Anna has the best chance of being selected," Frances said. "With her impeccable upbringing and good looks, she is the right choice for the prince. No doubt about it. He would be a fool not to pick her, and since he's not a fool, it's practically a done deal! So, here's what we'll do, darling," she said, turning back to Anna. "We'll go shopping tomorrow, after we've rested today. We'll buy you some more gowns and brooches—I think a nice blue color would be good. And we'll go to the library and brush up on your history. You'll need to know all about the history of your future family…"

Frances went on at some length about the plans she had for Anna in the upcoming weeks. The more she went on, the more Ellie wanted to gag. Thankfully they weren't subjected to much more of it, as Frances and the girls soon finished their breakfast and went upstairs. Ellie and Mrs. Tuttle cleaned up the breakfast mess and as soon as they were back in the kitchen, Mrs. Tuttle turned to her and said,

"Remember what I told you, Ellie?" she asked. "Don't ever count your chickens before they hatch!"

Ellie smiled. It was a good expression, and one that might have saved Frances a lot of money, and, Ellie hoped, disappointment.

Chapter Seven

By Royal Decree

NEARLY two weeks after the ball, Hartmere was abuzz with rumors and excitement. The royal family had issued a pronouncement from Penchester Palace—the prince would be marrying a commoner from Hartmere. He had already chosen his bride, leading many to conclude he had chosen her at the ball.

The only detail missing from the announcement was the most tantalizing of all—*who* had Prince Fillip chosen? For reasons unknown, the royal family had chosen to stay mum on that, only saying that there would be another announcement in a couple of weeks, once his bride had been safely secured.

"If she's a commoner, they'll want to protect her," Mrs. Tuttle explained, as they were out in the bramble, picking blackberries. "If they said who it was, without having her safe in the castle...well, you know how people are! There'd be blood in the streets!"

"There probably already is," Ellie remarked darkly. "I can't believe he's actually going to marry a commoner!"

"Well, we all figured that was the point of the ball," Mrs. Tuttle said.

"Yes, but *still*," Ellie said. "I mean, it's unheard of, isn't it? A royal prince marrying a commoner of his own country?"

"It's not like any of you there were low born," Mrs. Tuttle pointed out. "He didn't invite milkmaids and tavern wenches, did he?"

"Well, a servant showed up there anyway," Ellie said. "And who's to say I was the only one who snuck in?"

"You're not a servant," Mrs. Tuttle snapped. "You're only doing servant-like things because of that awful shrew in there. But this isn't who you really are, Ellie, and you know that. And I'm not saying it is, but *if* it turns out to be you, you stand up for yourself. Tell them who you really are."

"It won't be me," Ellie said firmly. "But I will stand up for myself if that happens."

"Good," Mrs. Tuttle said, nodding her head. "But I swear, if it's that cow Anna he's chosen, I don't think I'll be able to stop myself…"

"You'd better hold it in," Ellie warned. "They won't tolerate any talk against her, and they wouldn't believe it anyway, not coming from you."

Mrs. Tuttle grumbled. "*I'm* the one they should listen to, been emptying her chamber pot for years, waiting after her and serving her, and washing the nasty stains out of her clothes…"

"I know," Ellie said, smiling sympathetically. "Both of us have seen Anna's best and worst qualities. We would be the best judges of her character."

When they came out of the bramble, their baskets brimming with blackberries, Ellie's mouth started watering at the thought of all the pastries and tarts they could make. Even as they were walking back to the house, she couldn't help but pop a few in her mouth.

When she and Mrs. Tuttle entered the back of the house through the servants' entrance, they heard an awful din coming from upstairs. It sounded as though a bunch of cats were being slung roughly against the walls—there was a terrible yowling, caterwauling cacophony that seemed to be coming from the main hall or the dining room. Exchanging panicked looks, Mrs. Tuttle and Ellie ran upstairs and could not have been more surprised by what they saw.

Frances, Anna, and Emma were all standing in a circle in the hall, bouncing up and down, laughing, snorting, giggling, screeching, and making all manner of excited noises. Mrs. Tuttle and Ellie exchanged looks again, this time with furrowed eyebrows and slightly disturbed expressions. Ellie had never seen anyone so seemingly happy sound so ridiculously unhinged. From the noise alone, one would not have guessed that elation was prompting the response.

Squinting her eyes, Ellie could make out a piece of paper clutched in Frances' hand. Her stomach sank like a stone and fell so hard and fast, she thought it had landed with a thud on the floor. Almost as if she'd heard it, Frances became aware of their presence and broke away from her daughters. With a look of furious triumph, she waved the paper crazily in the air like a madwoman.

"See this?" she screeched. "It is proof! Proof that the prince has chosen Anna to be his bride!"

Ellie's heart sank this time, as she considered the implications. What would Frances do with her now that they would be moving into the castle? She certainly wouldn't let Ellie keep Maplecroft Manor. Would she send her away to serve another family? Or would she insist on bringing her to the castle, where she'd have to suffer the humiliation of waiting on her stepmother hand and foot until the day one of them died? Ellie couldn't bear the thought, especially running the risk that Evander would see her and know that she was a servant.

"What does it say?" Mrs. Tuttle asked.

"It says we are to expect a royal visit tomorrow!" she replied. "It says that we should comport ourselves with decorum and expect the royal party to call upon us. Read it for yourselves!"

Flinging the document, Frances waved her hands in the air and went back to celebrate with her daughters. Mrs. Tuttle rushed to pick up the paper from the floor while Ellie merely stood with her fists clenched, hot angry tears brimming at the corners of her eyes. She wouldn't be dragged off to the castle to serve her stepmother. She would run away and find somewhere else to serve. Refusing to think of this as defeat, Ellie had her mind made up. This royal proposal would be a way for her to free herself: to cut ties with Frances Hardwick once and for all.

"Can you read this, Ellie?" Mrs. Tuttle asked. "I can't quite make out the words with all the swooping letters..."

Reluctantly, Ellie took the small card and then read it once, then twice, then several times after. Her tears began to dissipate as a small well of hope began to bubble up within. The card was very vague and did not mention Anna specifically. It merely said: *A messenger from the royal family will be coming to Maplecroft Manor tomorrow. Please gather all the ladies of your household, comport yourselves with dignity, and prepare to receive the royal messenger and a small party of guards.*

"What does it say?" Mrs. Tuttle whispered excitedly.

"It just says a royal messenger is coming," Ellie said. "And it's addressed to Frances, but it doesn't mention Anna by name. It says to gather all the ladies of the household and prepare to receive the royal messenger."

Instantly, Mrs. Tuttle gripped Ellie's arm hard and fixed her with an intense stare. Pulling her off to the side, she whispered,

"So, it could be you?"

Ellie floundered and tried to wriggle out of Mrs. Tuttle's vice-like grip. She didn't want to admit that that was her hope, but she did eventually concede it to Mrs. Tuttle, who couldn't help herself. She let out a squeal and then a whooping laugh, drawing the attention of Frances.

"What's so funny?" she barked. "What are you two laughing about?"

"Nothing, madam," Ellie answered quickly, turning back around. "We were only reading the letter and...and expressing joy for Anna."

Frances' eyes narrowed like the slits of a cat's. Ellie was sure that she didn't believe them, but on this, the day of her assumed triumph and exultation, she didn't feel like pushing it. Shrugging her shoulders, she turned back to her daughters and

98

then led them into the sitting room, telling them about the grand lives they were soon to lead. Ellie tucked the letter in her pocket and followed Mrs. Tuttle back down to the kitchen.

"Well, it certainly doesn't seem as though Emma is upset anymore," Ellie remarked. "She seems to have gotten over her irritation at not being picked."

"She probably figures that she benefits just as much," Mrs. Tuttle replied. "She'll get to make a brilliant match if her sister is a princess, and she'll be rich. Besides, I think Frances would have popped her in the mouth if she had continued acting sour about it…"

Ellie chuckled. "You're probably right about that," she conceded. "Frances certainly doesn't tolerate other people being in a different mood than she is. She can't abide it."

"Ellie," Mrs. Tuttle said seriously. "Do you know what I think? I think that royal message is meant for you. I think when they come tomorrow, they're going to come looking for you."

Ellie waved a dismissive hand. "No, it's probably Anna. I didn't talk that much to the prince…"

"Doesn't matter," Mrs. Tuttle said. "You're more intelligent than she is, you're much more interesting to talk to, and you're far lovelier than she is by a hundredfold!"

"Yes, but she's higher born than I am," Ellie pointed out. "Her mother is a baronetess in her own right."

"And your mother was the daughter of a baron!" Mrs. Tuttle countered. "Your pedigree is as good as hers. And if the prince should choose you, then he would take control of your father's estate. You could make the baronetess a penniless servant if you wanted!"

"What?" Ellie said, confused. "Why would the prince take over? Wouldn't he have to pay out an annuity?"

"By any normal standards a man might," Mrs. Tuttle argued. "But he's the prince. What he says goes. And once he marries you, his status as son-in-law and only man of the household would entitle him to full rights over the estate. The baronetess wouldn't be able to lift a legal finger in her defense."

Mrs. Tuttle started cackling at the thought, and Ellie briefly relished in the vision of throwing Frances out on her fat bottom. *Fend for yourself,* she'd say. But in truth, she didn't know if she'd be able to do such a thing if it came down to it.

"Oh, I just know it's you, Ellie!" Mrs. Tuttle exclaimed. "Oh, I'm going to start cooking immediately! I'll make a blackberry cobbler—no, blackberry puff pastries! Yes, that way I can serve them easily to everyone! Oh, it's a day to celebrate— why not make both?"

Mrs. Tuttle immediately began rummaging for her bowls and pans. Ellie smiled and helped her. For several hours, they baked peaceably, the oven eventually filling the whole house with the warming smell of flour and sweet blackberries. Ellie tried not to think too much about the announcement. For all she knew, the entire scenario was moot because the prince had chosen Anna. There was nothing for it but to wait until tomorrow.

But as she went up to her loft in the attic, Ellie found that her mind would not stop racing with thoughts, and she tossed and turned all night in anticipation of what the next day would bring. As she finally drifted into unconsciousness in the middle of the night, her last thoughts, though, were of marrying Evander, and not the prince.

Chapter Eight

If the Shoe Fits

THE next morning, Frances and her daughters were all too nervous to eat their breakfast. And in that regard, Ellie found she had something in common with her stepfamily.

"Come, Ellie, you must eat *something*," Mrs. Tuttle nagged. "You don't want to go around all day on an empty stomach. It'll make things worse."

Eventually, she had eaten a small piece of toast and a few bites of egg, only to appease Mrs. Tuttle.

"At least drink your tea!" the older woman nipped. "The hot will do your belly some good."

She had been right in that, as Ellie began to feel a bit stronger, the warmth from the tea spreading through her belly and flooding her veins. All morning, she couldn't stop thinking about the royal messenger, and what information he would bring. Ellie's entire future hinged upon that one moment. Would she be the chosen one, or would Anna?

In a crazy moment of doubt, Ellie started to wonder if she had made a mountain out of a molehill. What if the royal message wasn't related to the prince's marriage proposal at all? What if it was just an offer for Anna and Emma to come to court? What if it was something pertaining to Frances' standing as a baronetess? Ellie had pulled out the card and went over the

102

wording again and again and again. It was so vague it could have meant any of those things.

Ellie could only hope that it *was* pertaining to the prince's proposal, given that they had received it so shortly following the royal announcement.

"Let's go over the protocol once again, shall we?" Frances said, once breakfast had been cleared out.

"Anna and Emma and I will be in the drawing room all day, waiting for them to come. Ellie, you and Mrs. Tuttle will go about your daily chores as normal until you hear me ring my bell. Once you hear that, you are to prepare to answer the door. Mrs. Tuttle, you should do that—you have more experience. Then, I will show them to the sitting room, and you both will stay here, just behind this curtain in the drawing room, should they need anything. Mrs. Tuttle, you said you had pastries for our guests?"

"Yes, madam, I do," she answered.

"Excellent. You will serve them after the proposal or offer of marriage has been made. And we will want champagne, for toasting, as well."

"Very good, madam."

"After that, I am not sure what will happen," Frances said airily, espousing a sort of aristocratic ennui. Ellie grimaced—it was sickeningly overconfident.

"But you must watch carefully for my cues," she continued. "Chances are we will retire to the castle for the night, in which case you will carry on normally here. Once Anna has settled in, we will visit the subject of your service. As mother of the princess, I will likely be gifted a far better settlement of land, in which case Maplecroft Manor might be sold or granted to someone else. So, we will decide what to do with you all in due time. Thankfully, there's only three of you to worry about!"

With a tinkle of laughter, she waved a hand to dismiss them and once they were a safe distance away, Mrs. Tuttle mocked her with a sour face.

"Who does she think she is?" she demanded. "Her daughter isn't even royal yet—might not be for all we know—and she's making all these grand plans and pronouncements. And ooh, it burns me up that she thinks she can just get rid of you! You're her stepdaughter, not just some servant! She'll have to provide better for you than *that*. She won't get away with it!"

"Calm yourself, Mrs. Tuttle," Ellie said easily. "Trust me, I have no problem with her trying to get rid of me. I don't want to be forced to live on her charity, if it comes to it. If Anna is made the fiancée of the prince today, I'm leaving Maplecroft Manor."

"What?" Mrs. Tuttle said, in shock.

"Yes, I've made up my mind. I won't stay and work for her, no matter where she goes. And if she won't let me stay here, then I've got to go."

Mrs. Tuttle closed her mouth, straightened herself up and said,

"Well, not without me, you're not."

And that was the end of it. Mrs. Tuttle wouldn't hear another word about it. So, it was settled that if the offer was made to Anna, the three servants of Maplecroft Manor—Ellie, and Mr. and Mrs. Tuttle—would disappear in the night, off to better lives.

FOR several hours, Ellie and Mrs. Tuttle went about their chores, but at some point, they were done for the afternoon, so they sat in the sitting room, on the other side of the curtain from Frances, Anna, and Emma. They could hear them bickering, but paid them no mind, instead choosing to play cards.

At about half past three, they heard the frantic ringing of Frances' bell, and they both sprang into action. Ellie felt her nerves return with a frenzied urgency.

"They're coming!" Frances shouted. "They're coming up the driveway! They're here! Mrs. Tuttle! Mrs. Tuttle!"

Ellie watched as Mrs. Tuttle disappeared around the corner to answer the door. Standing behind the curtain, Ellie pressed her ear as close to it as she could, and even worked up the courage to peek through the slit. She heard the door open, and then the booming, unmistakable voice of the Grand Duke of Talbany, Lord Robert Cecil.

She saw him greet Frances and her stepsisters. There were a few other lanky lads behind him, all his clerks and squires, no doubt. But the prince was not there, and neither were the king and queen. Their absence was noticeable, and Ellie could have sworn she saw Frances' face blanch with disappointment. When she motioned to lead them into the sitting room, Ellie darted away quickly, going back in the hallway that looped around to the main entrance hall.

Meeting up with Mrs. Tuttle, they waited until everyone had gone in the sitting room and Frances had drawn the curtain again. Creeping into the drawing room, Mrs. Tuttle and Ellie exchanged nervous glances. They didn't know what anything meant so far, so they crept as close to the curtain as they could, eavesdropping.

Once all the introductions had been made, they could hear the authoritative voice of the Grand Duke.

"I've noticed there are just the three of you," he said bluntly. "Are there any other ladies of the household?"

"Why, no, my lord, it's just me and my daughters," Frances replied tightly.

"Hmm," the Grand Duke mumbled. "Well, as you have probably gathered, His Royal Highness Prince Fillip has chosen his bride from a...uh, selection of ladies of Hartmere. You were all at the ball, I presume?"

"Of course we were, my lord," she said. "Anna was selected to speak to His Royal Highness and she kept him entertained for more than ten whole minutes!"

"Indeed," the Grand Duke said gruffly. "Well, the prince has chosen his bride from the ladies at the ball. His choice is a woman from this household, at Maplecroft Manor, which is why we are here."

Ellie could practically hear the sharp intake of breath from Frances and Anna. They were so sure their moment was about to come.

"The thing is...I'm not sure his intended bride is here among us," the Grand Duke said.

"What?" Frances blurted. "Well, that's quite impossible! My daughters and I are the only ladies of Maplecroft Manor, I assure you."

106

"The prince has decreed that a lady by the name of Eleanor Katherine Marchand become his bride and princess," the Grand Duke declared. "If she should choose to accept his royal proposal, of course," he added blandly. "He has requested that we come here on his behalf and extend his offer of marriage to Miss Eleanor Marchand. So, I ask you—where is she?"

Immediately, Mrs. Tuttle's hand shot across and grabbed Ellie's wrist in another vice-like grip. But neither of them dared to move a muscle. Ellie could feel her heart beat rising faster and faster—and then slowing...slowing to a standstill, as everything seemed to freeze for a moment. Even the dust in the air stopped falling and no one breathed as Frances Hardwick absorbed the full enormity of what the Grand Duke had said.

Ellie would have given anything to be a fly on the wall, to see her stepmother's face. Trapped and caught completely unawares, she would have to exercise extreme self-discipline to keep her composure in the company of the Grand Duke, his clerks, and the royal guard.

"E-Eleanor Marchand?" Frances repeated, dumbstruck. "Why, yes, that's my daughter here!" she let out a nervous laugh. "I introduced her as Anna, because that's what we've called her for years, short for Eleanor. But yes, her full name is Eleanor Katherine Marchand."

Mrs. Tuttle swore under her breath and Ellie knew that she was fixing to burst in and set the record straight, but she grabbed the housekeeper and held her fast. The Grand Duke wasn't an idiot—surely, he would see straight through her stepmother's pathetic attempt.

"Anna," the Grand Duke stated. "Seems an odd nickname for 'Eleanor'. But the prince asked that we do one other thing, to confirm the identity of his intended bride. He gave us the shoe she was wearing on the night of the ball. It seems that she must have lost it during the course of the evening. At any rate, he assured us that this slipper would fit the woman he chose. Shall we see if this shoe fits your daughter?"

"W-why, certainly," Frances fumbled. "Anna, go on, take off your shoe."

At this point, Ellie couldn't help but peek through the slit in the curtain. Anna was sitting on the far end of the couch, next to her mother and Emma. She leaned forward to slide out of her own slipper. Ellie had to suppress a snigger at her large feet. They would never fit in Leonora Marchand's shoe.

The Grand Duke seemed to know this as well, as he took the slipper from one of his clerks, eyeing Anna's feet dubiously. Nevertheless, he knelt and presented the shoe. Anna tried to put her foot in with some difficulty—her foot was not only longer than Ellie's, but wider as well. It was almost comical, seeing her whole heel hang off the edge, and watching Frances' horrified, panicked face.

"Well, Anna's feet tend to swell when she's under pressure," Frances said, in a last-ditch effort. "It's an unfortunate family trait, I'm afraid to say."

"Madam," the Grand Duke said sharply. "Come, her foot clearly does not fit this slipper, swollen or otherwise. That seems very clear. Now, where is Eleanor Marchand?"

"This *is* Eleanor Marchand!" she insisted shrilly. "It's clear what's happened! That's not Anna's slipper. His Royal Highness must have been mistaken and picked up someone else's shoe."

"Madam, enough of this nonsense," the Grand Duke said shortly. "It's quite clear that your daughter Anna is not Eleanor, and thus not His Royal Highness' intended bride. Now, where is Miss Eleanor Marchand? When she spoke with the prince, she gave this estate as her residence."

"The girl must have been lying!" Frances blurted. "There is no one here by that name, I can assure you! She must have been some sort of impostor. Is that really the kind of girl His Royal Highness should marry? Perhaps you should tell him of her deception and remind him of Annalise Marchand's virtues..."

"Madam, please!" the Grand Duke said, holding up an impatient hand. "That is enough. If no one else is here, then we will take our leave."

"Wait!"

Ellie was confused, as she heard two sets of voices yell this at once—one was Frances' voice, the other Mrs. Tuttle's. And before she knew what was happening, Mrs. Tuttle had thrown open the curtain and barged into the sitting room.

"My lord, please," she said. "But there *is* an Eleanor Marchand who lives here. She's standing right there. She is the daughter of the late Cornelius Marchand and Lady Leonora Penwhistle."

All eyes instantly whipped to Ellie, who stood on the threshold of the sitting room, her knees weak like jelly. She thought she would faint on the spot, but Mrs. Tuttle led her gently into the room and bade her sit in one of the chairs nearest to the Grand Duke.

"Ah, yes," the Grand Duke murmured. "Yes, I remember you."

Her throat was so tight that she choked on her words and merely swallowed, looking stupid and waifish, she was sure. The Grand Duke knelt again and held out the slipper. In one breathless moment, Ellie slid her foot in the shoe. It was a perfect fit. The Grand Duke looked back up at her beaming, as he doffed his cap.

"Miss Marchand," he said. "His Royal Highness, Prince Fillip Westenra of Trenway, would like to offer you his hand in marriage. Do you accept?"

Before Ellie could say anything, Frances burst forward, her face thunderstruck.

"Excuse me, my lord," she said hotly. "But this cannot be right. This girl is a servant in my household. She is not worthy to be a princess, and she attended the ball without my permission or knowledge. Worse than that, she tricked and deceived the prince by lying about who she really is! You would not want His Royal Highness to marry a *servant*, after all!"

The Grand Duke looked back and forth between Frances and Ellie, a shocked expression on his face.

"Is this true?" he demanded.

"No!" Ellie said quickly, feeling her anger and courage flare up. "With all due respect, Lady Hardwick is not being completely truthful. I am the daughter of Cornelius Marchand

110

and Lady Leonora Penwhistle. My stepmother forced me into servitude following my father's death. But I am not a servant by birth."

The Grand Duke looked back to Frances.

"Madam?" he prompted. "What do you have to say to this?"

Frances floundered, her mouth gaping open and shut, at a loss of what to say.

"Miss Marchand is penniless," she said. "Her inheritance is spent—there was nothing left for her but to serve in the house, to earn her keep."

Ellie was about to speak up for herself again, but the Grand Duke had heard enough.

"Gregory!" he shouted. "Gregory, what is the age at which a minor can control and access his or her inheritance?"

One of his clerks, Gregory, spoke up instantly.

"Eighteen, my lord," he answered.

"And how old are you, Eleanor?" the Grand Duke asked.

"Seventeen," she answered.

The Grand Duke looked back at Frances with a smug expression, having bested her.

"Madam, I think we've heard enough now," he said. "I will be taking Miss Marchand back to Bellbroke Castle. When she has settled in, I am sure she will contact you with further instructions."

"Further instructions?" Frances blustered. "What does that mean?"

"As closest kin of the future princess, it is up to Miss Marchand and His Royal Highness to determine where you shall live and what shall become of you. And if I may make a suggestion, madam, if I were you, I would try to get in your stepdaughter's good graces until then. By my account of the present situation, I would not want to be in your shoes."

He looked down at her feet, which were nearly as large as her daughter's.

"My lord, I must protest!" Frances cried. "This cannot be right! Ellie is not suited at all to be princess and..."

"Please, madam, enough," the Grand Duke said again. "It is not your place to determine who is and is not suitable to marry His Royal Highness. He is perfectly capable of making that decision himself. Now, if you will excuse us..."

The Grand Duke motioned for his clerks to follow him, and then instructed the guards to keep her stepfamily in the sitting room. Holding his hand out to Ellie, he escorted her into the drawing room where he told her to gather her belongings so they could leave.

"Strictly speaking, I had orders to leave you at your house until summoned to officially meet the royal family," he whispered to her as they walked. "Ordinarily, you would reside here until the wedding, but under the present circumstances, I think it best to take you from this place henceforth."

"I...I appreciate that, my lord," she said, her voice still shaky. "Could I perhaps ask one other favor, as a measure of safety?"

"Of course," he said, looking mildly puzzled.

112

"I would like to bring Mrs. Tuttle with me," she said, gesturing to the housekeeper. "She is my dearest companion and the closest I have to a family. Also, I am afraid of what my stepmother will do to her in my absence...for speaking out and revealing my identity. Her husband, Mr. Tuttle, our groundskeeper, should come as well."

The Grand Duke nodded his head without pause.

"Absolutely, of course," he said. "Whatever you wish, Miss Marchand. If they will pack their belongings as quickly as possible, we will leave forthwith to Bellbroke."

Ellie smiled and thanked the Grand Duke. Her nerves were still tingling as she climbed up the ladder to the attic for the last time. Looking around with a delayed sense of happiness, Ellie realized that her life had changed in the best possible way. It still felt surreal, but as she gathered everything she wanted to bring—which wasn't much—she kept forcing herself to accept it bit-by-bit.

She was going to be a princess. Prince Fillip had chosen *her* to be his bride, and instead of looking down the barrel at a life of endless servitude, she was now facing the dizzyingly joyful prospect of life at Bellbroke Castle.

Chapter Nine

A Royal Engagement

IT was as if she was floating in a bubble as they rode to Penchester Palace. Everything still felt surreal, as if it wasn't really happening, just a sweet fantasy she was imagining in the garden at Maplecroft Manor. Ellie looked out the window of the carriage and saw the churning gray waters of the River Morrow, saw the boats and barges bobbing on the surface as they tried to tie in before the storm hit. She had a sudden memory of her father, and how he used to be one of those men aboard the boats. She remembered his tall, proud ship *The Cromwellian*, and how he had brought her on the deck on a fine spring day when she was little and held her hands to help her steer it. They had gone down the river on his boat, all the way down the inlets that led to the open sea.

"Think of the ship like your life, Ellie," he used to tell her. "You are always the captain. You always get to steer and choose where you want to take your ship. Always."

She had to stop herself from tearing up. It was supposed to be the happiest day of her life. Her father wouldn't have wanted her to cry and make a fuss about him. She turned to Mrs. Tuttle, who would often play this game with her.

"If my father were alive," she started. "What would he say?"

The older woman laughed. "A few choice words of surprise, I believe!" she exclaimed. "No, he would say...*be careful.* Yes, that's what he would say."

"Exactly what I was thinking," Ellie answered. "He would want me to be careful with my head and my heart."

Cornelius Marchand wanted the best for his daughter, and Ellie knew better than anyone that he had equipped her to handle life's most daunting challenges so that she would be able to have the best. But he had always tempered pride with pragmatism, and always looked at life through the lens of caution.

Which was why, as they arrived at Penchester, in the same courtyard as she had on the night of the ball, Ellie began to view her drastic change in circumstance with more than just a grain of salt. The same question she had originally asked came back to haunt her: *why would the prince marry a commoner?* When she stepped out of the carriage in her tattered dress and old clogs, she knew that no matter the scope of the grandeur that she was about to walk into, she would have to keep her wits about her.

ALMOST as soon as she had set foot inside Bellbroke Castle, she was scooped up by maids and brought to a bedroom where they had immediately drawn a bath. Mr. and Mrs. Tuttle were taken to another area of the castle. The Grand Duke had explained that because they were servants, they would not be treated to the same degree as Ellie. Even though they were like her parents to her, birth mattered more to the royal family than affinity. Ellie's parents were dead—to them there were no substitutes, unless they had been born with the aristocratic silver spoon in their mouths.

While Ellie found this highly unfair and upsetting, she realized that even as servants of the castle, they would have a much better life than they had ever had at Maplecroft Manor. With so many other servants, they wouldn't have to work as much. And Ellie vowed that as soon as she was technically a princess, she would buy them a house where they could live in leisure. Perhaps she would send them back to Maplecroft Manor. After all, she certainly wasn't going to allow her stepmother and stepsisters to continue living there.

When she had been thoroughly scrubbed, and laced up in a dress, she was instructed to meet the Grand Duke in the corridor.

"Ah, yes," he said, extending his arm. "This is how I remember seeing you, Miss Marchand, on the night of the ball."

"Do you still think that I burst through the curtain on purpose?" she asked.

The Grand Duke chuckled. "That depends," he answered. "On whether you thought it would work. Yet...here you are."

"Your question is a trap," she declared. "I had no intention of interrupting the prince's interview with that girl..."

"Miss Scrimshaw," the Grand Duke supplied. "And don't expect to become fast friends with *her*. She's weaseled her way back into the court as one of the queen's ladies-in-waiting. As soon as she sees you, she'll recognize you."

"Great," Ellie muttered. "I suppose she'll believe my story the same way you did."

Chuckling again, the Grand Duke patted her arm.

"Probably," he admitted. "But you seem to be a sharp girl, Miss Marchand, if you don't mind me saying. You'll need to be sharp and strong to be a princess. Based on what I've seen so far, you'll do just fine. You'll learn how princesses deal with the Miss Scrimshaw's of the world."

They had walked through the ballroom where Ellie had danced twice with Evander, and multiple times with the other two courtiers. Her stomach twisted in knots as she wondered if she would meet Evander again. Would he be disappointed that she was to marry the prince? Part of her hoped he would be...it would be a sign at least that he felt as she did, for there was a part of her that was disappointed as well. She couldn't stop thinking about their kiss. It had been her first kiss, and she remembered it with such vivid detail that it made her knees weak and her head dizzy.

Once through the ballroom, they had entered the doors that the king and queen had come through on the night of the ball. Ellie had never been in this part of the castle before. Her palms were starting to sweat as her stomach fluttered nervously. They walked through three very large and ornate salons and then they came upon a massive set of double doors. The Grand Duke told her to wait as he went to announce her.

Ellie took a deep breath and smoothed the skirts of her dress. She felt as grand as she did on the night of the ball, but underneath the burgundy silk brocade she knew that she was just Ellie. This made her feel naked and exposed, even though she was layered in rich fabrics and jewels.

The great doors opened with a shocking lurch and the slow sound of wood creaking on the hinges. Ellie barely seemed to register the great boom of the Grand Duke's voice ringing through the hall, announcing her name. She felt a prod from behind, as if she was a cow, and like a cow, she stepped forward, following the scarlet runner of carpet that stretched out before her like the tongue of a serpent.

The thrones of the King and Queen were at the far end of the hall above her, and the room was empty to either side, light flooding in from the windows. She could see the glow of blue on the eastern side, and knew that the view of the lake from this room must be spectacular. Straight ahead of her, the King and Queen sat on their thrones, and a young figure stood on the stairs just below them, undoubtedly the prince.

As Ellie came closer, she thought she saw something vaguely familiar and unexpected about him, in the way he stood and in his visage. She bowed low, held her position and then stood back up and let her eyes wander up to the prince, to get a closer look at him.

She could not have been more shocked than if she were to stare in the face of a great lion or a monkey. And it took every ounce of self-control that she possessed not to gasp aloud and step back in surprise. By the grin on the prince's face, he seemed to be waiting for that exact reaction.

"Surprised?" he asked, coyly.

She looked him up and down, surveying his fashion and posture. There could be no doubt that he was the prince. But it was not the man she had met in the antechamber on the night of the ball. Not the man she had discussed cats and astronomy with. No, the man standing in front of her was none other than Sir Leopold Evander Wallingford.

"I wanted to make sure we met alone first," he said, gesturing to the empty room. "So that I could introduce myself properly. Or rather *re-introduce*," he added, with another boyish grin.

"Evander?" she echoed hollowly. "Y-you are the prince?"

"Yes!" he exclaimed, beaming. "A welcome surprise, I hope. Or did you, perchance, fall in love with my impostor?"

"No, I didn't," she assured him.

"Good. That would have been rather unfortunate and awkward," he said, his smile fading. "I hate to think that I tricked you in this manner," he continued. "Sadly, it was necessary, to see which girl was truly worthy. I needed to be able to mingle freely, and my status would not have allowed me to do so otherwise. You do understand?"

Ellie nodded her head, feeling dizzy and overwhelmed. For the past several hours she had felt conflicted by her undeniable attraction to Evander and the reality that she must marry the prince. Knowing that they were one and the same...it was almost too good to be true.

Seeing her white, shocked face, Evander came down and put his hands on her arms, steadying her.

"Ellie Kate?" he said softly. "Are you all right? Please say you forgive me. I did not mean to deceive you."

"Please," she said. "You have nothing to apologize for. It just...took me by surprise...that is all."

Evander continued to look at her directly, with concern in his eyes. After a moment, he smiled and nodded his head.

"Well," he said, turning back to his parents. "Now that the question of my identity is settled, please allow me to introduce you to my father, King Richard III, and my mother, Queen Adelaide."

Taking her hand, Evander led her up the stairs so that she could kiss the hand of his mother and father and bow before them. Up close, Ellie saw that Evander more closely resembled his mother. He had her coloring, the light hair and blue eyes, and overall his face favored hers. But he did have his father's strong jaw and chin. King Richard looked rather worse for the wear. Ellie did not know much about politics or the royal family, but she did know that King Richard branded himself a robust leader and experienced general.

Based on looks alone, Ellie assessed that it must have been true. His skin was tanned and leathery, his nose crooked as if it had been broken several times, and his black beard was peppered with sprinkles of gray...from stress, perhaps? Ellie knew it could not have been easy running a kingdom. Looking at both King Richard and Queen Adelaide, Ellie couldn't help but think they were an odd couple, a mismatched pair certainly by appearances alone. And while Queen Adelaide was very fair and beautiful, she still wore that sour look on her face that rather spoiled her features.

From that, Ellie wondered if the queen was happy in her role as wife to the king. If she had to bet, she would say not. After thinking this, Ellie had to stop herself for a moment. Perhaps she was jumping to conclusions. After all, this was a hasty assessment based on mere glances.

"We are pleased to meet you, Miss Eleanor Marchand," King Richard said in a low, gravelly voice. "My son sang your praises immediately after the ball. She is the only girl who is truly interesting and pure of heart, he said."

Ellie blushed, flashing a glance at Evander who grabbed her hand and squeezed it supportively.

"You are to be congratulated, Miss Marchand," the king continued. "We have been trying for ages to get my son to settle down with a wife. It has been…an ordeal…to say the least. Nevertheless, we are glad that he has finally made his choice and that he is happy in that choice."

Ellie felt a little uncomfortable by the implications in what he said. She had the feeling that the king and queen were not entirely pleased with her, despite what they said. It was as she had feared—this method of matchmaking was too unorthodox. A prince should marry a true princess, born to royal blood.

"Shall we take a walk through the gardens?" Evander asked her. "We will reconvene with my mother and father for dinner tonight, but I thought we should spend the afternoon together."

Ellie nodded wordlessly, and with that, they were dismissed from the imperious, intimidating presence of the king and queen. Ellie draped her arm on Evander's and the further they got from the thrones, the more elated she began to feel. The realization that Evander *was* the prince was beginning to truly sink in, and she couldn't help but beam and grin broadly.

EVANDER led her out to the hanging gardens, the ones she had seen on the night of the ball. There were a thousand questions on her mind, but she felt too nervous to ask a single one of them. Evander stood beside her with a beatific grin, the cologne from his neck and clothes sending shivers down her spine.

"I know all of this must come as a shock," he said, sitting down on the bench by the fountain. "I hope that you can think of me the way you did before…on the night of the ball."

"You have a different name," she said flatly. "Who was your impostor that night? Is he Evander?"

"No," he answered. "That man is named Julian Marnier. He is a courtier. Evander is one of my middle names."

"Fillip," she said, tasting the name on her tongue. "I think it does suit you better."

"Does it?" he said, beaming. "Well, different name or no, I am still the same person you met and danced with on the night of the ball. The same man you kissed…"

"Yes," she said, blushing. "And I got rather chewed out for it. My godmother, Lady Penelope, said I was spoiling my chances with the prince. Little did she know!"

Fillip laughed aloud. "Yes, little did she know you were sealing the deal with the prince..."

"Seriously, why did you pick me?" she asked. "Out of the hundreds of girls that were there...and you know about my past now. I'm not noble and I lived the past four years of my life as a servant."

"Ellie Kate, none of that matters to me," he said reassuringly.

"It might matter to your mother and father."

"They've agreed to my choice; there'll be no backing out now."

"So, there was some objection?"

"Ellie Kate, I chose you because you didn't come for a crown," he explained. "Out of all the girls I talked to, you were the only one who just wanted to have a good time. You weren't preening and simpering like all the rest. You were genuine. I could see your personality shining through, and that attracted me above all else. We may barely know each other, but you were the only one I wanted to get to know."

She blushed again. "Well, you certainly have a way with words," she said. "I want to get to know you too. I couldn't stop thinking about you after the ball."

"Really?" he said, flashing another grin. "Well, and then there's the obvious fact that you were the most beautiful girl at the ball. There was an undeniable attraction...a tugging, like a

123

pull that I just couldn't ignore. Do you know what I mean? Like sparks flying between us…"

"Yes, I know what you mean," she said faintly, as he reached out to take her hand. His lips brushed her cheek, and then her mouth, and suddenly they were kissing again as they had on the night of the ball.

"And that," Fillip said, pulling away. "At least we know *that* works."

Ellie smiled, the tips of her toes tingling. But she was not good in situations like these—at least she didn't feel as though she was. She had never really been in this position before, but she felt that every inch of her skin was burning and she had to do something to stop it.

"How does the castle float like this?" she asked, randomly.

"What?"

"How does it stay afloat?" she repeated. "It was one of the things I noticed at the ball. The castle is on the water and it doesn't look like there's any land beneath it."

"See, this is another reason I chose you," he said, laughing. "What other girl would ask a question like that? You're right, there is no land beneath the castle. It is built on a foundation of several stone pillars that are embedded deep in the clay at the bottom of the lake. There are wooden poles as well, to provide additional support. Every few months or so, divers are sent down to check on the moorings and repair any damages."

"Ah, I see," she said. "Stone pillars…it must have been very difficult to build."

124

"I'm sure it was," he said. "It was built over a hundred years ago."

"Over a hundred years!" Ellie exclaimed. "But why build on a lake? Why go through all the trouble when you could simply build on the land?"

"For defensive purposes," Fillip explained. "The more inaccessible a castle is, the better. That's why many castles on land will have a moat built around it, with water pumped in. Water is a very effective deterrent for invasions. The way that Bellbroke Castle is structured, it's virtually impossible for an enemy to take. You can't launch a siege on water, and while the distance is such that you could shoot from catapults on the land, there are still no good places to position. You'd have to take Penchester first, fire the catapults from the shore, and still find a way to take the castle from the water, which would be very difficult."

"But what if they launched the siege from the other side?" Ellie asked. "The back of Bellbroke nearly abuts the land; it's not directly in the middle of the lake. If they came from that side, they wouldn't have to take Penchester first and it would be easier to take the castle."

"Easier, perhaps, but by no means *easy*," Fillip countered, looking at her in a new light. "You have a strategist's mind. Are you always so analytical?"

"A bit, yes," she answered. "I suppose it comes from my cheekiness. My stepmother always said that my tongue and my cheek would always get me in trouble. *Don't be smart,* she'd always snap."

"What a horrid, odious woman," Fillip remarked, shuddering. "I had the distinct displeasure of meeting her on the night of the ball. She tried to bribe the Grand Duke, spewing crocodile tears and making a scene, and then she snapped her fingers at me and demanded I get her a glass of champagne."

Ellie snorted. "I wonder if she'll even recognize your face."

"Oh, I'm sure she will," he said. "I told her flatly that I wasn't her servant and that if she wanted a glass of champagne, she should move her fat arse and get it herself. And I advised that she quit wasting her time with the Grand Duke. You should have seen the look on her face!"

"I would've given nearly anything," Ellie said. "It must have been golden."

"Speaking of your stepmother, what are we to do with her?" he asked, pensively.

"Oh, please, let's discuss that another time," she said. "I can't give it proper thought right now, and I should like to make sure I do it just right."

Fillip nodded his head. "As you wish."

Looking behind her at the fountain, Ellie was suddenly reminded of the old man she had seen, the one who had known her name. His words came back to her with striking clarity: *You're the one he'll choose.* How could he have known that?

"Is there an old man who lives here?" she asked. "I saw an old man here on the night of the ball. He was sitting here at this fountain."

"What?" Fillip said, furrowing his brows. "An old man? Oh, it must have been old Terry, short for Tiresias. He's my great uncle."

"Ah," Ellie said. "Well...he said some very odd things to me."

"Oh, I imagine he did," Fillip said. "Terry is always saying odd things. My mother thinks he's blessed with the second sight."

"That may not be far from the truth," Ellie said. "He knew who I was. He said my name, even though we had never been introduced, and he told me that I would be the one you'd choose."

"He said that?" Fillip laughed. "How shockingly prescient of him."

"I suppose he could have said it to dozens of girls," Ellie said. "And the fact that he was right doesn't really mean anything. But how could he have known my name? He might have had access to the list of names, sure, but how would he know which face to put it to? I've never met him in my life."

"No, it is odd," Fillip agreed. "But Terry is known for saying odd things. You must take him with a grain of salt, though. Often, he speaks nonsense and sometimes his gibberish is so pronounced, you can't make out a single word! But then there are other times...when what he says is...unsettling."

"He became upset," Ellie continued, thinking back to that night. "After he said my name, he became upset and asked me to forgive him. He seemed to think that he had wronged me, somehow."

127

Fillip shook his head. "Don't put too much stock in it," he advised. "My father says that Terry suffered a terrible fall in his youth and he's had to be cared for like a child ever since. He was a burden on my grandparents, and while he's mellowed a bit in his older age, he's still somewhat troublesome."

"And what does your mother say?"

Fillip sighed. "My mother has unorthodox views about...well, many things. But essentially, she thinks that Terry exists and floats among three planes of existence—the past, the present, and the future. So, when he says mostly odd or bizarre things, he could be referencing the distant past and future—one that we can't know so naturally it confuses us, and the other may be so obscure we might not know it or couldn't remember anyway. And then when he says those things that strike us particularly, he is referring to the present, like his seeming to know your name."

"And his knowing that you would choose me, that was in the future," Ellie said. "His comment about forgiveness would have to be from the future as well. But what could he possibly have done? Or will do...I guess...it's a bit ominous."

Fillip waved a dismissive hand. "You're overthinking it," he said. "My mother has been obsessed with Terry's yammering for years, but it hasn't gotten her anywhere. Fixating on future prophecies can be self-fulfilling. If you go around looking for something, of course you'll find it, and you may inject meaning in something that would have been otherwise meaningless. If Terry misplaces one of your jewels or says something unkind about you, you'll think that's what he was referring to, and it might not have been. It might have just been a delusion from his addled mind..."

"Perhaps," Ellie conceded.

"Come," Fillip said, standing up. "Let's take a turn, shall we? There's a spot at the top where you can see the whole lake spread out around you. It's dazzling, like flying."

Unable to resist, Ellie took his hand and they walked through the gardens, up to the very top. Fillip stood behind her and wrapped his arms around her waist. Perhaps it was from being up so high, or perhaps it was Fillip's touch, but Ellie felt breathless staring down at the rippling water of the lake below her. The rays of the setting sun made the water sparkle, and Ellie felt as though she could see for miles ahead.

"How far does the lake go on?" she asked.

"Oh, for miles and miles yet," Fillip answered. "About seven miles south, the lake takes a turn, but right off the shore there is a town called Aschenputtel. Once it turns east, the lake goes on for another two miles or so."

Leaning against the solid frame of the prince, Ellie continued to gaze out upon the lake, but her mind was still churning, thinking about his great uncle, Terry. Old and addled he might be, but he had known her name, and that was something that Ellie's logical and analytical mind just couldn't get past.

Chapter Ten

The King's Justice

FILLIP led Ellie through the labyrinthine corridors of Bellbroke Castle to the main dining hall. Another massive room opened up before her, with a high vaulted ceiling, a large roaring fireplace, and the longest table Ellie had ever seen in her life.

"We're going to eat here?" she asked. "We'll have to shout to hear each other."

"No, no, we'll eat in the smaller chamber tonight," Fillip explained. "This will be the table we eat when we're entertaining large parties. And then there's the Trencher Hall where we'll normally eat when court is in session. There's a table up on a dais where we eat, and many tables below for the courtiers."

"It's all so complicated," Ellie said. "And to think, just yesterday I was eating on the wooden kitchen counter where Mrs. Tuttle and I prepared food. We didn't always have time to sit down and eat...mostly bites here and there."

"Well, you'll have plenty of time to sit and eat now," he said. "More time than anyone ever needs, trust me. You'll make up for all those years of standing. Court feasts can last hours, what with all the dancing and music and speeches. Even tonight's dinner has twelve courses."

"Twelve?" Ellie repeated, her mouth gaping. "Why would anyone need to eat *twelve* courses?"

"I don't know," Fillip said. "It does seem excessive, doesn't it? But that's the standard number for a celebratory feast. It's not always so many. A normal day is five."

"Five courses?" she repeated, again. "That's still a bit much..."

"The trick is to take small bites of everything, so you'll have room for it all, not that I've ever had such a problem..." he admitted, grinning. "Mother says I have four stomachs, like a cow. But you'll want to at least take one bite at each course. It'll be considered rude otherwise, and trust me, Mother will be paying attention."

Great, Ellie thought to herself. Fillip's mother was too intimidating already. The added pressure of her watching everything she did, just waiting to sniff out any secrets or point out any slights...it was overwhelming.

Leading her over to the side of the dining hall, Fillip pulled back a curtain, revealing a strange octagonal door.

"For privacy," Fillip explained. "You can imagine why sometimes the royal family wants to be aloof."

As soon as he had opened the door, a surging swell of voices greeted her as she realized that everyone was already assembled. The room behind the strange octagonal door was still fairly large, about the size of three rooms at Maplecroft Manor. But it was still much smaller and cozier than the hall they had just come out of.

The king and queen were seated at opposite ends of a rectangular table that seemed to seat eight or ten. No shouting necessary at this table, Ellie thought, as Fillip escorted her to her chair. There were four other people and Ellie only recognized one of them—Fillip's great uncle Tiresias, or Terry, as he was called.

"Fillip, how good of you to join us," Queen Adelaide demurred. "For a moment, we thought you two had gotten lost in the gardens."

"It wouldn't be the first time, eh?" the king said, and the two men on either side of him laughed at his lascivious insinuation.

"Richard, please!" the queen hissed. "That is hardly appropriate and they barely know each other!"

Distinctly uncomfortable, Ellie felt as though she should speak up and defend herself, but at a look from Fillip, she settled back in her chair. She had been informed about the relations between a man and a woman. Her father had deferred explaining anything until a woman could be brought in the house, so it had been up to Frances to give the talk. She had made a rather blunt and rushed stab at it, so that there were a lot of gaps in Ellie's knowledge and a lot of questions left unanswered. But she had been able to gather the main gist, and it was such that innuendo did not go over her head.

"Introductions are in order," the queen continued. "Everyone, this is my son Fillip's choice of bride, the future princess, Eleanor Katherine Marchand. Eleanor, allow me to present Lord Roland Haldane, Duke of Vestfold and Viscount of Alesund, the king's brother. To his other side, Lord Edmund Tyburn, Earl of Castlewick, the king's cousin. There is also the king's sister Lady Jehanne Westenra Pendlevere, Duchess of Corcoast and Countess of Marlborough. And finally, to my right, is the king's uncle, Lord Tiresias Westenra, former Duke of Vestfold, Baron de Villiers."

Ellie felt dizzy from the string of names and titles, but she tried to match the name to everyone's face. The king had a brother, a cousin, a sister, and an uncle who were important enough to attend this dinner. Did Fillip have any siblings? She felt foolish asking, and decided that she would ask Fillip later, when they were alone. She also noticed that the queen's family was absent, but then she remembered that her family was overseas, in Kronstadt.

It struck Ellie very suddenly, how alone Queen Adelaide must feel. And then, it struck her that she would probably feel the same way. After all, what family did Ellie have to stick by her through this? Only Mr. and Mrs. Tuttle, and when would she see them again? They certainly wouldn't be allowed to be at her side for any function or dinner. And as for her stepmother and stepsisters...well, she obviously wasn't going to have them anywhere near her.

Suddenly it felt as though Ellie was staring at a version of herself, in the distant future. That would be her someday: surrounded by her husband, the king's family. Ellie could only hope that she and Fillip would not grow apart as the king and queen obviously had.

She stood up and bowed to all of them, expressing her gratitude to the king and queen, and her pleasure in meeting all of them. Her eyes went to Tiresias first, as soon as she sat down, but the old man was oblivious to her, fixed in concentration on his napkin, which he was struggling to put over his shoulder.

The first course was brought out—a kind of strange soup that was orange, and the conversation vacillated between war strategy, diplomacy, and old family spats that were still being hashed out. As the conversation was mostly taken over by King Richard and his side of the table—his brother Roland, cousin Edmund, and sister Jehanne, Ellie observed quietly that they were like a power quartet. Adelaide was all but excluded from the inner circle, and Fillip, who interjected now and then, was still like a young pup trying to find his place in the pack. Richard boomingly acknowledged his son several times, and laughed at a few of the comments Fillip made, but he was still mainly enmeshed with the adult members of his family. Fillip remained on the fringes, eagerly trying to fit in, but shunted like he was still a child. Tiresias didn't utter a single word, but ate with a ravenous fury that was startling to Ellie. He was thin and frail, yet he ate like a young man in his prime.

One other thing that Ellie noticed was that King Richard was extremely loud. His normal speaking volume was abnormally high, and it was only made worse when he became excited. Then he would just start shouting and yelling, and the din was so loud that it started to make Ellie's head hurt.

She had lost track of the conversation, but suddenly the king pointed across the table at Fillip and yelled,

"Fiordiligi! Fillip, Fiordiligi!"

Fillip laughed and pointed back at his father, repeating the ridiculous word until King Richard erupted in a fit of laughter that nearly had him choking on his food. Ellie leaned over to Fillip.

134

"What is Fiordiligi?" she whispered.

"It's a joke my father came up with," Fillip said. "It's meant to indicate something that is strong and durable until the very end, then it shatters and cracks out of nowhere. It happens a lot here at Bellbroke," he explained. "You'll have to look out for it, but the glass here is like that, in the windows. It will randomly shatter if the wind blows too hard, or even sometimes when there's no wind at all—not even a gentle breeze!"

"But where does that word come from?" she asked. "Fiordiligi?"

"There was once a glazier named Fiordiligi," Fillip explained. "He was commissioned by the last Henlopen king to make all the glass here, which is why we call it that. So many windows have broken...we don't think much of the original glass is left, but then one day, a window will shatter and we'll say, *Fiordiligi*. It can be applied to other things too, such as the chair my aunt broke just by sitting on it, or this horse we once had that suddenly keeled over and died."

Ellie was intrigued by the idea of *Fiordiligi*, and she thought it was a funny expression, though it took a moment for her tongue to wrap around its pronunciation.

As a dessert course was brought out, everyone seemed to remember that Ellie was there and that they were supposed to be getting to know her. Ellie felt a bit discomfited by this turn of events, as she was happier to be blending in the background, observing everything. But the king's sister addressed her first.

"So, Eleanor, tell us about your parents," Lady Jehanne said. "My brother tells me that they are deceased. I am so sorry to hear that."

Ellie swallowed a bite of her cake and thought it strange the way that Jehanne had prefaced her question. *Tell me about your parents…oh, but they're dead, aren't they? Tell us anyway.*

"My father was a merchant," Ellie began. "His name was Cornelius Marchand. He was a self-made man. He never spoke to me of his family, or how he grew up, but I always assumed it was bad. I know he was poor, and I think he must have suffered a great deal. But eventually he learned to read, and that led to apprenticeships on the wharf, and then he finally landed a clerk's position in the merchant guild. From there, he saved his money, and gambled to earn a bit. With a few lucky investments and good friendships, he procured a ship, *The Cromwellian*, and began making a name for himself. He would go where no other merchants would, and because he had a natural affinity for languages, he was able to trade and deal more successfully."

"How fascinating," Jehanne said, with just a touch of overenthusiasm. "I always love stories of these self-made men. They're popping up more and more these days. Men who come from nowhere, who grow up in gutters and alleys and end up ruling the world! It's fascinating—just *how* do they do it?"

"Hard work and risk-taking," the king's cousin, Lord Edmund grunted. "Something you wouldn't know anything about, Jehanne."

"Oh, I know quite a bit about risk-taking," Jehanne countered with a wink. "And as for the hard work...well it depends on what qualifies as *work*."

Ellie noticed the queen blanch at yet another quip of innuendo. Ellie got the impression that Adelaide was very proper, and had grown up in a much less bawdy environment than the king and his peers. Even Jehanne was part of the bantering, and Ellie found that unusual for a woman.

"What about your mother?" Queen Adelaide asked. "Lady Leonora Penwhistle. I know she died when you were much younger, poor dear, did you get to know her well?"

"No, not well," Ellie said. "I don't really remember her much at all. Just flashes, you know...like if you're in the sunlight and you blink, you get just a small glimpse of things. That's what I remember. But she was the eldest daughter of Baron Windermere. Her family was originally from La Fôret, in the north. My father told me that she loved to read, that she played the harp, and that she had a streak of precociousness."

"My, my, what a heritage," the queen remarked loftily, taking a sip.

"Let's turn to the subject of your stepmother, shall we?" the king said, a topic that Ellie had been dreading.

To her side, she saw a shadow pass over Fillip's face and she saw him make eye contact with his father and give the slightest shake of his head. Ellie warmed when she saw that Fillip was trying to stick up for her. But the king either didn't notice or didn't care. He plunged ahead, and because he was the king and her future father-in-law, Ellie had no choice but to oblige him.

"My sources tell me that she is a baronetess, meaning that she holds a title in her own right," the king prefaced. "She inherited it from her late father. No brothers and only two younger sisters. She has two daughters of her own, Annalise and Emmeline, from her marriage to a man, now deceased, named Sir Umbert Hardwick. Did you know that she had a husband before that?"

Ellie looked up. "No, I didn't know that," she said.

"Yes, my sources investigated her past very thoroughly. It turns out that she was married before to another member of the landed gentry, Sir Nicholas Carew. There were no children from the union. Like his successor, Sir Umbert, Sir Nicholas died under mysterious circumstances. Both were relatively young and healthy, with no reported problems by their physicians, both suddenly took ill to their beds and died very rapidly...as did Lady Frances' father, Lord Gilbert Turenne, Baronet."

Ellie felt faint as the king recited his information. Four mysterious deaths, including Ellie's own father. His was the last in a string of strange illnesses that seemed to follow her stepmother like an ill-fated shadow. But Ellie knew that fate had nothing to do with it. There was coincidence and then there was intent.

"I always wondered," she said softly. "I always wondered if she had poisoned my father. He was relatively young also, and in good health. They say he was taken by a broken heart, for my mother, but it was years too late for that."

The table sat in silence for a long moment, and Ellie felt the burning stares of seven pairs of eyes upon her.

138

"Murder is a serious offense in this kingdom," the king proclaimed. "Even one count comes with a death penalty, but four! Well, four is enough to warrant imprisonment...and execution."

Ellie swallowed at the thought of execution. She had seen the barbarity of the king's laws before, at Tudor Square, the place of execution in Hartmere. Too many times had she smelled burning flesh, or seen the cobbled streets run red with blood from the execution block. Too many times had she seen severed heads impaled on pikes by Traitor's Gate, the entrance to the city. She knew what form the king's justice took, and while she hated her stepmother, she didn't think she could hate anyone like *that*. And besides, there still wasn't any *proof* that she had murdered her father...just the shadowy insinuation of three prior graves, three skeletons that haunted the corners of Frances' closet.

"I wish I could leave it up to you, Eleanor," the king continued. "After all, she is your stepmother and after the initial report that Cecil gave me, I had always intended to let you deal with her. Let her stretch her legs a bit, with her newfound power, I thought. I certainly never expected my men to discover what they did. As such, I will be ordering the prosecution against her. You may hire representation for her, if you wish. As a baronetess, she will have a right to a trial, ultimately judged by a panel of lords. Or you can distance yourself from it entirely, if that is your wish."

"Good god, Father," Fillip interjected. "Did you really think it appropriate or necessary to bring that up *now?* We're supposed to be having a celebratory dinner, for god's sake."

139

"She needed to know and I thought now was as good a time as any," the king replied.

"You have the tact of a tadpole, you know that?" Fillip asserted. "You could have told us privately, after dinner."

"I didn't think it would go over badly," the king said. "I thought she might even be pleased. The shrew forced her to work like a slave for years and killed her father. I thought she might be happy to see the woman executed."

"Richard, honestly," the queen muttered. "You can see by her face that she's not *happy*."

Ellie's cheeks burned red and she felt that she ought to speak up for herself. She didn't like that everyone was talking around her, like she wasn't there.

"I'm not happy," she stated. "It doesn't give me pleasure to think that my stepmother could be executed. I only wanted her out of my life, but I was thinking more along the lines of permanent banishment, not death."

"What about what she did to your father?" Jehanne asked bluntly. "Think—if she hadn't come along then he'd still be around. He might be sitting here at this table with us, and you would have never been a servant!"

"I can't think like that," Ellie said stiffly. "I can't think in hypotheticals, I've grown too used to seeing things as they are. That's the only way they can be. My father is dead and whether she did it or not...well, I still can't stomach the thought of her being...hanged...or beheaded. I understand if it must be done, and I'll make my peace with it. But as you said, Your Majesty, I would prefer to stay as far out of it as possible."

140

"There it is," the king said, waving a regal hand. "A girl after my own heart. Pragmatic and straightforward. As you wish, my dearest, I shall keep you out of it and sheltered from the entire proceeding. The only matter left, of course, is what to do with your stepsisters. They are innocent in the entire affair, I presume, having been only alive for the last two murders. You don't suspect them in any foul play?"

"No," Ellie answered, still thinking of Emma dangling Teacup out of the window. "I wouldn't describe them as innocent, but they are not guilty of any crime. I would like to have them permanently banished from Trenway."

"From all of Trenway?" the queen questioned. "Where would you send them?"

"I don't care," Ellie said flatly. "Anywhere but here. I don't want to chance ever seeing them again."

Underneath the table, Ellie felt a sudden hand squeeze her knee, and she looked up and saw Fillip staring right at her. He gave another squeeze and winked supportively. Ellie wished that they were alone. She felt as if she had so much to say to him, so much to explain. It was too odd, being here in this room, with all these strangers, discussing her life. She should have been able to tell Fillip first. He shouldn't have had to learn at the same pace with these other people, even his mother and father. He should have known first.

"One more thing," Ellie added, thinking quickly. "When she's imprisoned, make sure she's only given lentils."

The king snorted on his wine. "Excuse me?" he said, coughing and snickering. "Lentils?"

"Yes," Ellie affirmed, thinking of her stepmother's peculiar aversion to them. "She hates lentils. Used to dump them in the fireplace and then make me pick up every single one. The Crown can exercise its form of justice but this will be my vengeance. Let her eat nothing but lentils."

There was silence for a moment as everyone absorbed what Ellie had said. Fillip and the queen looked at her pityingly, as if imagining her picking out lentils from a fireplace. Edmund and Roland looked bored. Jehanne looked at her intriguingly, as if seeing her in a new light. And the king...well, the king was delighted by Ellie's words. He clapped his hands slowly, laughing at her straightforward, yet uncomplicated form of revenge.

"Brilliant!" he lauded. "So simple, but devilish. I just might consult you, dear Eleanor, on how to handle my enemies. Give them lentils...I love it!"

"It has a personal touch," Jehanne agreed. "That alone will probably have more of an effect than being locked in a dungeon."

"As you wish," the king said, scribbling on a piece of parchment. "So let it be written, so let it be done."

"Could you not show leniency?" the queen asked. Astonished faces turned to her, and realizing that she was in the minority, she quickly recovered. "Lock her up and give her lentils, yes, for dear Eleanor's sake. But must she be executed? She is a woman, after all, and a noblewoman at that, though barely. Is it usual for noblewomen to be put to death?"

"It isn't *usual* for noblewomen to kill four men," the king countered. "Mercy, even for the sake of dear Eleanor would be to set a bad precedent, one that I don't wish to set in this country."

"Ah, yes, we wouldn't want that," the queen remarked dryly. "Nothing as horrible as a bad precedent. I shudder to think..."

Ellie stiffened in her chair, almost afraid to look at the king. When she did caution a glance, she saw that his face had darkened like storm clouds. He was staring at the queen with barely concealed distaste.

"How many times have I told you, my dear, to keep quiet on things which you know nothing about?" the king said in a low voice. "You come from a country of garbled tongues, of wishy-washy policies, and of spineless cowardice. Your country has done nothing but set bad precedents and they now pay the price for it. Don't lecture me on mercy or leniency!"

"I didn't think *I* was the one doing any lecturing," she replied evenly. "Only trying to make a point."

"Well you should stop," the king grumbled. "You make yourself sound foolish. You look ridiculous."

"Brother, brother, please," Jehanne interjected in a soothing, dulcet tone. "Stop this bickering. It behooves no one to quarrel with your queen. We are here to celebrate the engagement of your son!"

Jehanne lifted her glass in a toast, nodding her head down the table at Ellie. The latter might have thought it a kind gesture, had she not been strangely disturbed by the disingenuous twinkle in Jehanne's eye.

"To Eleanor Marchand," Jehanne said, standing up. "The woman who captured my nephew's heart. She will make the loveliest bride and the most charming of princesses."

They all drank to the young couple's health and happiness. Almost as soon as their glasses hit the table, the king's brother Lord Roland made a bawdy joke about Fillip looking forward to the wedding night. Fillip smiled and laughed with his uncle but Ellie's stomach gave a lurch. With all the noise and laughter on the other end of the table, the queen took the opportunity to lean across and address Ellie in a quiet voice.

"Enjoy your engagement, Eleanor," she advised. "It passes too quickly. Marriage is the tomb of love."

She tipped her glass back, draining the wine and then lifted her hand to snap her fingers for a refill. Ellie's mouth gaped open but she wasn't quite sure what to say, and the queen didn't seem to want or expect any sort of comment. Looking around uncertainly, Ellie hoped that they were coming to the last course of the evening. She didn't think that she would be able to take another bite, even to be polite.

It was partly because she was genuinely full, but mostly because her stomach was unsettled by what had been said, and the instincts that were starting to kick in. Her father had taught her to be constantly vigilant and to always be prepared for anything. He had taught her to hone her instincts and to trust them. And right now, they told her that the castle was far more dangerous than Maplecroft Manor had ever been.

144

Chapter Eleven

The Glass Castle

OVER the next few weeks, Ellie came to understand how Bellbroke Castle had earned its nickname of the Glass Castle. As Penelope had hinted on that midsummer night, the castle was simply full of windows. Nearly every room she had seen boasted a stunning panoramic view of the lake, or the forest behind. Even interior rooms had large stained glass window panels cut into the stone walls. This often made privacy a bit hard to come by. Even though the stained glass was darkly colored in the form of pictures, one could still see shadowy figures through them, and few rooms were fully soundproof because of it.

Thankfully, Ellie's room was on one of the outer walls of the castle, and because she had four large glass windows, she didn't have any stained-glass panels. Still, there were things she didn't like about living in the castle. Mostly, she wasn't used to the sheer size of it, and she doubted she would become accustomed to it. Maplecroft Manor was large—there were twelve bedrooms and six rooms on the main floor. But she didn't need a ball of yarn to find her way around it. Seven weeks into living at Bellbroke Castle, and she was still dependent on her ball of yarn.

She had figured out the basic layout: the large ballroom in the center bisected the castle into two halves, the northern half and the southern half. The southern half contained most of the bedrooms and private chambers. It was where the royal family retreated—the inner sanctum of the inner sanctum that was itself Bellbroke Castle. The northern half was where the court reigned. The Trencher Hall, and even the dining room where Ellie had eaten on her first night were on the northern half. This was also, naturally, where the kitchens were—Bellbroke had six kitchens— and where the staff slept.

But there were many rooms that seemed to have no purpose at all or that were filled with random objects, and this applied to both halves of the castle. For instance, she found a room that had dozens of empty birdcages strewn about. The room had been furnished nicely enough with chairs, couches, desks, bureaus, lamps, and small tables. But there were birdcages everywhere—on the floor, on the furniture, hanging from hooks, and no birds. Not even a single feather.

There was also a small library in the northern half that seemed to have hundreds of books crammed on the shelves, but when Ellie went to look at them, she saw that all the pages were blank. Every single book had nothing but blank pages. It was maddening. And she had found at least two other libraries, all filled with books that *did* have written content. It was just that one library. What could possibly be the point of having such a library?

One other exhausting and tedious aspect of the castle were the staircases. Because Bellbroke was so large and so tall, there were staircases everywhere. One could hardly go through the day without climbing at least a hundred. The only good aspect of it was that Ellie hardly had to worry about her legs or figure—she'd get plenty of exercise just trying to go about her business. Many of the staircases were grand and spectacular, such as the ones that wrapped around the ballroom, but Ellie found that their effect was much diminished when they became a regular, habitual obstacle.

Of course, while the staircases were necessary and useful, there was at least one that wasn't. Ellie had discovered a staircase in the southern half that seemed to have no purpose at all. She had entered a large chamber that appeared to be some sort of musical room. It was filled with harps, lutes, viols, drums, and various other reed instruments. In the back, Ellie spotted a staircase that was shrouded in darkness, nearly obscure from the narrow entry. Sneaking through it, she followed the staircase up until she came upon a door.

Curious, she twisted the handle and quickly gasped for breath. The wind from outside had hit her forcefully as she realized that she was standing on a precipice of a cliff. Directly beneath her was the lake, about twenty feet down. Someone had built a staircase that led outside, and there wasn't a balcony or a deck or anything. Just a door that led into thin air. Again, Ellie found herself wondering: *what could be the purpose of that?*

Armed with her questions, Ellie was determined to ask Fillip about these strange features of the castle. She hadn't been able to spend much time with him following the engagement dinner. Like his royal mother and father, Fillip had a strict

147

schedule of public appearances and council duties that he was expected to perform, and this took up a great deal of his time. Not to mention, he liked to spend what free time he had riding out with his friends in the forest to hunt.

Ellie found his love of the hunt to be typical, but maddening. It struck her as odd that someone who never had to worry about food would be so obsessed with hunting. Likewise, Fillip found her perspective to be strange and incomprehensible.

"Don't tell me you feel sorry for the animals," he had said, scoffing. "You, who've wrung the necks of chickens and butchered animals with your own bare hands."

"Mr. Tuttle mostly did all of that!" she had protested. "I did learn how to do it, and I did kill chickens and pigs, but I didn't like it!"

"Did you need it?" he had countered. "Did you *need* to eat those animals to survive? Or did you perhaps like the taste of meat? Come, tell me there's nothing more delicious than a strip of bacon?"

She hadn't been able to refute that. Bacon was good. But it did make her wonder: if it had been up to her, would she still have slaughtered animals for the eating? It had never been a question worth pondering before. Frances expected meat on the table, and that's what she got. But while the taste of meat was good, Ellie knew that one could live without it. Her father had taught her as much. Ellie could remember what he had told her, when they tended the gardens together.

"Out in the wilderness, you must hunt just to get by," he had explained. "I know this. When I was a boy, I had to...survive by myself for a while. There's not enough you can forage, and the meat helps you to stay strong. Gives you more energy than mushrooms, berries, and leaves would do. But if you have a garden…well, if you have a garden, there's no need for meat."

They had planted nearly every fruit and vegetable you could think of at Maplecroft Manor. It was one of the few houses along the river that had an orchard, berry brambles, and a vineyard. Of course, with the death of her father and the shortage in field staff, the vineyard had not been maintained. But she and Mrs. Tuttle still collected fruit from the orchard and berry brambles. And while the vegetable garden had shrunk in size, they could still plant peas, potatoes, onions, green beans, carrots, turnips, and squash. Mrs. Tuttle had managed to keep her mother's herb garden alive.

"With variety such as this," her father had said. "You can live off the land. And you can have animals for milk and eggs, but you never need slaughter them."

Yes, Ellie thought that if she had been mistress of Maplecroft Manor, she would have hired back the field staff, maintained the gardens, built a proper chicken coop, and kept a few goats for milk. There would be no need for cows and pigs, and she wouldn't go to market and waste good money on fish and venison the way that Frances did. Meat had always been extraordinarily expensive—something the Crown could care less about, but something that had always been important to her father. *Cut your coat according to your cloth,* he had counseled. It meant: live within your means, and don't spend more than you have or need.

It had been the first argument that she and the prince had ever had. And what had started as a mere difference of opinion had turned into a principled stand that ended in hot words of anger. Ellie had called him a stubborn, spoiled boy and basically accused him of having no feelings or respect for life he deemed inferior. And he had branded her as an oversentimental, naïve girl who had unrealistic expectations.

Only afterward did Ellie feel completely foolish. And also scared. Realizing that her life literally lay in the hands of Fillip, she rushed to find him and quickly apologize for all that she had said. He must have caught on to her fear, because he tipped her chin up and gazed at her with those impossibly blue eyes.

"Ellie Kate, you needn't be frightened of me," he had said, with obvious concern. "People have disagreements. It happens all the time. We both said things we didn't mean, and I know I'm sorry for what I said. I don't actually think that about you—it just sort of came out. And since you did the same, it's understandable."

"I just...I just don't want to ruin anything," she had said. "My stepmother was right about my cheek. It gets me in trouble, and I don't want to have trouble with you. I owe you so much..."

"Ellie Kate, please," he had said. "Again, you don't need to be frightened. I'm not going to put you aside, or have you locked up for shouting at me a bit. I need to be shouted at every now and then!"

He had smiled, and Ellie couldn't help but laugh. He held her hands steady in his.

150

"I don't want you to apologize because you're afraid of repercussions," he had continued. "Repercussions that aren't going to happen. If you're sorry, be sorry from the heart. It's one of the things I admire about you—you don't walk around me in sycophantic awe. You've always treated me like an equal. There's bravery in that, certainly, considering my status, but there's also honesty in it. And that's what makes us special. Unique. I want us to be equals—I want you to always feel that way, even before I make you my equal officially."

"It's a bit hard to always keep that in mind," Ellie admitted. "Despite what I say and how I act, we're on different levels and we always will be, even after the wedding."

"I don't want you to think like that," Fillip insisted. "That is not how it is going to be. You will hold the title of princess, and when my father dies and I ascend, you will become queen. You will be my regent if I have to travel out of the country—you will be in charge, you will be my second-in-command, and everyone will obey you as if you were a princess of the blood."

Ellie had nodded her head, but she knew that she would never feel like a princess of the blood. Even if she could get used to this royal lifestyle, she struggled to picture herself on the throne. Struggled to imagine scenarios in which her judgment was sought, in which subjects prostrated themselves before her, in which she might have to mete out justice or make important decisions. Royals had councils, of course, but they were expected to understand the issues thoroughly and not rely upon their councils. They were expected to lead. Could she do that? She really didn't know.

"Can I confess something to you?" Ellie had asked. "Can I say what I truly feel without you becoming upset?"

Fillip had sighed. "Ah, what a loaded question," he had remarked. "Go on then, throw it at me."

Ellie had bit her lip. "I don't want us to be like your parents," she had said in a quiet voice. "I don't mean to be disrespectful at all, but...they don't seem happy. Everything is always tense between them."

"Caught on to that, have you?" he had asked, snorting. "Yes, my parents are the epitome of why arranged marriages are a bad idea. They were never well suited. Trust me, Ellie Kate, we won't be like them."

"It just frightens me a bit," Ellie had said. "Arguing over stupid things like hunting..."

"Well, I would rather argue over stupid things like that for years," Fillip had assured her. "They don't argue about stupid things. They argue about very important things. Things that can really hurt a person—that can break a person down. By all means, let's disagree on hunting or other lifestyle choices, or politics, or even religion. You can live with differences of opinion on those things. You can even be happy with it—I love a good debate; I love people who can challenge how I think. That's invigorating. But there's a difference between that and matters of the heart."

Ellie was curious to know what the king and queen argued about, what issue or issues had driven them apart. Fillip knew—it was in the downward curve of his mouth, in the creased lines of his eyes—he knew the wedge that had driven his parents apart, but he wouldn't say, and Ellie wouldn't push him. She thought that he would tell her when he wanted to. When he trusted her.

In the aftermath of their fight and reconciliation, Fillip sent her a special present and Ellie nearly squealed with delight. He had brought her kitten back from Maplecroft Manor, Teacup. The kitten had been delivered in an ornate and gilded cage, and underneath had been a note, from Fillip.

My dearest Ellie Kate,

We can disagree on hunting, but at least we can both agree on how cute and cuddly kittens are! I know you spoke with Julian Marnier about this furry gray cat, and I know you'd probably like to have her back, so I sent someone to fetch her. I hope she brings you happiness here, and that a part of your former home helps you transition into thinking of Bellbroke Castle as your home. I want you to feel comfortable here. Your position is secure and you have nothing to fear. I promise you that. And I will do everything in my power to assure you of it. I will not rest until you can.

Yours,

Fillip

Ellie had smiled, thinking of his graciousness and this thoughtfulness. Teacup had been a warm welcome from her former home. With the castle being so large, she was mostly aloof, but unlike Ellie, she seemed to have mastered the layout. She always came back to Ellie's room at daybreak for morning treats and naps, and in the evenings, she would lay on the sofa while Ellie read a book.

Even still, Ellie was struggling to think of Bellbroke Castle as her home. It wasn't as though there was anything obvious missing. It was just a feeling, an instinct that she couldn't shake. Perhaps part of it had to do with all the strange features of the castle. Perhaps it had to do with the shifting glances of the king and the way he always seemed to half-look at her, as though he was ashamed. Perhaps it was the look of unease in the queen's eye whenever Ellie was around, and her habit of whispering advice and warnings.

Whatever it was, Ellie simply couldn't relax. To make herself feel more at ease, she decided to invite Lady Penelope Talbot and her daughters to the castle for a visit. They had written to her almost immediately after the royal announcement had been made. Lady Penelope said they had been among the cheering crowd on that hot, summer day when the royal family stood on a balcony at Penchester Palace, presenting Ellie as the future Princess Eleanor of Trenway.

Not wanting to be left out, Fillip remarked that it was a wonderful idea, and asked if he could tag along. Feeling a surge of happiness and confidence, Ellie wrote out the invitation, and then when the appointed day arrived, she walked down the stone steps with Fillip at her side, to greet Lady Talbot at the dock.

"Ellie!" Penelope exclaimed, rushing forward to bring her in an embrace, kissing her on both cheeks. "Oh, how *wonderful* to see you," she gushed. "Ah, you look so happy and healthy!"

"I am," she said, laughing at Penelope's enthusiasm.

"Your Highness," Penelope addressed Fillip, bowing low. "Forgive me for not addressing you first. I allowed myself to be carried away with joy for dear Ellie."

Fillip smiled beneficently. "No apology necessary, madam," he assured her. "I completely understand. I, too, get carried away with joy for Ellie."

Ellie could see him looking at her from the corner of his eyes, a grin tugging at his lips. Penelope was touched by the sweetness of it, she clapped her hands together and let out another exclamation of happiness. Fillip and Ellie led Lady Talbot and her daughters to the hanging gardens, where a table had been set up on the far balcony, overlooking the lake. Ellie was thankful for the shade of a large oak tree that hung above them. It was the kind of summer day in early August where the heat seemed to bleach everything of color.

Once they had sat down, the servants brought a novelty item—iced tea. Ordinarily teatime would have been a steaming pot served with crumpets and scones, but given the extraordinary heat on the lake, it was a tradition at Bellbroke to serve iced tea with a variety of fresh fruits and cheeses in the summer. Once their refreshments had arrived, the last invited guest finally made her way through the tiered garden, muttering apologies as she came.

"I'm sorry, I'm sorry…had to explain to the scullery maid the difference between a pear and a turnip…*where* they get these girls is beyond me, but that they've never seen a blade of grass is sadly evident!"

"Mrs. Tuttle!" Ellie exclaimed, jumping up to greet her.

"Pathetic!" Mrs. Tuttle said, still referring to the scullery maid. "Can you imagine not knowing the difference?"

"No, I can't," Ellie replied. "But then again, I've always had trouble distinguishing between arugula and parsley."

Mrs. Tuttle scoffed. "They look practically the same…not like a turnip and a pear! I swear!"

Lady Talbot rose out of her seat as well, to embrace the older woman. They both bonded over how they had colluded on Ellie's behalf on the night of the ball, and then laughed and reveled in their unexpected success of it.

"Truly, I never thought it would come to this!" Penelope said, sitting down. "I just wanted to give her a night she wouldn't forget."

"And so you did," Ellie replied warmly.

"You gave me a night I wouldn't forget either," Fillip added, thanking them both. "Truly, it was such an unanticipated pleasure to meet Ellie Kate. Almost as soon as I'd met her and danced with her, I knew she was too precious to let go."

Everyone at the tabled cooed and fawned over his words, fluttering like doves in the rafters.

"I still feel terrible, by the way," Penelope confessed. "I had no idea that Your Highness was pretending to be a courtier at the ball. I shall never forget how coldly I addressed you…oh, I am burned with shame to think of it! I thought Ellie was ruining her chances with the prince!"

The whole table erupted with laughter, most of them remembering how Lady Penelope had acted when she'd interrupted Ellie and Fillip kissing outside the castle.

"But you couldn't have known either, did you, Ellie?" Penelope asked.

"No, I didn't," Ellie confessed. "From my perspective and yours, I was ruining my chances with the prince."

"No, you just had good instincts," Fillip maintained. "I think that deep down, you might have known, or suspected."

"Possibly," Ellie said, playing along. "I do remember feeling conflicted when the Grand Duke made the offer of marriage. All that night, I couldn't stop thinking of the man I knew as Evander."

It was Ellie's turn to look over at Fillip with a mooning, doting face that previously she had mocked in others. But there was nothing feigned in her expression, and she knew that Fillip could see that. He responded by placing a light kiss on her forehead.

"This is why I adore her," he said, turning back to the table. "That unwavering loyalty. It was the same for me too, once we had come together, there could be no tearing us apart."

Once again, the table cooed and fawned, and at the sound of sniffling, Ellie looked over and saw that Mrs. Tuttle was weeping into her handkerchief.

"Mrs. Tuttle!" she exclaimed, putting her hand on the woman's shoulder.

"I'm sorry," Mrs. Tuttle sputtered. "It's just so romantic...and so...*wonderful* that you've found each other, and now you'll be happy and taken care of. It was all your father ever wanted, and I wish he could have lived to see this day."

Ellie's face fell, remembering her father, and how he had died...the words he had said to her on his deathbed. Ellie blinked her eyes and shook her shoulders, trying to snap herself out of it.

"To Cornelius Marchand," Fillip had lifted his glass of iced tea, the rest of the table following suit. "The man responsible for bringing the most beautiful, intelligent woman into my life. Always remembered and honored, never forgotten."

Ellie and the others drank to Fillip's toast, but to Ellie the tea went down with a particularly bitter taste.

"I wish I could be in love like that," Helena said, randomly. "I wish someone would love me the way Prince Fillip loves you."

"You will," Penelope assured her, a bit impatiently. "Give yourself some time, Helena, you're only fourteen."

"Yes, give it time," Ellie said to her, smiling. "It can come so fast, and when you least expect it."

Visibly cheered, Helena began to nibble at her scone while the conversation turned to Ellie and her adjustment at the castle. Soon they began to talk of other things, such as the weather, recent sporting events held at the tourney grounds, and future dates. Lady Penelope was most curious to know when the famous wedding would take place.

Ellie turned to Fillip for this question, seeing as how she was curious as well, having been given no information yet. He bristled a bit uncomfortably, explaining that ultimately his mother and father were in charge of setting the date, and they hadn't yet determined one.

"But why not?" Penelope demanded. "Forgive my impertinence, Your Highness, but don't you have a say in the matter? I always thought autumn weddings were just gorgeous. Divine and inspired! Could there be an autumn wedding in your future?"

Fillip nearly choked on his iced tea, and transitioned it into a laugh.

"I think autumn is far too soon for a royal wedding," he said. "That would only give my mother a couple months to plan, and she simply couldn't do that with so little time. I expect that we'll settle on a spring date, at the earliest."

Lady Penelope frowned, but sat back in her seat, forced to accept that idea. Ellie didn't think it was so bad. Truth be told, the idea of an autumn wedding did seem far too soon. She liked the idea of having another nine months to get a feel for royal life.

"My dear, have you thought of who your attendants will be?" Penelope asked.

"My...my what?"

"Your attendants...the girls who will stand beside you on the day of the wedding. Tradition says you usually have at least three..."

"Oh," Ellie said, perplexed. "Well, I haven't given it much thought. I suppose I could have Helena and Maria, if they want..."

Both girls brightened up immediately, at the thought of being part of a royal wedding. They practically shouted their acceptance and eagerness for the opportunity immediately. Lady Penelope smiled, and then sharply told them to hush.

"That's very kind of you, dear," she said. "To include my girls. I promise you that I will get them in tip-top shape for this kind of event, and they won't embarrass you..." she added, flashing warning looks at her giggling daughters. "Have you asked your stepsisters as well? I wouldn't blame you if you didn't, but I just wondered..."

Ellie flinched and blanched at the mention of her stepsisters. She had wanted to forget them altogether, if she could be perfectly blunt, just as she wanted to forget Frances, and the awful fate that had been bestowed upon her by the king.

"No, I haven't," Ellie answered.

"Those girls are a bit of a sore subject with Ellie, I mean...Her Royal Highness," Mrs. Tuttle explained. "They're to be banished from Trenway following the trial of their mother."

Shocked, Lady Penelope gasped and covered her mouth, expressing her apologies to Ellie for bringing up such an unpleasant topic. Ellie assured her that it was fine, that no apologies were needed.

"I am so sorry," Lady Penelope repeated. "We didn't hear anything about it..."

"I think my father, the King, is trying to keep it hushed up," Fillip related. "He doesn't want a big fuss made over it, for Ellie's sake."

"Oh, my dear," Lady Penelope exclaimed. "I am so sorry. Of course, you shouldn't feel poorly about it...the woman was horrible to you. She was as bad as they come, and she deserves every minute of suffering."

Lady Penelope went on to detail her own unpleasant encounters with Frances following Cornelius' death, how she had tried to get word through to Ellie, how she had often stopped by Maplecroft Manor, demanding to see the daughter of her deceased best friend, and how Frances had coldly slammed the door in her face and returned all her letters unopened.

"She was truly a wicked woman," Penelope decreed. "And all her wickedness has finally been turned back on her. She deserves no less for how she treated you...making you a servant in your own home, spending all your inheritance, isolating you from your friends...it was abominable!"

"I didn't want this to happen to her," Ellie interrupted, becoming shaky with frustration and stress. "This wasn't some punishment I handed down, so I don't feel guilty. But I don't feel vindicated either."

Everyone was deathly quiet in the wake of Ellie's words.

"The Crown determined that she was guilty of murder four times over," Ellie continued. "It is for that crime that she is being detained and put on trial. I have no say in it. But I am almost glad that it is not up to me to determine her fate. Such a burden would be too...overwhelming...after all she's done to me, as you said."

"Of course it would," Mrs. Tuttle said quietly, rubbing her arm. "It is better this way, Ellie, dear. You were right, though, it looks as though she did murder your father. I remember when you first shared that with me. I didn't want to believe it. I always thought she was a nasty woman, but there's a fine line between that and murder. But now that we know she did it...well...she can rot in a cell until the end of time for all I care. For that and what she did to you..."

"Hear, hear!" Lady Penelope echoed somberly. "Cornelius Marchand became one of my dearest friends after he married Leonora. He was such a wonderful man. To think..." Penelope shook her head. "To think that his life was cut short by that vile woman...she deserves the axe."

Ellie knew that it was counterintuitive, but she felt an icy shudder at Lady Penelope's words. Her father had never counseled her to hold vengeance in her heart. She tried to remember the righteous anger she had felt when living at Maplecroft Manor, how desperately she had wanted Frances and her daughters to be held accountable, to be punished. But those feelings had vanished. Almost immediately upon entering Bellbroke Castle, she had ceased to think of them at all. No longer was she desirous for revenge, even if it was true that Frances had murdered her father.

Those things seemed long in the past, and Ellie wanted to move forward from it. She didn't relish the idea of Frances losing her head, or being burned on a pyre. Even in the heat of her righteous anger, she didn't think she would have enjoyed seeing that. She might have like to preside over Maplecroft Manor for an afternoon, forcing Frances to do all the chores and cleaning, barking commands over her shoulder as had once been done to

162

her. *That* had been Ellie's idea of revenge, not cold-blooded murder.

As the conversation shifted towards other less controversial topics, Ellie found her mind wandering and struggling to stay rooted in the present. As if sensing her discomfort, Fillip's hand found hers under the table, squeezing every few minutes to ground her. Ellie was grateful for his presence, and physically leaned into him when they escorted Lady Talbot and her daughters back to the docks.

She knew she was being ridiculous, but thinking of her stepmother's precarious position made Ellie worry about her own within the castle. It still disturbed her to think that the king could snap his fingers, and instantly alter a woman's life forever. He could doom her fully in the blink of an eye. Frances had never seen it coming. Why would it be any different if the same happened to Ellie?

SINCE the tea with Lady Talbot and Mrs. Tuttle, Ellie had continued to feel uneasy in the castle. And it came to a head one day late in the summer, when Ellie was up and getting dressed for the day. There was suddenly a loud cracking noise and then the abrupt sound of glass shattering. Jumping in fright, Ellie turned around, half-dressed and saw that the windows in her room had broken. All of them. Out of nowhere and for no reason, the glass had simply shattered, and as Ellie looked out at the vista of the lake, she whispered,

"*Fiordiligi.*"

In this context and setting, the word seemed more sinister than amusing. And the idea that something so perfect and stunning could crash and shatter in a minute for no reason at all seemed very ominous to Ellie, almost like a warning in and of itself.

Chapter Twelve

Madness and Murder

THE day could not have had a more portentous beginning. When the windows had abruptly shattered, Ellie had finished dressing and then called for the servants. Unfazed, they assured her that the glazier would be out within the day to fix it.

"The same glazier?" she asked. "Fiordiligi?"

"No, milady, a different one," he told her. "Fiordiligi is long dead."

"How many windows of his are left?" she queried. "How often does this happen?"

"It happens too often to count," he answered. "And it's hard to say how many are left. Hopefully not many…"

With the same bored expression, he had begged to be excused, and Ellie had wordlessly granted, still feeling puzzled by what had happened. She should have expected it—Fillip did tell her about the phenomenon, but still…she supposed that all the glass had been replaced by now, and she certainly didn't expect for *her* glass to be affected.

The whole incident left her strangely rattled, and she felt that the only proper cure was to go down to the apothecary. One of the more comforting places in the castle was the apothecary's den, next to the kitchens in the northern half. Naturally, there was always a physician in residence at the castle, and an apothecary. Bellbroke Castle was unusual in that its apothecary was a woman. Appropriately, her name was Hazel, and she was of an age with Mrs. Tuttle.

Initially skeptical of her interest, Hazel had been reluctant to let Ellie have much to do in the apothecary. But once Ellie had demonstrated a working knowledge of herbs and tinctures, Hazel delighted in finding someone who shared an interest. As she bounded along in the corridors, eager to work with her hands and focus on a task, Ellie was hardly prepared for the surprise that greeted her in Hazel's den.

Tiresias was there, muttering something to Hazel and chewing on a ginger root. Stopping dead in her tracks, Ellie stared at the both of them. She had not seen Tiresias since the engagement dinner, and had not spoken to him since the night of the ball. He had remained completely aloof. She wasn't even sure where he slept.

"Ellie!" Hazel exclaimed. "Come join us, we were brewing a tisane."

"Sorry," she said. "I don't fancy ginger."

"Really?" Tiresias exclaimed. "Oh, that's a shame. It has such wonderful health benefits!"

"That's what Mrs. Tuttle says," Ellie muttered. "I'm sorry, I didn't realize you were busy, I'll come back…"

"Nonsense!" Tiresias shouted. "Come back, dear girl. Hazel tells me you have an affinity for herbs, which I knew of course, but I should like to test your knowledge!"

166

Ellie didn't care much to be tested, but she was also curious about Tiresias. She still wanted to know how he had known her name on the night of the ball. But before she could broach that subject, Tiresias held up a brown stick and Ellie sniffed it.

"Cinnamon," she said.

"That was easy," Tiresias said, pulling a pink flowered herb, but Ellie knew it too.

"Yarrow," she said.

Not to be undone, he picked up a sprig that looked like a twig from an evergreen.

"Rosemary."

Tiresias chuckled. "You were right, Hazel, she does know a thing or two. But let's get something trickier…"

He picked up a bowl of chopped leaves. They were so finely chopped that one had to go by smell and partial appearance. It was much easier to tell herbs apart when they were in the garden. But Ellie sniffed it and then determined.

"Basil," she answered.

"Are you sure?" Tiresias teased. "Are you sure it's not oregano?"

"The leaves are darker than oregano," she said. "And the smell is minty, almost. No, I'm sure it's basil."

"Very good!" Tiresias said. "That's a tough one. Let's try one more, shall we…?"

He hummed a bit as he poked through Hazel's jars. The apothecary exchanged an amused look with Ellie. *Humor the old man,* it seemed to say. Finally, he settled upon one that he liked,

167

and brought it over with a grin, presenting it with a bow and flourish. It was a nice verdant stem with an explosion of small white flowers at the top.

"Valerian," Ellie stated. "Mix that in with your tea and you'll have yourself a nice nap."

Tiresias chuckled.

"Right you are!" he exclaimed. "Right you are and sharp as a sword! How did you come to know so much about herbs?"

"How did you?" Ellie countered.

Tiresias laughed a bit, in surprise at having the question flipped. But he obliged her curiosity.

"Oh, it's always been an interest of mine," he said. "You know, nature is a wondrous thing. The variety of life has always astounded me—just think of the sheer variety and you'll go dizzy with madness! And there's such a fine balance to it—there's an antidote for nearly every poison within nature. Sometimes one poison can be an antidote for another. Fascinating!"

"Like bladder beans are an antidote for nightshade," Ellie offered. "But by itself, bladder beans could kill you."

"Exactly! Yes, that's exactly what I mean! Now, don't shy out of my question…how do you know so much? I've been tinkering my whole life, but what about you, my dear?"

Ellie was puzzled by how rational he was, at least in this moment. He had been lucid and able to carry on a conversation for several minutes without rambling into something strange. It was like she was talking to a completely different man than the one she remembered from the night of the ball.

"Shouldn't you know already?" she asked.

"I beg your pardon?"

"You can see the past, can't you?" she prompted. "Can't you see in my past to answer your own question."

The smile faded from his face as he put the sprig of valerian away.

"Ah," he sighed. "I see you've been talking to some of my detractors. Those visions come and go, my dear. Nothing I can control, I'm afraid."

Ellie crossed her arms.

"Do you remember me at all?" she asked, a bit defensively.

"Remember you? Well, of course I know who you are, my dear," he said. "You're my great nephew's fiancée. Well done, by the way, snagging a prince!"

"We met before that," Ellie contended. "Don't you remember? On the night of the ball, I met you by the fountain and you already knew who I was."

The old man's eyebrows furrowed in bemusement. Ellie could see that he was straining to remember, but failing.

"No, I'm afraid I don't remember that…"

"You said my name," she insisted. "You asked me to forgive you and you said my name, Ellie. And you said that the prince would choose me."

Tiresias shook his head, seeming to become agitated. Hazel looked concerned, and Ellie should have known to stop, but anger was filling her veins for some reason, and she was taking it out on the old man. His failure to remember was irritating her. It was like no one in this castle would give her a straight answer.

"You begged me to forgive you for something," she pressed on. "What was it? Have you done something to betray me? Do you know that you'll do something in the future? You said that the mind was weak...did you mean yours? And then you told me to go across the sea, to where it's safe. What did you mean by that? Safe from what?"

Tiresias shook his head again, but Ellie raised her voice, commanding him to answer. Finally, he slammed his fist on the table, causing the mortars and pestles to rattle.

"Stop it!" he yelled. "I don't know what you're saying!"

Hazel reached forward to comfort Tiresias, who had retreated into himself like a little boy. He was putting his wrists over his ears and whimpering, like a dog that had been kicked. Ellie didn't need Hazel's chastising look—she felt bad enough already.

"I think you're upsetting him," Hazel said. "I'll make him a tisane and try to calm him down."

"I'm sorry," Ellie said. "I didn't mean to...I'll come back later."

"You know about his condition, don't you?" Hazel asked. "He suffered a head injury long ago. He's raving mad most of the time, except when he's down here. When he's around the herbs and plants, he's at peace."

Ellie felt a surge of guilt and regret wash over her. She had just sent him into a fit when he had been at his most happy. She hoped that he wouldn't have negative associations of this
170

place because of what she did. Resigned to leave, Ellie walked to the threshold, but Tiresias' aggrieved voice called her back.

"Ellie!" he called out, with a distinct change in tone, that of recognition. "Yes, oh yes, Ellie! There was something I meant to tell you...something I overheard through the glass window...then it shattered...Fiordiligi! What was I supposed to tell you...?"

Tiresias pressed his fingers against his temples, willing himself to remember. Ellie stood on the threshold, disturbed by his sudden change in affect. He was more like the man she had remembered by the fountain now, unpredictable and unhinged.

"Think, think, think!" he urged himself, now banging on his skull. "What was it? ARGH!"

In a moment of frustration, Tiresias rounded on the table and swept everything off it with a roar like a bear. Ellie watched in mute horror as the glass vials went shattering to the floor, as the clay mortars emptied their contents everywhere.

"The mind is weak!" he yelled. "I know what I meant by that now! The mind is weak! Why can't I remember?"

Launching into another fit of rage, Tiresias started to pull out his own hair and hit himself repeatedly. When he flung himself on the floor, Hazel yelled at her to call for help.

"I'm sorry," Ellie murmured, horrified by what she was seeing. "I'm sorry, I never meant to..."

"JUST GO!" Hazel shouted. "Go for help!"

Springing into action, Ellie darted through to one of the kitchens and enlisted the help of several young lads. Leading them back to the apothecary, Ellie watched again in horror as they helped Hazel grab hold of him and carry him to a makeshift cot, where they strapped him down so he couldn't hurt himself. Ellie saw angry red welts on his skin where he had pinched himself, and started to claw at his flesh. He was screaming incoherently, shaking his head roughly back and forth, almost frothing at the mouth like a rabid animal.

"He'll have to be brought to his bedroom," Hazel said to the boys. "I'll bring up a strong sedative."

Ellie's heart sank realizing that she had ruined Tiresias' brief spell of serenity. It had brought her peace too, to come to the apothecary and work. Now she wondered if Hazel wouldn't necessarily like Ellie coming down to work with her.

Shaken, Ellie returned to her room and lay down on her bed. To her surprise, Teacup was there waiting for her, and promptly jumped up to lay down. Ellie petted her and was soothed by the sound of her purring, but she still couldn't shake the memory of what had happened in the apothecary, and what Tiresias had hinted at. Once again, he seemed to assert that she was in danger. He had overheard something...but what? Something that he wasn't meant to, obviously, but it concerned her.

Ellie closed her eyes and tried to sleep, but all she could see were the twisted convulsions of Tiresias, the shifting expressions of the king, and that look of worry and warning that always seemed to cloud the queen's eyes. It was easy for Fillip to write that he would do all in his power to assure her of her position, but ultimately it didn't mean much to Ellie. She didn't think she would ever be able to shake the feeling that something wasn't right, and that she was likely in danger.

AROUND five 'o' clock, Fillip came to bring her down for dinner. They had to report to the throne room first, as King Richard had sent word that he had news for them. When Ellie opened the door to her fiancé, she saw that his face was as grim and ashen as hers.

"Knowing Father, it won't just be one thing," Fillip said. "He's a man who likes a knockout. Did you know that he loves to watch street fighting? His favorite champions are the ones who keep punching until the opponent falls down unconscious. Rapid fire, he calls it, and he gets so excited, he nearly foams at the mouth."

Ellie frowned, not wanting to think of anyone foaming at the mouth ever again. Vivid memories of earlier that morning resurfaced as she saw Tiresias destroy the apothecary and then turn on himself. Taking a deep breath, she decided to tell Fillip about what had happened. He was immediately sympathetic, pulling her into a hug.

"Oh, I'm so sorry you had to see that, Ellie Kate," he said, rubbing her back.

"See it?" she hiccupped. "I *caused* it!"

"Don't fret," he assured her. "Trust me, we've all set him off before. It was the first time, you didn't know his triggers, and you got carried away. It happens—you couldn't have known what his reaction would be."

"Still...I should have known...I should have been more sensitive..."

"And you will be," he said. "Next time. Don't worry, Ellie Kate, I'll help you smooth things over with him, but chances are he won't even remember what happened. Come, let's go see what my father has to say."

Holding her steady, Fillip led her to the throne room where King Richard's booming voice could be heard through the thick oaken doors. He was clearly angry, and though Ellie couldn't make out every precise word, she sensed that he was being very dictatorial.

"Sounds like he's still in there with his advisors," Fillip remarked.

"*That's* how he talks to his advisors?" she questioned.

"Oh yes," Fillip said. "It usually goes on like this for hours. He introduces some grand, lofty plan, they typically shut it down, and then he goes on a tirade about the absolute authority of a monarch."

"Goodness," Ellie breathed, feeling uncomfortable.

"The problem is that he's technically wrong, and he knows it, and that makes him all the angrier," Fillip explained. "You see, there is no such thing as an absolute monarchy in this country anymore. That power was stripped about fifty years ago by the nobles who threatened civil war if they didn't have more of a say in the rule. And that led the commoners to revolt as well. Ultimately, it was up to my grandfather to broker peace. And he decided to sacrifice some of his power to keep the country united. Now there's a Noble Council and a Commons House. Any measure must be approved by a two-thirds majority. The King himself counts as one unit, but the measure must also be passed by a majority within the Noble Council or Commons House. My father hates it because the others are usually in opposition with each other, and in this case, both are united against him on the matter of war."

"Surely the king still has the most power in the country, though," Ellie said. "Otherwise, why have a king at all? What's his function if not to have the final say?"

Fillip frowned. "And there's the rub. That's what people in the streets are saying too. It's a dangerous time. They say, if a group of men can rule us, why not rule ourselves? Right now, my father is a powerful figurehead. And he still has full control over the judicial realm of the kingdom. He dispenses judgment and resolves disputes. The council has no jurisdiction there, but it's not enough for my father. He doesn't like that type of ruling—he thinks it's child's play. More than once, he's had me preside over the court and listen to petitions for the day."

"Well, it's good practice for you," Ellie observed.

Fillip made a face that suggested he was dubious about the noble intentions of his father.

"He's done it to prove a point," he said. "And because he didn't want to do it that day. My father doesn't trust me with much. Thinks I have too much of my mother in me. But I'm his only heir, and I'm all he's got, so we're stuck with each other."

"That's terrible," Ellie said. "Is that how you really feel?"

"It's how he really feels," he countered. "He told me so himself. From the horse's mouth. Anyway, enough about that. Let's go in."

"But it doesn't sound like he's finished..."

"He'll never be unless we barge in."

Without any further ado, Fillip pushed open the doors and strolled in confidently. Ellie trailed by his side with much less confidence, and the king didn't even seem to notice their presence. He was leaning over a table that looked like it had a map pinned across it with several wooden figurines.

"You're going to sit here and LIE TO MY FACE?" he roared. "You're lying to my face when you say these things. We have the money! We have the resources! We have the men!"

"Your Majesty, begging pardon," one of the grey-bearded men interjected. "It's not only about possessing necessary resources, it's about timing..."

"WHEN'S A BETTER BLOODY TIME?" he shouted. "Do you think Grunwald will wait for a better bloody time?"

"I think they would, sire, with proper diplomacy," another one suggested.

The king blew a raspberry noise between his lips, shaking his great head back and forth like a mighty lion.

"Diplomacy!" he mocked. "Do me a favor: don't ever say that asinine word in here ever again. I don't want to hear about diplomacy. Grunwald doesn't even know what that word means. They won't wait to go on the defensive—they'll strike as soon as they're ready and it'll be sooner rather than later."

"Our intelligence suggests otherwise," one of them said calmly. "Operatives on the ground in Grunwald inform us that the land is much depleted from this summer's drought, that much of their fleet was destroyed in a storm, and that King Anselm is not angling to go to war with anyone, let alone Trenway."

"You really are dense, aren't you?" the king sputtered. "You're going to believe your *spies?* Yes, Master Caldecott, your slimy network of spies? What do you expect of those who slither like snakes? How would you know if they turned on you? How could you be sure of their loyalty when they lie for a living? Men like that are not to be believed. And most of them have been in Grunwald for so long, they've probably switched sides, feeding you false information."

"With all due respect, sire," Master Caldecott began. "While that's certainly possible, it's not *probable.* And we cannot wage a war based on the mere supposition that our intelligence is false because it's possible our agents have turned coat. Facts win the day, sire, not suspicions."

The king narrowed his eyes to tiny black slits and pointed a threatening finger at Master Caldecott.

"I want you to say that to the people," he said. "I want you to say that to grieving widows and families. I want you to say that to survivors of a military assault on our coast. I want you to repeat those exact words. And do remember them, Caldecott, because you'll be saying them soon enough. Mark my words— Grunwald *will* attack us."

"And when they do, we will most certainly go to war," the grey-bearded one said.

King Richard took a dramatic step backward, and then finally turned to Fillip and Ellie, as if he'd known they'd been there the whole time. He gestured toward the solemn figures of the council.

"Be my witness, son," he said. "And you too, Ellie. You heard them say it. They would rather see lives lost before they lift a finger to prevent it. Incredible."

And then the king clapped his hands together in slow, mocking applause, stepping closer and closer to the council until they were flinching from the noise of his hands so near to their faces.

"Is that all you have for us, Your Majesty?" one of them asked, interrupting his clapping.

"Yes, begone!" the king snapped quickly. "You disgust me. Each and every one of you. I cannot bear to see your faces any longer. Go!"

The council members filed out and when they were alone, the king leaned over his table and flicked one of the figurines over. Ellie thought it was rather childish.

"Father, you said there was something you wanted to tell us?" Fillip prompted.

Straightening up, the king whipped around, his hands behind his back and his face suddenly clear as if he had been in a perfectly good mood the whole time.

"Yes, I do," he confirmed. "Your mother wanted to be here to announce it as well, but she was too ill. We have chosen a date for your wedding. It will be next spring on the first of May."

"But that's only a few months away!" Ellie blurted.

"Fillip, your bride looks a bit panicked at the prospect," the king said, laughing. "Hopefully you two haven't fallen out!"

"No, we haven't," Fillip assured him. "At least I hope we haven't!" he added with a boyish wink, and he and his father laughed. "I think we are just both surprised by the...speed with which this was determined."

"Why drag it out?" the king countered. "The queen and I figured that it would be better to see you two married quickly—that way the nobles have less time to protest against Ellie's non-royal and non-noble status. The common people love you, Ellie. They're still celebrating in the streets. Don't believe me? Go out and experience it for yourself. You've been holed up here at Bellbroke Castle. Make Fillip take you with a few guards to see what it's like. They can't wait for you to be a real princess."

"Really?" Ellie said, trying to picture it in her head. The king was right, though, she had been holed up at Bellbroke for the rest of the summer. Autumn was almost upon them. It had been so long since she had been able to relax and while her days away—and Bellbroke was so large. She could easily spend another ten months here without leaving and keep herself entertained. But she also knew that she couldn't retreat from the real world forever. Bellbroke Castle was like her bower, but she couldn't stay locked within.

"Oh, yes, they love you," the king affirmed. "It's incredible, really. They haven't been this excited in ages, especially not over anything *we* do. It truly was a brilliant idea to host that ball. Anyway, now that the date of your wedding has been announced, preparations will begin immediately."

"Fantastic," Fillip said, a bit dismissively. "Well, is that all you had to tell us?"

The king's face darkened. "No," he admitted. "Ellie, I have news about your stepmother."

"Oh?" Ellie said, wondering if she had been arrested or tried yet. She had wanted to stay out of it, and she hadn't regretted her decision, but the subject did float around in the back of her mind, and had for the past month or two.

"She was executed yesterday," he said.

At first, Ellie thought she hadn't heard correctly. But at the grim look of the king's face, and at Fillip's shocked reaction, it began to sink in that she *had* heard correctly.

"Father!" Fillip shouted. "H-how could you? This is low, even for you."

"Careful, son," the king growled. "You're dangerously close to testing my patience and becoming disrespectful."

"She's...d-dead?" Ellie repeated hollowly.

"Yes," the king affirmed. "She was executed yesterday morning at ten 'o' clock. Beheaded. I commuted her sentence from burning. Women are usually burned."

Ellie's hands went instinctively to her neck as she tried to swallow. It was too much to take in. Frances was dead? She couldn't imagine it. She didn't want to, but the images came unbidden. Frances in a dark cold chamber of a dungeon, Frances being walked down a flight of stairs, Frances being led to the scaffold. And then...then what? Ellie had never seen someone get beheaded. She understood what it meant, of course, but the imagery eluded her. It seemed too drastic...it seemed too terrible a thing to do, it couldn't possibly happen in real life.

Ellie wasn't a naïve girl. She understood murder and crime. She had seen a dying man bleeding in the streets. Her father had taught her the basics of fighting, and therefore the basics of anatomy—how best to hurt someone, where to strike the best blows and so on. But there was a difference between that and this cold, calculated murder by the Crown in which life was quickly taken, the body casually mutilated.

To the court, it was like a spectator event—the entertainment of the day. And that was what she struggled to imagine. She struggled to think of Frances, someone who had been a close and prominent figure in her life, being slaughtered before a crowd of people yesterday at ten 'o' clock in the morning. It beggared belief.

What were her last thoughts? What did she think about when she had been confined to her cell? Had she known the hour of her death? Did knowing make it worse? Ellie thought that it certainly had to be worse. She preferred to be in the dark about the hour of her own death. What grim turns could the mind take when it knew such information? And when it knew also that there was no possibility of getting out of it?

"How can you be so callous?" Fillip demanded.

"What's callous? Ellie said she wanted to stay out of it, and I kept her out of it. But now that it's been done and it's all over, I thought she ought to know."

"Did you have to couple it with the news of our wedding date?" Fillip asked. "Does that seem normal to you? Give us happy news and then prattle on about her stepmother's execution?"

"I thought that would be happy news as well," the king said, innocently. "I thought it would be just as welcome as news of the wedding date."

Fillip swore under his breath and made a whistling noise between his teeth, shaking his head and coming over to console Ellie. She wasn't crying or anything, but she was struggling to breathe and her head felt heavy and dizzy suddenly.

"It's just so soon," she said faintly. "I didn't think it would be so soon..."

"The king's justice is swift," King Richard chirped. "It's the one thing my council will allow me to do, so I make sure it is done efficiently."

"D-did she have any last words?" Ellie asked.

"Perhaps you shouldn't know," the king said ominously. "In an effort to be sensitive, there are certain details of her execution that might be too disturbing."

"Tell me!" Ellie demanded. "Now that you've told me she's dead, I need to know everything."

The king's eyes flicked to Fillip's, as if seeking permission, and when it seemed to be granted, he shrugged his shoulders.

"As you wish," he said. "Before she died, she was allowed to make a final confession and speak her last. She chose to maintain her innocence and insist that wrongful prosecution had been made against her. After that, she cursed your name, at which point the crowd began to go mad with rage. They began

182

chanting for her death, throwing things at her, and so on. The executioner stepped forward and Lady Hardwick became frightened and tried to run away. The constable had to hold her down to the block, and even still, she tried to dodge the blows. All in all, it took seven blows to cut off her head. My sources tell me it was a bloody mess, and the crowd had gone wild with mania. They turned on her the moment she spoke ill of you. What did I say? They love you!"

Ellie listened in horror while the king described the scene in an almost bored, detached manner. And then his tone had abruptly changed toward the end, when speaking of the crowd's hysteria for her. He had become excited thinking about it, totally unfazed and unconcerned by the violence her name had sparked. But Ellie was disturbed by it. She was not pleased by the idea that people wanted to kill for her. She was not pleased that her cause had started a mob scene, or that people were so eager to exact their brand of vengeance on her behalf. She had never asked for that, and didn't want it.

"My dear girl, are you quite all right?" the king asked, suddenly catching on to the fact that she was becoming ill.

Ellie was leaning over with her hands on her knees, trying to take a deep breath, but her throat was locked up and her chest was tight. All she could do was wheeze.

"I j-just need a minute," she stuttered.

Fillip lifted her up by the elbows and slung her arm over his shoulder, helping her to walk out of the throne room. Her hearing was starting to fade and her vision was becoming cloudy around the corners. She had the vague feeling that Fillip was trying to talk to her, but she had no idea what he was saying.

She couldn't stop thinking about her stepmother's fate. Couldn't stop picturing it in her head, in her mind's eye. This was Bellbroke Castle. This was the royal life. One minute, the king was shouting madly at his advisors, the next minute talking about a wedding, and the very next describing a grisly murder scene with relish. Even Fillip wasn't shocked by the execution; he just protested his father's delivery of it.

Ellie thought back to that summer night when the Grand Duke of Talbany had rescued her from Maplecroft Manor. She could still remember leaning against the back of the carriage, blinking her eyes lazily, and feeling relief flood over her skin like the lapping waters of the lake. How naïve she had been. How foolish to think that all her problems were over? How could she not have thought that royal life would come with its own set of problems—problems that were infinitely more complicated and inherently dangerous?

As Fillip continued to lead her up the stairs and through a series of corridors, Ellie was still vaguely aware that he was talking to her. But it was not his voice she heard in her head, it was her father's. *You must wake up, Ellie,* he seemed to say, *you've had your eyes wide shut, and it's time to wake up.* She knew what she had to do. She would allow herself this one moment of weakness; this one opportunity to grieve for her former way of life, for the conception of how she thought this new life would be. And once that was finished, she would remember what her father had taught her. He had endowed her with many skills, but most important of all, he had taught her to survive.

And Ellie was determined to do just that.

Chapter Thirteen

The Second Ball

SOPORIFIC heat flooded the patio where Ellie lounged with the queen and the king's sister, Jehanne. Despite fanning herself for nearly an hour, Ellie felt her skin getting hotter, felt beads of sweat drip down her forehead, and despaired when she looked to her side and saw that her glass of iced water had sweated itself dry and was now warm. The queen must have seen her look of gloom for she quickly snapped her fingers and ordered a servant to bring another fresh glass of water.

"You're at the castle now," the queen explained silkily. "Don't forget—you can have anything you want."

Ellie resisted the urge to roll her eyes. *Anything?* What she really wanted was to lie down in her room with a cool cloth on her forehead, the shutters closed, the curtains drawn and experience the peace and quiet of the dark. Instead, she was obligated to spend time with her future in-laws. Due to the customs of polite royal society, Ellie had not been allowed to decline the invitation to sit and do nothing outside on the hottest day of the year.

"Honestly, this is better than being cooped up inside though," Jehanne remarked. "There's a slight breeze and when it passes every few minutes, it is refreshing."

To Ellie, there was nothing refreshing about hot, humid air being blown in one's face. The problem with living on the lake in the summer was that moisture rose from the surface of the water and lingered in the hot air. This humidity was far worse than hot, dry air and made it feel ten times hotter. The breeze, despite Jehanne's position, did nothing to mitigate the effect of being steam cooked.

The lynchpin of the situation, the cherry on top of the cake, had been the bugs. Lakes were also notorious hosts of the most annoying insects. Ellie had seen them buzzing in hordes, hovering just above the surface of the water, but they flew higher too, high enough to reach the balcony where they feasted upon the bare skin of the royal women.

About fifteen minutes in, Ellie had slapped thirteen mosquitoes on her legs and decided that enough was enough. If Jehanne and Queen Adelaide insisted upon torturing her in this way, at least she could do something to get rid of the bugs. The heat and humidity was beyond her control—the bugs were not. Ellie had asked the servants to fetch her some supplies from Hazel's apothecary. Within minutes, both the queen and the king's sister were mesmerized by how Ellie had solved their problem and created a nice ambiance to the afternoon.

She threw everything she knew at it—she burned sage leaves, cedar bark, and rubbed lemon balm on her skin. Eventually the queen remembered that they had special nets for these kinds of things that were down in the boathouse and she ordered a servant to bring one and string it up along the outside edge of the balcony. Protected by the net and the burning herbs,

187

they were no longer plagued by bugs. But as with the heat, there was something else beyond her control—the plague of inane conversation.

Jehanne and Adelaide had lived their entire lives within the cocoon of royal wealth and privilege. As such, they did not realize how ridiculous they sounded to those who were not born with a silver spoon in their mouths. Perhaps they had never even spoken with someone who did not share their background, so they remained oblivious. But to Ellie, the topics they chose to discuss were petulant, insipid—downright mean in some cases— and utterly stupid. Ultimately, Ellie decided that she would rather stick a thousand pins in her body than be forced to listen to another word.

"Ellie, do you mix your lip pigment from red ochre, madder, or vermilion?" Adelaide asked, trying to bring her in the discussion.

Before she could answer that she never mixed pigment to paint her lips, Jehanne interrupted.

"Oh, why bother asking *her?*" she said, a bit tetchily. "Ellie has perfectly natural rosy lips, not like the rest of us who have to bother with pigments. Must be nice to be born with good looks!"

Ellie fumbled for a response, not sure if she could even think of one that would satisfy. It was why she sometimes hated being around Jehanne and the queen, and even other women. There was always a not-so-subtle element of complimentary backstabbing undercut by a layer of jealousy and self-deprecation. What was she supposed to say to Jehanne? *Oh no, you were born* *with good looks too...*because of how Jehanne had introduced it, any nice response Ellie came up with would sound disingenuous.

"Well, if I were mixing up a lip pigment, I wouldn't use vermilion," she decided, going a different route. "It's poisonous and damaging to the skin."

The queen gasped and held her fingers up to her lips, as if poking around to detect any scarring.

"Really?" she asked, panicked. "I've been using vermilion for years. My ladies in Kronstadt swore by it."

Ellie shrugged. "Depending on how much you use, you might get away with it, but I would switch to ochre or madder. I'm not sure if they'll produce the same quality as vermilion, but they're not toxic, so there's that..."

"Vermilion goes on smoother," Jehanne noted. "And it stays on longer than ochre or madder, but I certainly wouldn't want to risk skin problems. I have enough of a job trying to keep the wrinkles at bay!"

Adelaide laughed alongside her and they both launched into the woes of middle age from a woman's perspective. Ellie allowed her mind to wander again, thinking that both Jehanne and Adelaide were foolish for fighting such an uphill battle. Why bother with it? *The wrinkles are inevitable,* she wanted to say, *no matter how much ointment you rub into your cheeks or how many kinds of toxic tinctures you mix up, the wrinkles are still coming for you.* Chances were that Adelaide and Jehanne were doing more damage to their skin with all their so-called remedies. If they would just leave well enough alone, and accept the realities of life, they'd be better off for it physically and mentally.

But Ellie knew that if she ever worked up the courage to voice such an opinion, it would fall on deaf ears anyway. She could have told Jehanne that the reason her hair was thinning was because she spent too much time trying to bleach it in the sun, and had washed it too many times with saffron and sulfur. Naturally dark hair like Jehanne's wouldn't ever become the golden and sunny blonde that she wanted—it was a waste of time trying to force it to be something it wasn't. And the result—a strange muddy straw color—was certainly worse than her natural hair color.

"Just remember, Ellie, a woman without paint is like food without salt," Jehanne said, wagging a knowing finger.

"Sounds like something a man would say," Ellie muttered.

Jehanne laughed. "Perhaps a man did say it," she said. "They set the standards for us women, after all."

Ellie tried not to choke on her own bile. As much as she wanted to challenge that idea, once again she said nothing, realizing that mounting such an argument would be futile. And it could get ugly—they would turn pedantic on her, lecturing her about royal expectations and so on. After all, it was Ellie's job to be married to Fillip. She didn't have a role in and of herself, she only stood as a reflection of her husband. So, in a sense, what they said was depressingly true. The royal men set the standards, and even though Ellie hadn't grown up in that environment, she would have to get used to it.

Frances had been the same way—overly concerned with her appearance. Ellie suspected it was a symptom of idleness and purposelessness. Without anything to *do*, or *be* why focus on anything else? Ellie frowned, determined that she would not let herself fall into that trap. Fillip respected her. He would give her a meaningful role. Something still unsettled her, though, and she realized that it was the fact that even if she had a meaningful role, it would be one that Fillip assigned to her, not one that she could choose or carve out for herself. And whatever duties she had wouldn't be taken seriously by anyone else. It would just be seen as a diversion for her until her true purpose came along—motherhood.

"So, Ellie, as I was saying, we'll have to order you a new gown," Queen Adelaide said, roping her back in the conversation.

"What?" Ellie blurted. "Why?"

"We shall be hosting another ball here at Bellbroke, in three weeks," the queen answered. "A final hurrah to summer, and an official party to mark your entrance into society. Don't worry—it'll mostly just be courtiers, people you've already met. But the nobility from the far reaches of the kingdom will be coming as well, earls and countesses that largely stay holed up in their tiny estates in the country. It's the king's way of introducing you to the powerful elite, of garnering their loyalty to you, and communicating unequivocally that fealty will be expected and enforced."

"That sounds tense," Ellie remarked. "Is there a sentiment amongst the nobles already—that they don't accept me?"

The queen opened her mouth quickly and her eyes flicked to Jehanne uncertainly.

"Not that they don't *accept* you, per se," Jehanne interjected. "Just that they...well, *some* of them, mind, have expressed...*concerns*...at a commoner being made princess."

"Ah."

"It's these country knights and barons," the queen said dismissively. "Trying to be uppity, always insisting on the old, proper way. Here in the capitol, the courtiers embrace change readily and are more open and accepting. And as Jehanne said, it was only a *few* nobles who expressed concern."

"It's nothing personal," Jehanne said.

"Well, obviously," Ellie snapped. "They don't even know me."

"Which is exactly why we're hosting the ball," the queen said excitedly. "So they can get the opportunity to meet you and to see why you're the perfect choice. Don't worry—you'll dazzle everyone and it'll be perfect!"

Ellie didn't share the queen's optimism. Instead, she felt a sinking weight in her stomach like the dropping of an anchor. If there was already opposition to her being made princess, there was a possibility, however slight, that the king would bow to pressure and have her dismissed and the engagement dissolved. What if he made such a bargain to procure support for the war he wanted? It wasn't such a farfetched idea. The nobles might promise to sway the council in favor of war and in return ask that the king betroth his son to one of their daughters instead. Ellie had to bet that the king would agree to such terms in a heartbeat, spelling doom for her and Fillip and the prospects of her future.

SEVERAL days later, Ellie found herself standing on a stool in the middle of her room while maids fluttered around her carrying sleeves and fabric, and a pompous dressmaker walked round her in circles complimenting her frame and complexion whilst intermittently shouting commands at the maids. Ellie might have found it comical were her stomach not twisted in knots at the prospect of yet another ball. Only this time she was not getting ready in the relative comfort and peace of Maplecroft Manor with a night of stress-free luxury ahead of her. Tonight, she was expected to dazzle and shine and win over a hundred or so nobles who were already set against her.

"Lovely, lovely," the dressmaker purred, cosseting her hair. "Like spun gold! I have seen women rub egg yolk in their hair and lay out in the sun for hours to achieve this shade. No! Bring the pearls, I said, bring the pearls, not the diamonds!"

Pierre Louis Perrault was an import from one of the southern islands that lay off the coast of Trenway. Ellie had only to hear his accent to determine that, but she also suspected that much of it was exaggerated and put on.

"We will make you into a *masterpiece!*" Perrault promised her. "Anyone who sees you will know that you are royal from your head to your toes! The overskirt," he said, snapping his fingers. "Put the overskirt on her!"

Ellie bent down a little to slip her arms through the holes in the top of the gown and then stood up straight as the maid fastened the two sides of the dress over the bodice.

"Made of figured emerald green velvet," Perrault explained. "It will flow elegantly when you walk and dance so that you can move like the goddess you are! Sleeves now, girls, sew on the sleeves!"

Perrault did not lift a finger to help the maids, who busily set about sliding Ellie's arms through the elaborate puffy sleeves, instead he continued to pace around her in circles, his ridiculous red heels thudding hollowly on the floor.

"The sleeves are my *pièce de résistance!*" he exclaimed, clapping his hands. "Three separate puffs around the elbow striped with green velvet and rich brocade sewn with thread of actual silver and gold. You'll notice—it matches the material of your underskirt, and with the real gold and silver, you'll shimmer like a jewel!"

Ellie did have to admit that the gown was stunning. She didn't doubt that she would make a favorable impression based on appearance alone. She just hoped that that would be enough because she wasn't sure if her wit would be nearly as extraordinary as the dress.

"You're probably wondering why I chose green," Perrault continued. "You must be questioning my fashion credentials, probably wondering why I would sabotage you with such a mediocre color. Don't worry, my dear, I'll explain myself. Initially, I wanted to swathe you in purple. I thought—it's the color of royalty. It's such a rare and difficult dye to make and

194

she'll stand out. She will make a bold declaration of her power and position.

"But then, you see, that's what ultimately convinced me that purple was the wrong choice for tonight. Queen Adelaide explained the significance of the night to me, and I realized that brazenly marching you out in royal colors might further ostracize you from the nobles you're trying to win over. We don't want that, obviously, and then she also informed me that you wore purple to the last ball, the one where His Royal Highness chose you to be his princess. Well! That settled it. A girl mustn't wear the same color twice!"

Perrault scoffed and flashed her a look that seemed to want validation of his assessment, or gratitude, perhaps that he had saved her from such a faux pas. Ellie found herself overly puzzling on his words—how could anyone manage to wear a different color every single day of their life? It seemed impossible, but Ellie certainly didn't want to ask the question aloud, because then Perrault might expound upon all the varieties of color and make her head spin. Therefore, she smiled weakly at him, but this seemed to suffice as he went on.

"So, what color to pick, then? I thought to myself, I should make her a gown of crimson and gold. With her fair hair, she will be the perfect portrait of a princess. Red makes just as bold of a statement as purple—it's extravagant and memorable. She will stand out of the crowd brilliantly. Red is vivacious, audacious—salacious! And that!" he exclaimed suddenly, snapping his fingers. "That word caught me and spared you yet another humiliation. Red can make a woman seem salacious.

Whores wear red so that they stand out in the streets. A princess of the blood might get away with wearing red and the same connotations would never dare be insinuated. But, no offense to you my dear, you were not born to power and prestige. The nobles will be looking for a reason to dislike you. So…with that in mind, better dead than red."

Ellie swallowed nervously. She had never given the color of her gown this much thought. She would have never worked out all the implications that Perrault had. She was glad that he had done all the reasoning, but it was yet another example of the utter absurdity of royal life—that so much thought could be put into something as meaningless and arbitrary as the color of one's gown.

"Next I considered blue," Perrault said loftily. "Blue to reflect the heavens above, to associate you with the lake and assert your position here at Bellbroke Castle. But blue is so uninspired these days. Everyone who wears blue is forgettable. It's a shade that people wear so as to blend in. It's a safe choice—practically no one looks bad in blue, and as I said, it's not memorable. I still wanted you to stand out. And, as a wise man once said, to win without risk is to triumph without glory."

As he was talking, the maids had finished sewing on the sleeves, and another came bearing an elaborate gilded box. She bent down before the stool and when she opened the box, Ellie nearly gasped. Inside were the most beautiful shoes she had ever seen in her life.

"Ah, you've noticed the slippers, I see," Perrault said. "It is a luxe mule made of white leather with green welt and green embroider completely encrusted with pearls. When I saw these slippers, I knew then and there that pearls simply *must* be the featured jewel of your gown. What do pearls symbolize? Innocence and youth. Are these not the valued ideals of Trenway? Are these not the prized virtues of the court? So once I saw the shoes, it all came together. Green would be the color of choice, to go along with the pearls. Green, as you know, also symbolizes youth and innocence, as well as chastity and temperance.

"A future princess must possess these virtues and more, especially a princess plucked from the low branches of obscurity. You are the champion of the commoners right now, my dear, and whether you wish to or not, you represent them. You are their ambassador in this court. And what you wear is more important than what you say. As I often tell my clients, let the clothes do the talking. If they're made by me, they'll do a much better job of it anyway."

Ellie wasn't sure that she agreed with that, but she let it go, choosing to delight in sliding on her new slippers. The soles were silky and smooth, but the lining on the inside was velvety, which had the effect of keeping her feet firmly secure.

"Our clothes, more than anything else, communicate the most about who we are as people," Perrault insisted. "It is the first thing that everyone notices, and trust me, those initial impressions of attire tend to stick the most stubbornly. Why else do you think His Royal Highness chose you on the night of the ball? Word has it that you were the most stylishly dressed, and I also heard that the prince kept your slipper clutched to his chest for days after the ball, rendered nearly feverish at its exquisite craft."

Ellie wanted to snort and chuckle aloud at the thought of Fillip lying dramatically on his bed, wet cloths on his forehead, his hand gripping her shoe like a drowning man hanging onto a rope. It was so farcically comical and absurdly far-fetched, but such was the fantasy world that a man like Perrault inhabited. He truly believed all the nonsense he spouted, the most ludicrous of it being that a man could change his stars and destiny if he wore the right kind of boots.

"I'm serious," he had averred, wagging his finger at their first meeting. "That boy was the son of a miller, he wore the right boots, and then married a duchess. Fashion is all you need to become rich and powerful. You, of all people, should know this."

Perrault had never been able to let go of the idea that Ellie had gone from rags to riches because of her choice in gown. He didn't understand that Fillip had chosen her for a different reason, a more meaningful reason. To him, there was no more meaningful reason than fashionable clothing.

"And the final touch is your jewelry," Perrault said, bringing her back to the present moment. "I went with simplicity to fit with our theme."

At his beckoning, a maid brought a necklace and fastened it around Ellie's neck. It was a pearl choker with a pendant in the shape of a clover with four emeralds set in gold. After his speech, Ellie was surprised to see the same maid come back with another necklace. This one was longer, but it was just a plain gold braid that hung down to her chest.

"The gold braid gives a shape and balance to the pearl choker," Perrault explained. "It will draw the eyes to your chest and ample décolletage, if I may be so bold..."

Ellie tried not to blush, but she saw the flush of rose tinting in her cheeks and cursed herself for being so susceptible to flattery. The truth was that it was in Perrault's natural personality to be a big flirt. In fact, flirtation was the primary currency of the court—flattery could get you anywhere and everywhere. Most courtiers had learned the art of flirtation in the same way that Ellie had learned her manners. It was so natural for them that the romance had been sucked out, in a way. It didn't really mean anything anymore—that was what happened when mystery was made mundane.

"Ah, my dear, you are perfect!" Perrault exclaimed, standing back to look at her. He clapped his hands together. "You are like a juicy pear, ripe for the plucking, a gem of the late summer! Ah, I cannot stand to look much longer. Remember what I said, my dear, and let the dress do all the talking!"

He kissed her on each cheek and then took his leave, strutting ridiculously in those iconic red heels of his. Ellie took one final look at herself in the mirror. She had to agree with Perrault. In some ways, she did look like a portrait of a princess in late summer. She didn't know that she resembled a pear ripe for the plucking, but that was one of Perrault's eccentricities—wild analogies.

Ellie's only reservation regarding her appearance was her hair. She had worn it up in a net for the first ball, but Perrault had decided that she should wear it down and loose for this one, with only a green velvet headband studded with diamonds at the top of her hair like an understated tiara. He wanted to emphasize her youth and beauty.

"A woman's hair is a symbol of her sensuality, of her distinct womanhood," Perrault had said. "For this reason, it is permissible for an unmarried woman to wear her hair down, to attract a man."

He had reasoned that she would have plenty of time to tie up her tresses once she was married to Fillip, but he urged her to wear it down as much as she could before her wedding day. Ellie had few complaints regarding her hair—she didn't think of it much, really. And when she had been a servant, she'd had no choice but to pull it up every day.

This was why she had reservations about wearing it down. She was used to tying it up, pushing it out of the way. Wearing it down, having it displayed long and loose…it seemed too flashy and showy, in Ellie's opinion. And because she wasn't used to seeing it like that, she wasn't even sure that it looked good. She asked the opinion of her two ladies-in-waiting, but they just brayed obsequious compliments and Ellie wasn't sure that she could trust them.

Instead, she went down to the kitchens where she had made friends with some of the scullery maids. Mrs. Tuttle liked to joke that they were all air-headed and out of their depth, but deep down, Ellie knew that Mrs. Tuttle had grown fond of many of the girls, as had Ellie.

"What do you think of my hair, Lindy?" she asked one of the maids.

"Oh, it's absolutely gorgeous, milady," she answered. "But what are you doing down here, all dressed up like that?"

Ellie frowned. "You can be honest," she urged. "Go on. Take a nice, long look at it and tell me truthfully—is it a tangled mess? Does it look wild and untamed? It feels out of control."

"Well, begging pardon, but it will be, milady, unless you get out of the kitchens!" Lindy cried, trying to shield her from the puffs of flour lingering in the air.

"I need you to be honest with me," Ellie pressed. "Tonight is very important and you're the only ones I can trust!"

Lindy looked truly shocked and let out a little laugh, turning back to some of the other scullery maids.

"Do you hear that, girls?" she called. "In a castle full of fancy ladies who know all about hair and perfume, we're the ones she trusts?" Turning back to Ellie, she added, "You must be off your rocker, you know that?"

"Hush," Ellie admonished. "Just tell me what you think."

"I think it looks like a waterfall!" one of the girls, Nell, called from the back.

Ellie smiled. "A waterfall?" she said. "Well, that's good, right?"

Lindy nodded her head, smiling. "It's very good," she said softly. "You look like a princess. A princess to do us proud."

"Well, I'm not so sure I'll make the king and queen proud...or Fillip," Ellie said, biting her lip. "I don't know why I'm so nervous. I shouldn't care what these people think. I'll probably never see half of them again, or if I do, I won't remember them."

"Don't you fuss and fret," Lindy assured her. "Once they see you, they'll have no choice but to love you. Just as we do."

Ellie glanced down at Lindy, seeing the girl in a new light. For her part, the maid's eyes flicked up and met hers shyly.

"We all look up to you, milady," she said in a quiet voice. Ellie looked around at all the maids, who had stopped fluttering about, to listen to her and Lindy's conversation. Ellie made a point to look at each one, to study the features of each face.

"You give us hope," Lindy went on. "You give us hope that maybe one day we can do better for ourselves, and rise out of the muck and mire. At first, we didn't believe that it was possible; we thought it was a lie that you had been a servant, a kitchen girl. None of us thought it was true; we just assumed they had said that to win people over or something. But then we saw you, and we started attending to you, and well...we just knew it was true then."

"I knew it was true when I saw the rough calluses on your hands," Nell chimed in.

"I knew it was true when you helped me clean up a broken vase," another said, Marie.

"I knew it was true when you showed me how to get a grass stain out of one of Prince Fillip's shirts," another said, Corinne.

Yet another maid came forward, this one Ellie recognized as Yvette, one of the first maids she had met at the castle.

"And I knew it when you helped Cook make one of the best rhubarb pies I've ever eaten in my life!"

All the girls smiled and emphatically agreed that they had never tasted rhubarb pie so good, but despite prodding, Ellie wouldn't relinquish her secret ingredient. Others came forward still, saying they recognized Ellie as one of them when she peeled potatoes faster than anyone they had ever seen, or when she knew how to sew on a button, or when she showed them how to clean a mirror with gin and a silk handkerchief.

"I knew it was true when I saw you empty your own chamber pot!" Meg said, to uproarious laughter.

Ellie laughed along with them. "I've been doing these things for years," she said. "It seemed foolish to stop just because I was here. A lot of it was just out of habit. It runs deep."

Corinne snorted. "Oh, you can bet that if I marry a rich man, I'll settle myself on a sofa that first day and not move a muscle!"

The other girls agreed, saying they would cleave to a life of luxury and have no trouble being idle.

"You all deserve it," Ellie said. "We all deserve to live richly. I think that maybe you'd become bored after a while and your hands would itch to do something like mine did, but you all deserve better than this...better than what you have."

"We're all very grateful," Lindy said. "We know that serving you is an honor and a position in the castle is already far beyond what most of us expected. But you do give us hope, milady, that we can dream of going even farther. Even if it never happens for any of us...the fact that it *could*...that it did happen to one *like* us...well, that in and of itself is enough."

Ellie reached down and squeezed Lindy's hand, and the girl rewarded her with a warm smile. In some ways, Ellie felt a bit sad. She would have rather spent every afternoon with these girls instead of the royal courtiers of her age. She looked again at every face around her—*these* were her peers, these were her people.

"You know when I knew it was true?" a small voice said, from the back window. It was Jane, one of the more quiet and reserved maids. "I knew it was true when you learned all of our names. That was the first thing you asked me: my name. And then you remembered it. You've never mixed us up—not once."

"Well no," Ellie said, laughing. "You're all very different and distinct!"

Her face fell as she looked around at them, at their downcast faces and realized that not everyone saw them as individual and distinct the way she did. That to many at the castle, they blended and blurred together.

"We've all been called each other's names," Lindy explained. "That is, when they manage to remember our names at all."

"I've been called Laura," Marie said. "There's not even a girl who works here named Laura."

Ellie frowned and clenched her fists, thinking of Jehanne and the queen, who had undoubtedly done some of these things. Ellie hated thinking ill of the queen who, more than anyone else in this castle, did seem to have a good and noble heart. But she had been born to privilege, had been immune to the struggles of poverty and hard work, and had always been surrounded by interchangeable faces. Doubtless she had seen hundreds of maids in her lifetime.

The queen often tried to temper the king's ill humor by championing causes that he preferred to abandon, such as the plight of the poor. The queen always advocated for those in the lower classes. It was a trait that Ellie had much admired until this moment. Adelaide claimed to care for the working class, but she couldn't even be bothered to learn the names of her maids. It smacked of hypocrisy and that was something that Ellie hated above all—saying one thing and doing quite the opposite.

Looking around at all the maids, Ellie felt bolstered and uplifted. This was more inspiring to her than anything Perrault had said. This feeling of support and admiration from her maids gave Ellie the courage to go to the ball with confidence and poise. She would do it for them. Everything that she did from now on would be for the maids, and all the other girls like them who dreamed of a better future, who looked to her as an example. She would give them something to live up to; she would make them proud.

Chapter Fourteen

The Many Shades of Green

ONE of the worst things about the second ball was that Ellie had to make a grand entrance by herself. Unlike the previous ball, where she had navigated the huge half-spiral staircase whilst swimming in a sea of anonymity, this time she would have to descend it alone with all eyes watching her from below, waiting to see her trip or stumble. Fillip would be waiting for her at the end of the staircase, where he would tuck her arm in his and then take her around the room, introducing her to the various noblemen and their wives. That would be unpleasant in and of itself, but Ellie was most anxious about the walk down the staircase.

She had never counted each step, but she was sure there were over a hundred. And given that she was already nervous, and given that she had not eaten much during the day because of it, Ellie was terribly afraid that she would stumble on one of the steps, which would be bad enough, or worse that it would cause her to fall. A tumble down that staircase would mean death unless she fell very close to the bottom of it.

Looking at it both ways, Ellie hoped that if she did fall, she fell right from the top. She would rather have died than stand up after tripping and falling in front of hundreds of people who were already looking down their noses at her. She could imagine the sniggering and staring that would linger all evening...what a nightmare. Ellie wished she could hole herself up in her room with a hot toddy and a good book.

Instead, Ellie made her way out of her room, lifting her skirts and practicing walking in her slippers in all sorts of odd ways. If she could get a good feel for the shoes, then she'd have a better chance navigating all those steps in them. Luckily for her, Pierre Louis Perrault really was the best fashion designer in all of Trenway, and the shoes he had made for her were flawless not only in appearance, but in composition as well. The mules were delightfully easy to walk in.

As she came closer to the grand ballroom, she could hear the din of the party below. All that separated her from them was a thick velvet curtain that had been draped over the balcony. Ellie could remember this balcony from the night of the first ball. She had looked out over it, onto the milling crowds below. But tonight, she was not allowed an outsider glimpse in. The curtain was there so she could make a dramatic entrance. She approached the herald who stood at the top of the staircase waiting for her. He stood solemnly, with his feet shoulder width apart, a long staff held in his hand, his face stoic and marble-like.

They made eye contact briefly, and Ellie gave the slightest nod of her head. It was his job to pick up on the most imperceptible shifts in the royal family. He saw that she was nervous, allowed her another moment to compose herself, and then at another quick nod from her, he banged his staff loudly on the stone floor three times. A sudden hush fell over the room below as the herald's voice boomed magnificently throughout the chamber. Ellie knew that he had been placed there strategically—it was an acoustic spot for his voice to carry naturally.

"The Duchess of Hartmere and future Princess of Trenway, Lady Eleanor Katherine Marchand," he announced.

Ellie was suddenly reminded of the ceremonial title that had been bestowed upon her almost immediately after arriving at Bellbroke Castle. It was yet another way of cleverly legitimizing her claim to royalty, by suddenly inventing a title and making her a duchess. As Fillip had explained to her, the king's powers were severely limited by his council, but he still had the ability to arbitrarily create and dissolve titles.

There was nothing else to be done for it. Ellie had been announced, and so she took a reeling step forward, clutching the banister for support. She took each step slowly and carefully, as though she were a toddler again, learning how to navigate the stairs at Maplecroft Manor, her little hand clutched around her father's finger. Ellie knew that they would have to wait for her, and besides, Queen Adelaide had told her that making people wait was a regal trait.

Resisting the urge to look down and match her foot to each step, Ellie forced herself to keep her chin held high, and to look down upon the courtiers below with a detached, chilled expression, as if they were figuratively beneath her as well. Ordinarily, Ellie would have never relished in such snobbery, but with these people, whose entire lives revolved around being snobbish to servants, Ellie delighted in every minute of it.

Before she knew it, she had made it to the very last step, and was rewarded with the sight of Fillip beaming at her, his arm

208

outstretched to take hers. As soon as she had linked arms with Fillip, the crowd erupted in massive applause and Ellie felt almost breathless. Walking down the stairs was hardly an accomplishment, but Ellie felt a flooding sense of relief, as if the worst part of the night was somehow behind her.

When the applause had died down, Fillip whispered in her ear,

"You look absolutely beautiful."

She blushed, looking downward. "It's not too much, is it?" she asked. "The hair? They spent hours curling it just to leave it down and it feels a wild mess back there."

"No, your hair is perfect," Fillip said, touching one of the tendrils by her ear. "You look exactly as I've always dreamed my future bride would look. Any man would feel humbled to have you by his side...just know that I feel doubly humbled."

"Doubly?" she said, laughing a bit. "Why is that?"

"Because you are like an angel, fit for a prince of the heavens and I am a mere mortal."

"Oh, stop it," she said teasingly. "I would settle for simply looking like someone who could be a princess."

"Well you do," Fillip assured her. "You look the part of a princess and more. Come, shall we meet these vipers?"

"I suppose we must," she said, allowing him to lead her. And with Fillip by her side, the ordeal of meeting dozens of people one after the other didn't seem such a grim prospect anymore.

AFTER about twenty minutes, all the names and the faces began to blur together, leaving Ellie with the impression that she really didn't remember who she had met at all. When she and Fillip took respite from the introductions to grab a bite to eat, she confessed this to him, whispering it as quietly as she could in his ear. Fillip, upon hearing it, burst into loud peals of laughter.

"Hush!" she chastised. "I don't want it getting about..."

"Don't worry, Ellie Kate," he told her. "Trust me...I wouldn't know half these people if Mother hadn't made me study their names and portraits for these last few days. I remember some of them, naturally, and you will too, for various reasons. Some people just have a way of sticking out. But you'll forget most, especially the old country nobles who only come out for these sorts of things."

"How many noble families are there in Trenway?" she asked. "This seems like far more than I ever imagined."

"There are seventy-one noble families in Trenway," he answered. "Each with a distinct motto and coat of arms. They each inhabit a castle or manor house somewhere in the country with a sprawling estate. Most have command of the area in which they live with an ability to call men to arms should their King require it. Other nobles have less power than that...there are tiers of nobility. You'll learn that."

"I've already picked up on some of it," she said. "A duke is the highest peer next to a prince, which is why Jehanne is a duchess, and why Roland and Edmund are dukes."

"And why you're a duchess," Fillip said.

"Well...yes..." she said, blushing again. "And after a duke there's a marquess, then an earl, then a viscount, then a baron, and then a baronet. But baronets are like knights—they're landed gentry, but they aren't considered to be part of the nobility."

"Correct," Fillip said.

"But what about Lord Robert Cecil?" she asked. "He's a Grand Duke. What does that mean?"

Fillip shrugged. "It's an invented title, I guess you could say. He's not above Roland or Edmund or anyone with royal blood. But he is above other dukes of non-royal blood. The Cecil family has always been closely intertwined with the Westenra family. Long ago, in the days of civil war, the Cecil's were fiercely loyal to the cause of Henric Westenra, my ancestor. Many say it was because of the Cecil's that Henric eventually took the throne. Almost immediately after Henric's coronation, he created the title of Grand Duke for his closest friend and ally, Lord Percy Cecil. The title has been passed down father to son ever since."

"Interesting," Ellie hummed.

"Oh no," Fillip swore. "Here comes my father, with the Marquess of Marsden. Three guesses what he wants..."

"What?" Ellie said, puzzled.

"The Marquess of Marsden is an old battle-axe," Fillip said. "He's fought in so many wars, he can't keep them straight in his head. Used to fight as a mercenary, that's how much he loved combat, only he didn't do it for the money. Would have volunteered his services. Now, he's so old and addled, it's a

211

miracle he hasn't died, but he's been forced into retirement. He was getting feeble, and in his last battle, his dementia caused him to turn on his own side, starting to slice apart the men he was fighting with. It's a wonder no one killed him for that! But after winning the battle, they dragged him off the field, and brought him back to Trenway with ropes around his wrists. His family had to take him in disgraced. I'm surprised he was invited here."

"What is your father doing with him?" Ellie asked. "Doesn't seem politic to be associating with someone like that..."

"My father doesn't care about his reputation," Fillip spat. "Not when it's his reputation that he wants. My father loves to talk war, and with the old Marquess, he'll get hours of conversation. But now he'll want to drag me into it."

"Well, he can't!" Ellie snapped. "You have to stay here with me."

By this point, the king had made his way over with the Marquess of Marsden. Curtly nodding to Ellie, he quickly complimented her on her gown and beauty, and then turned almost fanatically to his son.

"Come for some brandy and cigars, son," the king urged, clapping Fillip on the back. "We've got a regular war council set up in the other room. And you've never properly met the Marquess of Marsden, have you?"

"No, I haven't," Fillip said, standing up and acknowledging the old man. Ellie observed that her fiancé had been right—the marquess was shockingly feeble, especially given the picture Fillip had drawn of his earlier exploits. But such a life took a toll, and Ellie found that she was staring at the results of a life spent wasted in senseless violence.

"Come have a drink," the king urged again. "It's less stuffy in the other room...not as many people."

"Not as stuffy?" Fillip questioned. "In a small room filled with cigar smoke? No, thank you, Father, but I must stay with my lovely fiancée. Tonight is her party, after all."

"Exactly, so let her to it!" the king reasoned, like a child. "She'll need to learn how to deal with all this on her own eventually."

"Father..."

"Your mother did!" he protested. "When she first came here, she didn't speak a lick of our language. You think I was doing her any favors by huddling around her every hour of the day, constantly translating, helping her navigate everything? No, I let her learn to swim for herself and she's done a decent job of it. Still a lot to be desired..." he said, frowning, "but better than if I'd constantly been there to do everything for her."

Ellie panicked, sensing that Fillip's resolve was weakening. The king was a notorious pusher, and Fillip's deep desire to please his father would always come out in the end. The king was fickle, though, and if he didn't want something bad enough, he would leave after one or two declinations. But if he remained persistent enough, Fillip's walls would come tumbling down.

Fillip hazarded a brief glance out of the corner of his eye at her, gauging her expression and reaction to the developing situation. Ellie felt her chest heave and fall all at once. What choice did she have, ultimately? If she insisted that he stay by her side in front of the king, she would look weak in the king's eyes and she knew she couldn't risk doing anything to contradict her future father-in-law. All ways were his ways. He was like a baby throwing a tantrum when he didn't get his way, only he wasn't a baby. He was a large grown man with the command of hundreds at his fingertips. And Ellie knew for certain that she didn't want any of that man-baby wrath directed at her, nor did she want either man to think of her as some sort of helpless little girl.

"I'll be fine, Fillip," she lied, as convincingly as she could.

"Are you sure?" he said quickly.

"Absolutely, go ahead, I'll be fine," she repeated.

"Well, all right," he said, kissing her forehead. "I'll be back in half an hour or less," he promised, squeezing her hand.

She nodded her assent and then watched him walk away, feeling suddenly bereft and clueless as to what to do next. She supposed that she could go and find the queen or Jehanne. Glancing around the room, she didn't see them immediately, and the last thing she wanted to do was walk without purpose through a room of strangers, so she stayed put. It only took a few minutes before someone found her, and suddenly Ellie found herself staring at a vaguely familiar woman who took a smug sip from her goblet, her dark eyes flashing maliciously.

"Remember me?" she said, almost like a taunt.

"You look familiar," Ellie admitted. "I am sorry, please remind me of your name."

The woman tilted her head back, licking her lips.

214

"Cecelia Scrimshaw," she said, and to Ellie it sounded like nails scratching down a chalkboard. There was something sinister about her name. But it immediately rang a bell. On the night of the first ball, Ellie had interrupted this woman's meeting with the fake prince by drunkenly stumbling in the antechamber. She could still remember how Cecelia had bumped past her, skirts rustling angrily.

"I see you remember now," Cecelia said. "Great. Now that the introductions are over, let's move on, shall we?"

Taken aback by her tone, Ellie realized that Cecelia was still harboring a grudge over the incident on the night of the first ball. Then she recalled the Grand Duke's warning about her: *don't expect to become fast friends with her. She's weaseled her way back into the court as one of the queen's ladies-in-waiting. As soon as she sees you, she'll recognize you.* Well, that had certainly been true. Ellie looked around, wondering if the Grand Duke was witnessing this tense tête-á-tête.

"Strange how life turns out, isn't it?" Cecelia said. "To think—I would have been standing in your shoes had it not been for you and too many goblets of wine."

"Well, that's not the only…"

"It really beggars belief," she continued, "that your little drunken stumble into *my* interview was enough to alter my destiny. How could that be? I've spent weeks trying to puzzle it out, and lost hours of sleep that, trust me, I'm going to demand you pay back. I was just…*bewildered!* But then I figured it out."

"Look," Ellie interrupted. "I'm sorry for barging in on your interview with the prince. It wasn't intentional, and I tried to leave…"

"Oh, did you?" Cecelia demanded. "Did you try to leave? I don't remember that. In fact, I remember you doing the opposite. I remember *you* staying, while *I* had to do the leaving. That's what *I* remember."

"I'm sorry for doing that," Ellie said again, trying to remain calm. "It was an honest mistake."

"Honest?" Cecelia snorted, crossing her arms.

"You do realize that wasn't the prince you were meeting with. Technically, I didn't interrupt anything."

Cecelia repeated her words in a high-pitched mimic, and then turned nasty again.

"Of course, I realize that wasn't the prince!" she exclaimed. "I'm not an imbecile. I am a courtier. I was born and bred for this world, and I'd been living in the court for two whole years before the ball. I knew who the real prince was."

"All right, well, then I'm sure you realize that my interrupting that wasn't as dire as you thought it was," Ellie said defensively. "Did you even speak to the real prince that night?"

Cecelia mimicked her again, and Ellie resisted the urge to slap her across the face just to shut her up.

"You are so dumb, you know that?" Cecelia said. "And no, I don't care if you're a duchess or whatever trumped up fake title they gave you to make you feel more important than you are. I don't care that I'm speaking so disrespectfully to a future princess of Trenway. You know why? Because you're nothing.

And I've got nothing to fear from you. You can't do anything to hurt me...you couldn't lift a finger to touch a hair on my head. I'm protected in this court, and even if you tattle on me, just know that nothing will come of it."

Ellie's eyes narrowed into slits. There was plenty she could do to Cecelia Scrimshaw that didn't involve tattling like a four-year-old. The endless possibilities played through her head. She could sneak a garter snake in her bed, or she could slip some senna in her evening wine and watch her soil herself at dinner in front of the whole court. Best of all, none of it could be traced back to her.

"The prince would have been mine if it hadn't been for you," Cecelia sneered. "Fillip and I go way back, farther than you know and farther than he'll be willing to tell you. We have a shared history, he and I. Relationships like ours don't just...fade away."

"I don't know what you're talking about but I suggest you stop," Ellie warned.

"Or what?" Cecelia laughed. "You can't do anything to me. They chose the perfect color for you, didn't they? Green...what a laugh!"

Ellie looked down at her dress self-consciously. What had Perrault said that green connoted? She couldn't remember. All the color associations were so idiotic and convoluted anyway. But now she was suddenly worried that green connoted something negative, and it figured that Cecelia Scrimshaw would be the one to pick up on it.

"It just proves that you're totally inexperienced for the role of princess," Cecelia said pompously. "You're as green as a young boy heading to war. Naïve, foolish, completely unprepared...green. And soon you'll be green for another reason...green with envy."

"I doubt that," Ellie asserted. "I've never been envious a day in my life. You'd be surprised how low maintenance I am."

"Oh? Are you as copacetic when it comes to Fillip?" Cecelia asked. "Is that an open invitation to share him?"

"What?"

Cecelia grinned wickedly. "I didn't think so," she said. "No, your feelings for Fillip are real. Too bad his aren't for you. He's a good actor, always has been. We used to play-act together when we were younger, so I would know. He probably likes you, no doubt desires you. But those feelings tend to fade fast. That which burns hot always cools fast. Soon he'll want to move on to better things."

"And you think yourself better?" Ellie scoffed, looking her up and down. She was horribly bony and angular, with no figure to speak of and a face like a dog's. Literally, her face featured a squished looking nose that resembled one of Adelaide's dogs. What with her horrible attitude to go along with her appearance, Ellie couldn't fathom at all what attribute Cecelia could possibly count in her favor.

"I do," Cecelia claimed. "You're not even married and already his eye wanders. Don't believe me? Watch him when he comes back. Suddenly you'll see all the other girls he notices. And once you're married and maybe even crowned queen, he'll

218

be expected to have affairs. Trust me—I'll be the first one he goes after, I'll make sure of that."

All she could do was seethe inwardly at this pale slip of a girl. Ellie was practically shaking with rage from her head to her toes. If this had happened in the yard at Maplecroft Manor, Cecelia would have been on the ground by now, getting a mouthful of grass and sharp punches to the ribs. There would have been no way she'd suffer even a tenth of what the vile creature had spewed forth.

But here...locked in the rigidity and decorum of the castle, Ellie was powerless to retaliate in the way she wanted.

Cecelia picked at something under her nail. "Mistress is hardly the title I was going after, but it'll do well enough. Some mistresses can last for *years*. And if they're loved more than the queen, they get more gifts and more time with the king. Best of all, they can lounge in luxury without all the hassle and obligation of royal appearances. But don't be fooled—I would have been better at all of that than you, and I still want the glory. Well, only time will tell. As I said, you're not even married yet. Engagements can be undone..."

"And people can drown in two inches of water," Ellie muttered under her breath.

"What?"

"Nothing," Ellie said sweetly. "It was a pleasure to meet you again, Cecelia. I hope you have a lovely evening."

Without waiting for any reply, Ellie turned her back on Cecelia and walked away, hoping that other people had taken note of her public snub. It was one of the nice things about royal life that was ordinarily so stupid and tedious—the fact that people were always watching with hawk-like eyes, waiting to make massive inferences from the slightest gestures.

As she walked away to join Jehanne and Queen Adelaide, whom she finally spotted, Ellie knew that it would be best for her to shake off everything that Cecelia had said. She knew that it was just poisonous lies and exaggerations. Cecelia was jealous. Envy inspired bragging untruths more than anything else, and it prompted unwarranted cruelty, as Cecelia had demonstrated. Still, though, Ellie was bothered by her words, and despite herself, had a nagging urge to ask Fillip about it when he returned.

Chapter Fifteen

For Love of One's Father

FILLIP had still not emerged from his father's impromptu 'war council' after nearly two hours, and Ellie was starting to become worried. What if he stayed there all night? The ball would likely last until dawn, or at least that was what Jehanne had said. That sobering fact alone had made Ellie want to throw up, a desire which had probably been exacerbated by the copious amounts of wine she'd drunk just to make it through two hours. Feeling a bit sick, Ellie made her way to the outer balcony, on the western side of the castle. The view on this balcony wasn't great. It was of the forest on the shore that Bellbroke Castle abutted, but Ellie wasn't interested in a good view. And she knew that the lapping waves of the lake water would likely unsettle her stomach further.

Stepping out into the slightly chilled night air, Ellie closed her eyes and took a deep breath, relishing in the sweet pine scent from the trees on the shore. Perhaps it was the lingering effects of the wine, or perhaps it was the late summer night breeze that triggered a wave of nostalgia, but all alone on the balcony, Ellie began to hum a melody that she thought she had forgotten. It was a somber, mournful tune that her father had often sang to get her to sleep. He told her that it was a sea shanty he had learned from a pirate. Ellie smiled, remembering having teased him that it

221

couldn't be true—pirates didn't sing! *This one did,* he had told her matter-of-factly, *this one sang all night long to keep the nightmares at bay.*

Ellie couldn't have known it then, but she would turn back to this song, when her father had died, and she had been left alone with her hateful stepmother. When she had first been exiled to the attic, she could remember curling up on the cold floor, singing the words to the song faithfully, childishly believing that they might bring her father back. And then she had kept singing it occasionally throughout the subsequent years, as the pirate had, to keep the nightmares at bay.

Closing her eyes, lost in the song, Ellie didn't even flinch when she heard another voice join hers, one much lower in tenor. For a moment, her mind addled with drink, she thought it was her father. As she held on to the last notes of the song, Ellie reasoned that she must have imagined the voice of her father singing along with her. That was why she suffered a bit of a shock when she opened her eyes and saw a real man standing beside her.

"Mercy!" she swore, jumping back.

"I am sorry, milady, I did not mean to frighten you," he said, in a low-pitched, comforting voice. "I just heard you singing from inside, and it was so lovely, I thought I would join you. *Luna Lacrimae* is one of my favorite songs," he added, winking.

"My father used to sing it to me," Ellie confessed. "Said he learned it from a pirate."

The man chuckled. "Yes, it's a very old sea ditty, one of the more ancient ones I believe, plucked from the sea scrolls of

222

Charteris. Sailors have been singing it for at least a thousand years."

"Really?" Ellie said, incredulously. "A thousand years...I'm sorry, who are you?"

"Forgive me," the older man said, bowing his head. "My name is Alastair de Vere, Earl of Mortimer."

"I'm Ellie," she blurted. "Well, Eleanor Katherine Marchand, but you can call me Ellie."

He grinned in amusement. "Thank you for the liberty, milady, but I think I should prefer to call you Lady Marchand, which I knew by the way, as this is your party."

"Right," she said, a bit embarrassed. "It is. I quite forgot. I'm not ordinarily so forgetful," she added. "I suppose I just introduced myself out of habit."

"Understandable," he granted. "It must be a bit odd to be thrown in this mix, coming from your background."

"It's very daunting," Ellie agreed. "And very different."

"How are you getting along?" he queried. "If you don't mind my asking..."

"No, not at all. I think it's going well. All the protocol and decorum is a bit confusing, and apart from me feeling like there isn't anything useful I can *do*, I think I've been settling into my new life."

Lord de Vere grinned again. "Forgive me, milady, but you are quite a different mold."

"How do you mean?" Ellie asked, feeling a bit insulted. Lord de Vere picked up on it.

"Oh, no, I don't mean it in a bad way," he assured her. "It's just that…most women in this sphere, in this echelon, don't necessarily itch for 'useful' things to do."

"Well, that's how I was brought up," Ellie said, a bit defensively. "I'm not used to doing nothing all day."

Lord de Vere stumbled over another chuckle, which he tried to mask as a cough.

"And pray tell, dear lady, what have you been doing with your days?"

"Well, I've been reading, and I've been out riding with the prince. I've gone out on the lake, I've explored the castle and I think I've finally mapped it out. I've been working in the apothecary, and I've also been annoying the king's alchemist, trying to break into his laboratory."

As she listed her activities, it seemed as though Lord de Vere had been trying to stifle a great laugh, and as soon as she had finished, it appeared he couldn't help himself. A great boom of laughter erupted from his chest, and Ellie felt her ears bristle like that of a cat's at his obnoxious amusement.

"And pray tell, sir, what is so funny?" she demanded.

"The king's alchemist!" Lord de Vere wheezed, between breaths. "You've been annoying the king's alchemist…" and then he burst into another peal of laughter.

Ellie crossed her arms, waiting patiently for him to finish, and when he did, he very sincerely apologized for his uncontrollable mirth.

"I do apologize, milady," he began. "But once again, I must reiterate that you are a different breed entirely, and I find

224

that to be...utterly spectacular. Moreover, I've met the king's alchemist—a completely sour and disagreeable fellow, a pompous popinjay with more words than wit, and I think you could probably teach *him* a thing or two. It would be hysterical to see him showed up by a woman!"

Ellie couldn't resist smiling a bit, knowing that he wasn't laughing maliciously at her, or poking fun at her expense.

"Well, for my part, I hope you are incorrect, sir," she said. "For I do not know much regarding alchemy, and I should like to learn so I would hope that the alchemist is worth his salt."

"I'm afraid not," Lord de Vere proclaimed. "At least not by my estimation. But, as I'm sure your father told you, alchemy is less of a science and more of a bizarre sort of treasure hunt."

"I am more interested in the properties of the metals and liquids that they use," Ellie explained. "My father taught me how to use aqua regia, but we didn't have a chance to experiment with some of the others—aqua fortis, and aqua vitae—before he passed away."

"I am sorry to hear that," Lord de Vere said. "I am sure you will have your opportunity."

"I hope so," she said, a bit glumly.

"I hope that I do not presume too much," Lord de Vere began. "That is to say, I hope you do not think me impertinent, but I venture to say that your father would be very proud of you, if he could see you now. I know that I didn't know the man, though having met you, I do wish I could have. However, I have to think that anyone who could have raised such a thoughtful and intelligent young woman would be proud to see her standing on the mantle of change. You are a different sort of woman, as I've said, and I believe wholeheartedly that such a woman is what this kingdom needs. We need a queen of intelligence, integrity, and sensitivity."

Ellie blushed. "Thank you kindly, sir," she said. "But with all due respect as well, I don't know how you can say such things with confidence. You barely know me."

Ellie observed him, the way his silver beard seemed to sparkle in the moonlight, his blue eyes twinkling like the stars above, and instinctively knew that he was a friend.

"I barely know you, and yet..." he said, softly. "And yet, when I came upon you, you were singing one of my favorite songs, *Luna Lacrimae*, a song of deep longing and sadness. Anyone who sings this song in the dark of night has known pain and loss. And anyone who can feel so deeply is a person of sensitivity and integrity."

Reminded of her father, Ellie bowed her head, trying to hold back tears. She had not thought of him in such a visceral, child-like way in a long time. She had grown to be strong, and independent, yet seeing this older man in front of her, so reminiscent of Cornelius Marchand, reminded Ellie that the scars of childhood never fully went away.

"As for your intelligence," Lord de Vere continued. "Well, that was evident from the moment you opened your mouth. I am afraid I must go, but I bid you good night, milady, and it was a pleasure meeting you."

"It was a pleasure meeting you as well, Lord de Vere," Ellie said, watching him go with a bit of a heavy heart.

226

As much as she didn't want to go back inside, Ellie knew that if she stayed out on the balcony, looking up into the night sky and singing *Luna Lacrimae*, she would eventually start crying and fall to pieces in the middle of a very important ball. Knowing she couldn't do that, and unwilling to confront the demons of her father's death on this night, Ellie swallowed the lump in her throat, held her head high, and marched back into the ballroom, hoping that Fillip had finally come out of his father's 'war council'.

As it turned out, Fillip remained in the clutches of his jingoistic father for another three hours, so that by the time he stumbled out, he reeked of cigar smoke and brandy, and his face was flushed red with the heat and excitement of testosterone-fueled banter. By this point, the sky was beginning to lighten with the coming of dawn, and Ellie was utterly and completely exhausted. She had never stayed up so late before. And she could hardly call it late—it was now early, around the time that she would have been rising to start her day at Maplecroft Manor.

Completely overwrought from the night's events and conversations, when Fillip finally staggered out, Ellie glided over to him immediately, catching him by the arm.

"What have you been doing?" she hissed. "You were in there for over five hours!"

"ELLIE KATE!" Fillip boomed, bombarding her with brandy breath. "Oh, my darling, I'm so glad to see you!"

He wrapped his arms around her waist and planted a wet kiss on her cheek. Despite the ardor behind it, Ellie was less than thrilled to have brandy drool dripping down to her chin, and quickly wiped it away with her handkerchief. Already irritated, she was starting to become snappy at his obnoxious behavior.

"Great," she muttered. "You're slobbering drunk, literally. What an excellent way to end the evening."

Never having been around Fillip when he was drunk, Ellie wasn't entirely sure whether he would be able to pick up on sarcasm. Some drunks could, others were far too happy to think anyone could say anything negative whilst they were inebriated.

"Oh, Ellie Kate, you're so beautiful," he crooned. "Even when you frown. Why are you frowning? Don't frown, Ellie Kate..."

"I thought you said I still looked good with a frown," she snapped, walking him over to the refreshment table.

"What?" he said, confused. "Oh, look! Crumpets! *And* sweet honey rolls!"

Fillip made a beeline for the food table, nearly falling into it and causing the plate of honey rolls to crash to the floor. Ellie stood from a distance, watching him make a fool of himself, wondering if she had looked so ridiculous on the night of the first ball. But then...no, she couldn't have. She hadn't been a tenth as drunk as Fillip currently was.

She almost jumped again as she felt a hand on her shoulder. Turning around, she relaxed as she saw it was the queen.

"Don't worry, my dear," Adelaide told her. "Fillip has a love for drink like his father before him. But he's a young man still, and his father never drank to excess."

"You don't call *that* excess?" Ellie questioned.

"Well, it could be a lot worse," Adelaide prevaricated. "Trust me, I've seen worse. Anyway, I wanted to tell you that it will be all right. Just talk to him later today, once he's sobered up, and you've rested."

"Talk to him?"

"Yes," Adelaide said, patting her back again. "I've heard about the row you had with Cecelia Scrimshaw...well, we all saw it. As Fillip's mother, I can assure you that there was no formal relationship or betrothal between them...not ever, despite what Cecelia thinks. I can't speak to anything...informal...or if there was ever any...*understanding*...between them, or adolescent dalliance. I doubt it—Cecelia is not Fillip's type at all, and there was a great stretch of time when she wasn't even at the castle. I'm sure you've heard of her mother's indiscretion..."

Ellie felt her stomach twisting in knots as Adelaide continued. She knew that Fillip's mother meant well by saying these things, but what she didn't realize was that by speaking to the rumors at all, she was validating what Cecelia had said, in some ways, and that made it all the worse. If there was truly nothing to worry about, why say anything at all?

"Dreadful business," the queen continued. "Goneril Scrimshaw was an abhorrent woman and in the end, she got the retribution she deserved. Women like her, and Cecelia always do. Give them enough rope, and they'll hang themselves. You won't

229

have to lift a finger, you can just watch from your tower above and laugh coldly when they try to placate and plead with you. Just wait. Cecelia is my lady-in-waiting. I've had ample time to observe her, and she's just like Goneril—the rotten apple didn't fall far from the tree there."

Ellie continued to watch as Fillip chewed loudly through his crumpet, and then demanded some water from one of the servants when his mouth was dry. She couldn't help but wonder, in that moment, what kind of man he truly was. She knew that this wasn't an entirely fair observation—drink had a way of rendering a man abnormally stupid and silly. But her objection was to the kind of man who lent himself to drink's stupefying influence too often. There had to be some kind of flaw in that.

"Everything will be better in the morning," Adelaide said again, soothingly.

"It is morning," Ellie said stiffly.

Adelaide let out a little laugh. "Well, yes, but I meant the afternoon, I suppose. Everything will be better once you've both slept the night off. It always is, you know, better after sleep. Don't pester him with Cecelia's nonsense until later…"

Annoyed, Ellie had the nagging feeling that Adelaide wouldn't stop pestering her until she had assured her that she wouldn't bother Fillip about the issue of Cecelia until after he'd sobered up. Why was that? Was she afraid that he would let something slip in his uninhibited state?

"I won't," she promised, a bit half-heartedly, crossing her arms. "We'll talk later…but I am worried about it."

"Of course, you are," Adelaide gushed. "All right, well, good...as long as you'll talk later, that's good to hear. Everything will be fine," she said airily, walking away. "The ball was a complete success—you were a smashing hit! Everyone simply *adored* you."

Ellie gave a weak smile. "Good," she said softly. "I'm glad everyone else had a good time."

Still frowning, she continued to watch as Fillip guzzled his goblet of water in one gulp and then pulled it away from his face, gasping for air as he shoved it toward the servant, demanding a refill. There were a dozen things she admired about Fillip. In many ways, he was very mature. But in other ways, he was still immature, and she couldn't help but think that her annoyance was partly her own fault. Hadn't she been attracted to his boyish charm? What did it say about her that his youthful swagger, playful banter, and carefree, come-what-may attitude had been very attractive to her? She had to remind herself that there was a dark side to every personality—people weren't so cut and dried, good and bad.

This—this was the dark side to Fillip's boyish, youthful larks. He was still a young man at heart, with all the weaknesses and near-sightedness of his youth and social class, in particular. Having never had to struggle or work for a living, life was just a big party for Fillip. Day in and day out, he'd had the freedom to do whatever he wanted. Yes, there were some strings, and his days were beginning to fill up with royal duties, but he had never been plagued with worry—with the gut fear of survival.

In truth, Ellie never had either. She had never truly faced down the fear of starvation, but living on a farm, it had never been far from her mind. What was it that made Ellie and Fillip so different? After all, Ellie had imbibed too much...even she could feel the after-effects of the wine in her belly, though her mind had sobered up by this point. Why was she judging Fillip so harshly?

Perhaps it was because Ellie didn't like to lose control. Even when she drank too much, she was never beyond controlling her actions. She had never pushed past that point of losing awareness, of blurting whatever came to mind, or barreling through several hours, passing out, and then awakening with no memory of what had come before. Ellie was afraid that Fillip was heading toward that state of intoxication, and judging by the look of it, he was a familiar traveler down that road.

Even though she wanted to push the issue of Cecelia Scrimshaw, even though she wanted to see what revelations would come from Fillip's mouth when he had little to no control over his responses, Ellie knew that she would keep her promise to the queen. Not necessarily because she *wanted* to, but mostly because she knew that she needed to...for the sake of her and Fillip's relationship.

THE last day of summer dawned pink and orange, ripening into a spectacular blue with the sun a distant orb, hanging perfectly alone in the sky, its rays unimpeded by any trace of a cloud. Ellie stood on the balcony of the outer wall of the gardens, waiting for Fillip to come and see her. She had left word with his valet, arranging a time for them to talk. They had not seen each other since the day before last, the night of the ball. Ellie had slept her way through most of that following day, and due to the exertions of the night before, dinner was a solitary affair. The King and Queen still presided over a formal dinner with the court, but Ellie's attendance was optional. She wasn't sure if Fillip had opted out either, and she found that she didn't much care. When she took a moment to evaluate her feelings, she realized that another day of introspection might do them both good.

But on this day, a warm day in late September, Ellie knew that they need to talk, and it couldn't wait. Cecelia's words still bothered her, and she was finally willing to confront Fillip. She had also considered ways to retaliate against the Scrimshaw girl, more childish antics and possibilities playing through her head. The maids, particularly, had enjoyed this game. Corinne and Lindy suggested peppering her bed with thorns from a barberry bush, as well as putting the spiky leaves in her pillows. Marie said they ought to crush up poison ivy leaves and mix them in her skin ointment.

"I know she lathers it on daily," Marie whispered, conspiratorially. "Got dry skin like a dragon, that one. And she puts it *everywhere*...no man would want to get within twenty feet of her if she was red with poison ivy!"

Other tantalizing suggestions had been made, such as sneaking a skunk into her room to spray her clothes and bedding, covering the floor by her bed with butter, and adding coal tar dye to her shampoo. Ellie had nearly laughed herself silly imagining the last one. What would Cecelia Scrimshaw do when she looked in the mirror and saw scraggly wet black hair instead of the fake red tresses she had worked so hard for?

But as fun as it was to fantasize about taking revenge for how Cecelia had treated her, Ellie knew that she couldn't go to such lengths. Even if Cecelia identified the real culprit behind it, she would take out her anger on one of the maids who would have helped Ellie to achieve it. That wasn't a fair risk to ask them to take. Besides, it was immature, and Ellie was trying to grow into the role of a princess, which she imagined was very serious and dignified. A princess didn't need to resort to such antics to assert her dominance. She would have to find a different way.

Sighing, Ellie turned around and wondered if Fillip had received the message, or if he had decided not to come. Just as she was about to turn around and head back inside, she heard footsteps. Fillip came into view moments later, wearing a somber expression, his hands behind his back.

"Ellie Kate," he said, giving her a soft smile. "I heard that you wished to speak to me."

"Yes," she said, stiffening her spine. "I think there are some things we should discuss."

"First, let me apologize," he said, coming towards her with arms open, as if in surrender. "I behaved like a cad at the ball. I don't know what came over me..."

"Drink," Ellie answered, snorting. "Brandy by the smell of it."

Fillip's face fell, suitably chastised. "Yes," he admitted. "My father has always had a weakness for brandy. Looks as though I've possibly inherited it..."

"It's not so much that you got drunk," she explained, "but rather that you left me alone for five hours when you said you'd only be gone for thirty minutes."

"Yes, and I am so sorry for that, Ellie Kate," he said quickly. "I completely lost track of time, but that's my fault. I should have been more cognizant, I should have refused the glasses of brandy that Father was handing me one after the other...I should have been less selfish."

Ellie gave him a rueful smile. "But you were having a good time with your father, weren't you?" she affirmed quietly. "He was treating you like an equal, sharing plans with you, laughing and joking. It was nice, wasn't it?"

Fillip looked at her in astonishment, as if seeing her for the first time, and then his shoulders slumped forward. The movement was so small, but Ellie saw a glimpse of the child Fillip had been in that motion. As he bowed his head, Ellie could have sworn she was looking at a tiny seven-year-old, desperate for the love and approval of his father.

"You don't have to explain that to me," Ellie said. "I know what it's like to love your father, to enjoy spending time with him. You should relish it while you still can."

"Yes, but by all accounts, the feelings between you and your father were mutual," Fillip grumbled, and Ellie noticed that he was clenching his fists. "Your father liked spending time with you. He was proud of you. He taught you things from the time

235

you were little, always trying to take care of you and teach you for the future. My father has never been like that. I've had to snatch time with him when and wherever I could take it. He always determined when he would deign to see me, and I had to be ready to jump or else suffer his ill humor, wondering if it would be another month before he would seek me out again."

Ellie didn't know what to say, so she averted her gaze and looked down at the stone steps. She had identified the root of Fillip's struggle to personhood. He lacked and craved his father's approval. Until the king gave it, there was nothing to be done for it. And Fillip could learn to live without it, could become strong despite it, but it was a visceral, instinctive yearning that would never really go away.

"Ellie Kate, I am so sorry," Fillip said again, softening and coming to take her hand. "I know that's not your problem, and I should be focusing on you now. I am to be your husband, after all. I should act like it, and stop sniveling like a child."

"You're not sniveling," she murmured. "And you don't have to dismiss it. As your future wife, it is my problem. I don't know how to solve it. I don't know where to begin to make it better, but I will try to help you with your father, if I can. I promise to do that."

Fillip smiled beatifically down on her, tucking a curl behind her ear and caressing her cheek.

"You are wonderful, do you know that?" he asked, leaning down and kissing her. "What did I ever do to deserve you?"

"It's not about deserving," she said, leaning into his chest. "If we all got what we deserved, we'd be miserable."

Fillip laughed, wrapping his arms around her and running his fingers through her hair. Ellie knew that she could either bury the subject of Cecelia forever, or bring it up and cause him more distress. Just when she decided to let it go and trust that whatever had been between them was over, Fillip mentioned the unsavory scene.

"I heard you had a run-in with Cecelia Scrimshaw," he said, and Ellie pulled out of their embrace, looking up at him.

"Where did you hear that?" she asked.

"Mother. She seemed worried about you, and said that you were white as a ghost after Cecelia basically attacked you."

"She was very...vitriolic," Ellie admitted. "But she's harmless. Just a lot of bluster...nothing I can't handle."

"Are you sure?" Fillip questioned. "I wouldn't describe her as harmless. She can be very vicious. You've heard about her mother, I presume? If she threatened you, I can force Mother to dismiss her as a lady-in-waiting. Ladies have been permanently exiled for less..."

"No, I don't think that's necessary...yet," Ellie said. "She didn't threaten me, per se, she just...well, she told me that she was coming after you."

"Coming after me?" Fillip said, a bit lightly. "What did she mean by that?"

Ellie rolled her eyes. "She said that princes were expected to take mistresses, and that she would be the first one you had, she would make sure of it. And then she alluded to prior history

237

with you, saying that you would have chosen her for your bride had it not been for me."

Fillip stared at her for a moment, absorbing everything, and then let out a full-bellied laugh, one that echoed out onto the lake.

"She said that?" he asked. "She said that I would have chosen her? What a foul joke! What an imagination she has…although I suppose all the Scrimshaw's have been plagued with an overestimation of themselves. It's what gets them into trouble. Trust me, Ellie Kate, I wouldn't touch that viper with a ten-foot pole."

"So you weren't considering marrying her?"

Fillip shuddered, as if for effect, but Ellie found his distaste to be genuine.

"By the gods, no!" he said emphatically. "That woman is anathema to me. A completely loathsome creature. If she manages to bag anyone, I'll be surprised."

Ellie should have been reassured—she *wanted* to be reassured, but there was still something that bothered her, like a nagging feeling.

"What did she mean, then?" Ellie demanded. "When she said that you and she had a shared history?"

Fillip shook his head. "No idea," he answered lightly. Ellie squinted her eyes, scrutinizing him. It was almost *too* lightly.

"Well, she can't have just made it up," Ellie insisted. "She seemed the type to exaggerate, but not to out-and-out lie."

Fillip shrugged. "I don't know what to tell you," he said, looking directly in her eyes. "She was at the court when we were

238

both younger. Maybe that's what she's talking about. Her mother disgraced herself when Cecelia was a baby—for that reason, she practically grew up at the castle. But then her mother became ill and Cecelia was called away. I didn't see her for three years until she came back to serve my mother."

"She said she's been at the court for two years since," Ellie added. "And nothing has happened in that time? You don't have to be afraid to tell me, Fillip. That was long before we ever met. If there was something between the two of you...I'd rather know."

"But there wasn't, I swear," Fillip maintained. "We grew up together, if you can even call it that. I grew up around so many courtiers and their children. If all of them were to claim a close relationship with me, I'd have a dozen lovers and a dozen closer friends. But those ties mean nothing to me. I never had any attachment or relationship with Cecelia, she was just someone to hang around, like all the others."

Ellie bit her lip, wanting fervently to believe everything he was saying. It wasn't like *she'd* had any sort of prior relationship hanging back at Maplecroft Manor. Her exposure to boys and men had been pathetic, but much of that had been strictly enforced by Cornelius Marchand, who had desired above all else to build an impenetrable bubble around his precious daughter.

Frances had unintentionally and unwittingly continued to bolster this bubble by forcing Ellie into servitude. Stuck at the estate doing manual labor for much of the day had severely limited Ellie's contact with the outside world. And what little contact she did have—going out into Hartmere on market day—

was not exactly a ripe opportunity for meaningful or regular encounters.

Ellie's childhood had not been as Fillip's, surrounded by friends and playmates. Ellie had only had her father, the Tuttle's, and then her stepmother and stepsisters. She wanted to believe him when he said that he'd had no romantic attachment to Cecelia, or any of the other girls he played around with. Why should he, if they were children? Children didn't think about those sorts of things...but even with her limited exposure, Ellie knew that children *did* think of such things. She had certainly wondered about boys, much to her father's chagrin. Add to that the perversions of the court—Ellie knew that girls could become mothers as young as thirteen. And Cecelia had been sent away to attend her mother when she was fourteen...a physical encounter was certainly possible, even if it was utterly distasteful to Ellie's sentiments.

"Don't listen to anything that wretch has to say," Fillip continued. "Don't put any stock in it. She's just saying whatever she must to make you doubt us, and our relationship. That's how she thinks to tear us apart. But you mustn't surrender to it. It's a tactic, like everything else in this court. These people are full of venom, and they know how to manipulate people. Don't let her manipulate you."

Ellie wasn't a fool. She knew what a diversionary tactic felt like, and despite the nobility of his speech, Ellie wasn't entirely sure that he wasn't using one on her. 'These people' that he so disdainfully referred to included him by their very definition. He might have liked to see himself set apart, and in

240

many ways he was, but in terms of social interaction, he had learned the same lessons alongside them. Ellie closed her eyes tightly, trying not to think of him that way, trying to just *believe* what he told her. Was it so hard? Was it so difficult to put such trust in one's future husband? But every time she was on the verge of just accepting what he said, she thought of Queen Adelaide's face, and her tone on the night of the second ball. She had been so worried about what Cecelia had said to Ellie, had insisted Ellie wait to talk to Fillip until he was sober, had even warned him as soon as she could. Had the queen coached him on what to say to her? Had she advised him against telling Ellie the truth?

Ah, but there was the rub. The truth? What was the truth? Where was it? It was like an undulating snake, weaving its way in and out of the rooms at Bellbroke Castle, slithering up and down the staircases, always just out of Ellie's line of sight. Ultimately, she had to cling to what she *thought* was true. She knew that in order to survive this treacherous court, she would have to pick a person to trust, and then trust them fully until she was capable of surviving on her own. She was in unfamiliar territory—until she learned to operate on the same level as these people, she had to find a mentor. Fillip was the only person who could fit this role. But it gave her pause to think that she couldn't really be sure of him...

"Ellie Kate," he said, breaking her concentration. "Do you hear me?"

"Yes," she said faintly. "Yes, I do hear you."

He was bending down a bit, his hands on both her shoulders, his blue eyes fixed intensely on hers. It was hard not to be dazzled by him. *Or bamboozled,* she thought dully.

"Can we forget about what Cecelia said?" he asked. "Do you trust that there's nothing between her and me? Nothing ever before?"

Ellie nodded her head. "Yes," she answered. "Yes, I do believe you, and I do trust you."

Fillip rewarded her with a smile, and then held her close.

"I would never do anything to hurt you," he whispered. "You are far too precious to me. As my wife, I will treasure you always, and I will always put you first. I promise you will never live to doubt that."

Ellie closed her eyes and cradled her cheek against his chest again, inhaling his wonderful scent of amber and bergamot. She knew that it wouldn't be hard to trust him. But that was possibly the most dangerous part of it all.

Chapter Sixteen

Nothing Ventured, Nothing Gained

AUTUMN settled upon Bellbroke like a fairy's spell. Every morning, the lake was misted over with fog so thick it obscured the horizon. By noon, the sky would clear and the sun would shine as brightly as it could, in an attempt to compensate for its diminishing warmth. Scarlet and ochre leaves fell spectacularly from the trees, dotting the surface of the water, and littering the garden with brilliant autumn rushes.

The date of her wedding was fast approaching, but Ellie's thoughts had drifted far away from matrimony. In fact, she hardly had time to think of it, and when she did, she pictured it as some sort of deadline. The queen was constantly hinting that her free time as a married woman would fly out the window, and Ellie was afraid that she wouldn't be able to continue sleuthing as she was, trying to crack the code of Bellbroke, to put the various puzzle pieces together.

In the past month, Ellie had achieved one breakthrough: she had discovered the reason for the blank books in that strange library. She had gone there several times before, walking around slowly, observing everything, pulling the books out and looking at the shelves behind—were there false backs? Was there an entrance to a secret passageway? She even analyzed the stone tiles, using a solution of brine acid and water to dissolve the mortar. Mr. Tuttle had taught her that trick, having had to remove excess mortar from the newly replaced brick exterior at Maplecroft Manor. She was looking for anything that was under the stone tiles, but she had found nothing.

When she had finished that, she realized that she had completely torn up the floor and the mortar would have to be replaced. Thankfully, Mr. Tuttle was still residing in the castle, and after procuring some mortar for him, she quickly set him to work. The library was finished up within the day and no one was the wiser.

Having failed to find any architectural secrets, Ellie turned back to the books themselves. There had to be some *reason* as to why someone would fill shelf after shelf with empty books. She checked every last book in the room, maddeningly flipping the pages for the tiniest pen stroke. It would have been clever to hide a written book within a room of empty ones. The odds were in one's favor that it wouldn't be picked up.

It was during this search of every single book that Ellie made her breakthrough discovery. When she flipped through the pages, she noticed that they were crinkly, like they had been slightly wetted and then dried. She flipped through some other books to confirm. And then it hit her: something her father had told her many years ago, on a night when he'd returned from one of his stranger voyages.

"We shipped ten crates of honey to a very powerful man, the Duke of Carta," he had told her. "I just thought he liked honey, but after we'd delivered it, Lukas told me why he'd wanted it—invisible ink."

A mixture of honey and water could be used as invisible ink. Quickly, Ellie sniffed the pages and detected the slightest hint of honey. Grabbing as many books as she could hold, she ran to her room. Her father had told her that the writing could be rendered visible if exposed to heat. But it had to be done carefully otherwise the pages would be burned. Ellie could remember writing secret codes with her father in invisible ink, the two of them looking over their handiwork with a heat lamp, a convenient device her father had brought back from his travels.

But Ellie didn't have a heat lamp, so she'd had to improvise. Shoving coals in her bedpan, she laid it on the ground, and then carefully opened one of the books, flattening the page on top of the bedpan. It only took a few minutes, and then almost as if by magic, writing began to appear in a dark brown hue, almost as if burnt on the page. Glowing with her success, Ellie settled in to decode for the rest of the night.

It was slow, laborious work, but Ellie eventually revealed the invisible ink on all the pages in the four books she'd taken. After she had slept and eaten, she pulled them out and started to read them for content. And that was when she realized *why* they had been written in invisible ink.

One of the books contained the entire architectural structure of the castle, including a distinct labeling of rooms as well as tips on how to infiltrate, where the weaknesses were, and a description of the stone pillar foundation. Ellie understood why the king would want such information available, but invisible.

The second one appeared to be simply a list of names and dates from the reign of King Henric the Great. It contained a very long and rambling preface about the founding of the current dynasty and the achievements of the Westenra line of kings. What followed in the pages after had to be for genealogical purposes only. Names and dates of births, marriages, and deaths. It was very boring and tedious, but Ellie did learn quite a bit about her fiancé's family through it.

The other two volumes were very strange, and gave Ellie a tingling sensation down her spine. Reading them, she became aware that the Crown engaged in a large web of espionage, and the sheer scope and reach of its power frightened her a bit. These two volumes were spy journals. It was page after page of detailed, mechanical entries about the country of Grunwald. There were maps and diagrams of certain key places in the capitol city, observations about the people, inferences about the royal family, and transcripts of interviews with high-ranking officials who had been 'tricked' by the spy into divulging secrets under the effect of black henbane.

Naturally, Ellie could understand why the spy had written such information in invisible ink. And she reasoned that once Master Caldecott had singed the pages and read the ink, he ordered it to be copied once more in invisible ink, stored in the secret library; the original copy burned. They would want to have the information on hand, but in a sneaky way. Lest it fall into the wrong hands, it should be invisible.

Shortly after her investigation, Ellie began to panic. What if Master Caldecott periodically checked the library for the spy volumes? What would he do when he found out they were missing? For the time being, Ellie stored the books underneath her mattress, but that seemed such an obvious place to hide them. So she moved them behind a false back in her clothes bureau. She cleverly asked Fillip to buy her four blank books so that she could keep a journal, and then set about recreating the books she had nicked, writing in invisible honey ink by night.

The only flaw in her plan was the handwriting, of course, but she simply had to hope that no one would notice. As she copied, it made her desperately curious. What other forbidden knowledge was in the library? What other secrets were kept there? She told herself that if she ever did have free time when she was married, and if she got bored or decided to take a risk, she could always steal another book, decode it and copy it out again. It might be a fun hobby. And it would be a useful one too— knowledge was power, and the more she knew about the castle, the more secure she would feel.

JUST as the weather began to turn crisp with autumn, Ellie invited Mr. and Mrs. Tuttle up to her room to give them what she hoped would be a welcome announcement. Shortly after noon, the older couple made their way up to the southwestern tower and knocked on her door. Showing them in, Ellie beamed at the older woman, who looked less than thrilled and still had a smidge of flour on her cheek.

"What do you look so happy about?" Mrs. Tuttle barked. "I'm sorry, Ellie, I don't mean to snap. That scullery maid Yvette is as dingy as a bat! This morning I had to show her how to make dough. It's one of the simplest tasks in the world, and she didn't know where to start! How did she get hired on as a scullery maid, I ask you?"

"I don't know," Ellie answered. "But I do know that you won't have to deal with her much longer!"

Mrs. Tuttle frowned. "What do you mean?" she asked.

"I mean that I've found you a place to live!" Ellie exclaimed. "It's a beautiful seaside cottage with three bedrooms, an upstairs loft, and a nice, big kitchen. Fillip found it for you. It's on the eastern edge of the country, near a port town called Castine."

Both Mr. and Mrs. Tuttle looked astounded as they absorbed Ellie's news. She had hoped that they would erupt into happiness and laughter, but instead Mrs. Tuttle looked sad.

"We'll have to leave you?" she said, almost pathetically.

"What's wrong?" Ellie asked. "I thought you'd be pleased. You don't have to work anymore. Fillip and I have set you up with the deed to the cottage, and we'll give you enough money to live on for the rest of your days. It's my way of saying thank you, for everything you've done."

Mrs. Tuttle looked a bit choked up with emotion.

"Well, thank you, Ellie," she said. "We're very touched by the offer...but I don't want to leave you here. You can't be here all alone..."

Ellie reached out and took Mrs. Tuttle's hand.

"I'm not alone," she told her. "I have Fillip, and my maids as companions. I must learn to be independent here. And I can't bear the thought of you and Mr. Tuttle toiling while I sit around in leisure. It's time you retired to the country and lived a quiet, easy life."

Mrs. Tuttle scoffed. "When have we ever lived a quiet, easy life, Mr. Tuttle?" she asked. Her husband shook his head. "How could we get used to such a thing?"

"You will," Ellie said. "Trust me, it becomes a bit *too* natural after a while."

"Well…when are we to go?" Mrs. Tuttle asked.

"In two weeks, if that pleases you," Ellie replied. "Oh, come, don't look so upset. I'm not trying to get rid of you…I'm just trying to do right by you, to look after you, as you've always looked after me."

Mrs. Tuttle collapsed in tears, dabbing at her eyes with her handkerchief, and Mr. Tuttle patted her shoulder consolingly.

"It isn't right," she moaned. "It isn't right for you to look after *us*. That's what we ought to do…what we promised your father…"

"And you did," Ellie assured her. "You have. If it weren't for you, we wouldn't be sitting in the castle right now. There comes a time when the tables turn, and the younger look after the older. I'm in a position now to take care of you, and that's what I intend to do."

Mrs. Tuttle nodded her head sadly. "I know," she sputtered. "I know it's how the world works. Little ones grow up before you know it and the old keep getting older. Doesn't mean I like it, mind," she said, fixing Ellie with a sharp eye. "But I understand it. And we appreciate it…it'll be nice, getting out of service. It'll be nice to just have to work for the two of us."

249

"Yes, it will," Ellie affirmed. "And it's not like we'll never see each other again. Fillip tells me that we'll go on a royal progress next year through all the counties, and they always go through Castine. We'll make sure to visit you, and I'll write letters."

"You had better," Mrs. Tuttle said. "I'll try to write back, but you know I struggle making my letters."

Ellie smiled, squeezing Mrs. Tuttle's hand.

"This isn't good-bye," she insisted. "It's simply a short and sweet farewell. And think—you'll be rid of that irritating scullery maid!"

Mrs. Tuttle laughed, squeezing her hand in return.

"Yes, there is a blessing in that," she agreed.

Feeling a sense of satisfaction in helping Mr. and Mrs. Tuttle, Ellie spent the rest of her afternoon with the last reminder of her past, and her life at Maplecroft Manor. She had managed to remain calm and composed, happy for her friends throughout the entire conversation, but as soon as she had laid down for bed that night, she surrendered to a sudden onset of tears. The grief at losing her last vestige of home dealt a wicked blow she hadn't anticipated. She knew, of course, that Mr. and Mrs. Tuttle would be better off, far away from the machinations of Bellbroke Castle, safely ensconced in their cottage at Castine, free of manual labor. But she still lamented their loss, realizing that besides Fillip, she was losing her last true friends at Bellbroke Castle.

MR. and Mrs. Tuttle had departed in mid-October, the leaves a brilliant red and ochre. Ellie had tried not to cry as she helped them into the boat, and they, too, had been struggling to maintain composure. In that one last, long hug with Mrs. Tuttle, Ellie promised the older woman that she would stay in contact, and thanked her again for everything she had done.

"No need to thank me, dear," Mrs. Tuttle had said, caressing her cheek. "Gratitude is for those whom kindness isn't expected. But you've been like one of my own from the day you were born. Everything I did for you, I did out of love."

This had made Ellie blubber like a baby, so much so that she hid her head in Fillip's chest as the oarsmen rowed Mr. and Mrs. Tuttle away. She couldn't bear to see them go, so she had closed her eyes. But when she finally opened them, and saw that they were on the other side of the lake, out of view, Ellie regretted not watching them go. Regretted not hanging on to every last glimpse that she could.

Despondent in the days that followed, Ellie determined that she needed a distraction. And so she decided to visit Tiresias, to try and make amends for that day in the apothecary, and to try once again, to glean information from him. Tiresias was the oldest living resident of Bellbroke Castle, and she knew he had overheard something he wasn't meant to. He could give her insight into the past as well as the present: two of his specialties.

Having made up with Hazel, Ellie made a steaming pot of ginger tea and brought the tray up herself one morning, to

Tiresias' room. Knocking on the door, she waited until his servant had informed him of her arrival and showed her in.

When she walked into his room, Ellie realized that he had been given one of the smallest, dampest rooms in the castle. It was nearly a quarter the size of her room, and closer in appearance to the servants' quarters. Dust seemed to hang and linger in the air, and the wood paneling in the room was very dark and faded, giving an overall appearance of decay.

Tiresias was propped up in an ancient looking four poster bed that was made of spindly black wood and had dark curtains that had been tied up with old rope on the posts. But despite all the gloom, Tiresias sat snuggled in his bed with a cheerful grin and a happy white cap on his old head. Ellie couldn't help but smile at his infectious joy.

"What a marvelous surprise!" Tiresias exclaimed. "I was not expecting to see you, my dear."

Ellie was glad that he didn't seem to remember how she had upset him last time. She offered him the ginger tea, pouring him a cup, and he wrapped his hands around the porcelain to warm them, took a delicate sip and then hummed in delight, his shoulders relaxing.

"Nothing like warm tea on a brisk, fall morning," he declared. "Now, tell me, what's a pretty girl like you doing up here with an old man like me?"

Ellie smiled, feeling bad for being so obvious. Was she really so transparent? She had not inherited kindness from either of her parents, not kindness in the sense of going out of her way to just help others or spend time with them. It was not her natural way. Everything had always been a give and take, especially with Frances. Tit for tat, you scratch my back, I'll scratch yours. Ellie had learned the art of manipulation, and she felt bad for using it on Tiresias, bringing him ginger tea in exchange for information.

"I was hoping you could tell me about the castle," she said. "You've lived here for so long. Surely you know its layout, its secrets..."

Tiresias chuckled. "Oh yes, Bellbroke Castle is like an old courtesan: full of secrets, and desperate to keep them. Many of them will go to the grave with my death. So you want to take advantage, do you, before that blessed day comes?"

Ellie blushed with embarrassment.

"Yes," she answered straightly. "Well, I'm not trying to *take advantage*, in a bad way. If you don't want to tell me, that's fine, I'll go along my way."

Tiresias sniffed his ginger tea sharply. "No hint of black henbane," he said. "So I see you're not trying to trick me."

"How do you know about black henbane?" she asked.

"How do you?" he countered.

"I read about it," she confessed. "In one of Master Caldecott's spy books. The writer mentioned he used black henbane to wrest information from someone."

Tiresias cocked his eye at her.

"How did you read one of Master Caldecott's spy books?"

"If I tell you, will you promise not to tell anyone?"

The old man laughed and then wheezed a bit.

"See there? Another secret trying to worm its way into existence. This is how they all started, at Bellbroke. No, keep your secret, lass. It's safer with you than with me. My mind is addled, you know, and I'm not good for keeping anything. It's like a sieve up there—one day it'll all come through like thin, undercooked noodles. Besides...this is not a room for secret keeping," he said, gesturing up to the ceiling. "There are no roses up there."

"What do you mean?" she asked.

"There are certain rooms at Bellbroke, too few, really, that were made for the explicit purpose of secret keeping. Council rooms. Places where there are no windows or glass panels. You can imagine the importance of such rooms. Each of them has beautiful frescoes of red roses in the full bloom of June painted on the ceiling. Under the rose, you can be certain of confidentiality, or so the saying goes."

, "Tiresias, can you tell me why there is so much glass in the castle?" Ellie asked. "It seems rather odd to me."

The old man snorted. "You and me both," he commented. "But to answer your question, it's simple. The glass was put in to prevent secrets from forming. You see, there was once a very jealous king. He was old and decrepit, but he had married a young and pretty wife. His queen had passed away, his children were adults, and yet he lingered on with all the fleshly appetites of a young man. So, he married again, and his wealth and power attracted the most beautiful of maidens. Ultimately, he married a high-born lady from Wulster, an upstart region in the west. His marriage served a political purpose, as well as a

254

personal one and for a while it seemed as though he found joy in his new bride.

"The king, who was my great-grandfather, King Frederick, married Gwyneth but soon became very jealous of her. She had always been flirtatious—it was how she'd caught the king's eye. But once the myopic effect of new love had dissipated, he began to notice how other men's eyes lingered upon her, and how she began returning those amorous stares. And thus, he sought to remodel Bellbroke Castle, and ordered that walls be torn down, that holes be made for the new craze that was spreading all over Hartmere. He declared that windows would be brought in, ostensibly to brighten up the dreary old fortress.

"The best glazier in Hartmere was hired, a foreigner by the name of Pietro Fiordiligi. For several months, Fiordiligi installed glass windows on all exterior walls and glass panel frescoes on most interior walls. The work was hard and long, but Fiordiligi was diligent and precise in his work. Which was why it came as such a shock when King Frederick refused to pay him for it. It was one of the greatest commissions a tradesman could ask for, and Fiordiligi had accepted because of the prestige it would bring and the gold that was sure to be paid. When it wasn't…well, things got ugly.

"Before the glass installation had been finished, King Frederick's plan had worked—or backfired, considering on how you look at it. He had discovered his young wife cheating on him with one of the young courtiers. To be publicly cuckolded in the twilight of his life was intensely humiliating for King Frederick. And, as a way to transfer some of the blame, he turned a black eye on Fiordiligi. The glazier reminded him of his wife's infidelity, and he didn't want to pay for the glass that had exposed such a painful affair.

"As you can imagine, Fiordiligi did not have much sympathy for the king, at least not such that he was willing to forgive such financial exploitation. He didn't receive a single gold coin from the royal coffers, but as he stepped onto the boat, he cursed the king and the glass that he had so painstakingly put in. King Frederick died within the year and some say the glazier's curse is why Fiordiligi's glass always shatters."

Ellie sat for a moment, absorbing Tiresias' story. It certainly was interesting. She didn't know that she believed in curses, but it did have a nice ring to it, an explanation that would satisfy fanciful minds.

"You said you heard a secret," Ellie broached. "Through the glass. It was about me. Do you remember what you heard?"

Tiresias looked puzzled and then lifted a shaky hand to his brow. He emitted some small noises, and Ellie was suddenly afraid that he would regress into another fit. But he regained his composure and looked at her as if she hadn't said anything.

"Have you found the birdcage room yet?" he asked. "That's a delightful story, or at least it would be if it hadn't ended so badly."

"Yes, I've seen the birdcage room," she said. "But I want to know what you heard about me."

"I had a sister once," he continued, happily as a lark. "She was very pretty and very sweet. The sweetest princess that ever lived at Bellbroke! But she was born funny—never right in

256

the head, always slow to learn and such. They say it was from birthing trauma, her head was squeezed too tight in the birthing chamber for just two minutes too long. It can cause lasting damage, you know. Anyway, she loved birds, my sister. Her name was Ava. My father felt sorry for her and tried to make up for her sad lot in life by buying her anything she wanted.

"So, he bought her these birds. Hundreds of birds. She had an aviary in the castle, there in that room with all the birdcages. They used to be full of all kinds of birds of every color you can imagine. Ava loved it. She would spend hours with the birds, chirping to them, holding them, prancing around while they flew. Nothing gave her greater joy. It smelled awful in there and it was as noisy as could be…it was a terrible mess keeping all those birds. But my mother and father wouldn't hear of getting rid of them. They indulged Ava as none of us had ever been indulged. We all understood…well, at least some of us did.

"My other sister Parthenie resented the extra attention showered upon Ava. Mother and Father always blamed her for what happened. I never thought she did it on purpose, but certainly she wasn't doing what she was supposed to be doing, and her neglect led to the tragedy that occurred. It was a hot summer day and Ava wanted to sit out on the dock and put her feet in the water. She wasn't allowed to swim like the rest of us were—she couldn't master it. Someone had to be out with her the whole time to make sure she didn't get in. Ava liked to break the rules because she didn't understand why they existed and someone was always there to shield her from any consequence.

"But on this day, Ava was alone. Parthenie must have left her. To this day, I don't know what she was doing. Her story varied so much in the days that followed, I think it must have had something to do with that servant boy she was fooling around with. At any rate, Ava was left alone. She either fell in the water or jumped in. Because she couldn't swim, she drowned. One of the gardeners said he heard shouting and flailing in the water, but by the time he made his way down to the dock, it was too late. Ava was floating limply in the water. When they pulled her out, her face was blue and her eyes were glassy. She was dead.

"In her grief, my mother opened all the windows of the aviary, and released the birds from their cages. They flew away, gone as quickly as Ava was gone. She kept the cages in that room as a memorial to Ava, and ordered that they never be thrown away. But she kept them empty because she couldn't bear to see another bird. Every time she would hear one tweet or whistle during the day, she would sniffle and cry, thinking of Ava. My sister Parthenie was sent away shortly after that. Married off to some minor nobleman in a completely different country. Grunwald, I think. It was clear that my parents blamed her for Ava's death and after that, they didn't want anything to do with her."

"That is very sad," Ellie remarked. "You said she was sent away to Grunwald? King Richard wants to go to war with Grunwald."

"Yes, not surprising," Tiresias grumbled. "My nephew wants to go to war with any country, he's so hungry for power and glory. He looks back to the days of his great-grandfathers when war brought prestige, when troubadours would sing ballads named after the victorious kings. He wants songs sung about him, the cocky lion. He's always been a preening prince. Vainglorious is what they call it."

Ellie thought she'd give it one more shot.

"Are you sure you can't remember what you overheard?" she asked. "It was something to do with me, Eleanor Marchand. Something bad..."

A shadow passed over the old man's face, but he still remained quiet. After a moment, he reached out and gripped her wrist rather forcefully, maintaining an eerie sort of eye contact.

"Aschenputtel," he said. "There's a cottage in the woods by Aschenputtel. Go there when you must, and wear furs when you go."

"What?" Ellie said. "Wear furs? What do you mean, 'when I go'? Go where?"

Tiresias shook his head and turned over on the pillow.

"Please leave," he said. "I am an old man now, and I don't have the strength that I used to. All this talking has left me exhausted."

"B-but won't you tell me anything else?" she demanded, becoming frustrated. "Am I in danger?"

"I don't know," Tiresias mumbled. "Hasn't Fillip explained? It comes and goes in flashes. All I see is that you'll leave, and it will be cold when you do, so wear furs when you go."

Ellie gritted her teeth and stood up, grabbing the tray of ginger tea. She didn't understand how he could prattle on about

Fiordiligi and his sister's death forever and then drop hints like breadcrumbs about her own fate. He couldn't elaborate just a tiny bit? She knew that he was withholding information from her, she just couldn't decide if it was intentional or not. Either way, it frustrated her all the same.

Chapter Seventeen

Target Practice

"WHERE did you learn to shoot like *that?*" Fillip asked laughingly.

They were out on the tournament grounds near Penchester Palace, on the mainland in Hartmere. It was the first time that Ellie had been across the lake since June, and it felt strangely good to be out of Bellbroke. The royal family was having a semi-exclusive day of fun, to celebrate one of last nice days of fall. Winter was coming and it would bring the bitter cold. It was mid-morning and they were rounding out the archery contest, at which Ellie was winning.

She shrugged, grinning at her fiancé. "My father taught me," she answered.

"That's your response to everything!" Fillip protested. "How did your father manage to go out sailing as a merchant when he was teaching you how to ride, how to shoot, how to fence, how to read, how to handle dangerous substances..."

Fillip's aunt, Jehanne had just taken her shot and was within hearing distance. She looked over at them with interest.

"What?" she said. "Dangerous substances?"

Fillip laughed. "Yes, just the other day she demonstrated this. My father's bloody idiot of an alchemist spilled aqua regia all over the floor and was struggling to clean it up. Burned his hands and was throwing sugar all over the place, which was apparently making it worse..."

Ellie shook her head, lifting her bow to take another shot. "Bloody idiot," she said, letting the arrow fly straight to the middle circle of the target.

"And somehow Ellie Kate burst in on the scene, saw the burning pool of aqua regia, and immediately went down to the kitchen. I caught up with her down there, while she was madly mixing up water and what was it...?"

"Lye," she said, loading her bow again. "An aqueous solution of lye will neutralize the acidic aqua regia."

"Your father taught you that?" Jehanne asked incredulously. "What was he, an alchemist as well as a merchant?"

"He had to learn some of these things the hard way," Ellie replied. "Sometimes he shipped containers of acid. He had to know how to neutralize them in case there was spillage on the ship. You don't want to be at sea with acid burning through the wood..."

"True," Jehanne remarked, laughing. "Very true!"

"So she runs back up to the alchemist's room," Fillip continued. "Carrying this heaving bucket of lye water, and I had to carry some too...and then she carefully pours it over the acid. It made an awful noise, and the stench was terrible. But then...after a few minutes, the sizzling noises stopped and it seemed harmless."

"The servants still had to be careful mopping it up though," Ellie said. "I showed them how to do it properly. I've
262

had practice...not with aqua regia, particularly. We were never dissolving gold at Maplecroft Manor, but we've had to neutralize acids."

"Truly incredible," Fillip said admiringly. "My fiancée is truly incredible. I don't think we've ever had such a credit to the royal family."

"Careful now," Jehanne said. "I'm not just some pretty peach. I know useful things too."

"Of course," Fillip said. "But now my father will have to find a new alchemist. The other one was a bloody disgrace. He might just appoint Ellie Kate! Wouldn't that be hysterical?"

"I would have to respectfully decline," Ellie said, loosing another arrow into the target board. Jehanne cursed under her breath.

"How did you do that?" she demanded. "You split my arrow in twain. How is that possible? Damn! And mine was dead center..."

There was booming laughter from behind them, recognizably the king's, and the sound of thundering applause.

"Congratulations, my dear girl!" King Richard called out. "Jehanne has been the champion of archery for years. It's about time she was dethroned!"

"Says you, the sore loser," Jehanne scowled. "You've always been dreadful with the bow and it's made you sour."

"I only see one person who's sour here," the king remarked, looking at her pointedly. "Besides, the bow was never my weapon of choice. I like to be in the thicket, amid the fighting, not tucked away somewhere sniping from a safe distance. In that way, archery is the perfect sport for women. Ellie, my dear, once again you demonstrate skills and abilities much beyond what was expected."

Ellie thanked the king for his compliment, but couldn't help but feel that it was slightly backhanded.

"It's time for the real sport now," the king announced. "The joust! Men, let's leave the fair ladies to their cushioned seats and don our armor."

Frowning, Ellie walked to the edge of the lawn and handed her bow and quiver of arrows to a servant. She didn't appreciate how the king had dismissed archery, contending that only the joust was a 'real' sport. She didn't see how. It required skill, of course, but no more than archery. They both required strength and aim.

Pushing past it, Ellie went to take her seat with the queen and Jehanne, but not before she felt Fillip catch her by the wrist and whirl her around. Sweeping her into a kiss, Ellie literally felt as if her breath was taken away.

"Wish me luck," he said, winking.

"Of course," she replied. "Good luck."

He cleared his throat loudly as if trying to attract attention and bowed low before her.

"My lady, will you do me the honor of wearing your favor?"

Ellie rolled her eyes at his theatrics and pulled a silky handkerchief from the inside of her sleeve. She had almost forgotten to bring one, but the queen had reminded her before they left. Her initials had been stitched into the cloth, as well as her own personal sigil of roses, to symbolize when Fillip had chosen her and proposed. Every time Ellie saw them, she was reminded of what Tiresias had said about the roses on the ceiling, connoting secrecy. It was a fitting sigil for her, considering that she felt at all times to be tiptoeing around secrets, practically suffocating from the web of lies around her.

Fillip took her favor gratefully. "I will tie it around my lance and I know that it will bring me victory."

After kissing her again, Fillip loped athletically over to where the other men were getting ready. Ellie climbed the wooden stairs of the royal box and took her seat beside Queen Adelaide. The entertainment would hopefully be a rather short one. Fillip was going up against Lord Edmund and the king would go against his brother, Lord Roland. The winner of each match would then joust the other and that would be the end of it.

Ellie honestly hoped that Fillip would lose to Edmund so that he wouldn't have to joust against his father. Roland would surely cede his match to the king, because it was common knowledge that the king was not to lose. He prided himself especially on his athletic ability and no one dared challenge him seriously because of his royal status. It was treason to harm the king.

But Fillip would see himself above such laws, and because of his underlying rivalry with his father, he would try to beat his old man to prove his worthiness as heir. But this would not impress King Richard. Instead, the king would howl with defeat and become even more embittered against his son. Ellie had only seen the king lose at something once and it had been truly shocking.

One of the courtiers had bested him at a game of chess, and the king had thrown a massive tantrum. Ellie had been in the same room, sewing with the queen, and had watched it unfold. Her perception was that the courtier wasn't actively trying to win, but the king's strategy was so poor that his own loss was inevitable. When his king pawn had been taken, he had roared with anger, flipped the board over, and sent the pieces scattering. That hadn't been enough. He had verbally abused the poor courtier, and then knocked over the table and both of their chairs. Ellie had seen children who were better behaved.

"The king did not ask to wear my favor," the queen said quietly, turning to Ellie. "He hasn't worn it in years," she snorted. "I imagine he asks his concubine to provide him with duplicates of her snotty rags."

Ellie was often put in this kind of situation with the queen where she didn't know how to respond without sounding like a complete idiot. And the queen had a way of introducing these topics expecting...what? Ellie wasn't sure what the queen wanted. It wasn't sympathy—Ellie had already tried to play that card and all the queen had done was laugh at her.

So Ellie chose the only safe thing to do: ignore it and change the subject.

"I hope this will be over quickly," she said. "I sense a rain storm coming."

It was true—Ellie felt a distinct chill in the wind, and she saw clouds brewing on the horizon. Late autumn rain showers were always the worst. At least in a summer downpour, you weren't covered in cold water that brought with it the threat of an ague.

But that wasn't the only thing that Ellie felt in the wind. As it blew cold against her skin, she also felt a shiver travel down her spine, completely unrelated to the weather. Her stomach lurched as she looked around, surveying the field. She couldn't think what was setting off her instincts, but she had the feeling that something bad was going to happen. Her thoughts immediately turned to Fillip as she suddenly became very afraid that he was going to fall or get injured.

The first match was between the king and Lord Roland. It followed predictably, as Ellie thought it would. Roland held steady and hit the king on the first run, then he took a hit and broke a lance on the second run, and then finally allowed the king to unhorse him on the third run. It was a little anticlimactic and honestly a bit farcical. At the last minute, he had thrown his lance right before the moment of impact, and then just before the king's lance made contact, he flung himself sharply to the side, landing unimpressively in the dirt.

The king removed his helmet, shouting and laughing triumphantly. In addition to being a sore loser, the king was also a sore winner. He taunted Roland and wanted to go over each run play-by-play in an obnoxious litany of his skills and moves.

As Fillip prepared to go against Lord Edmund next, Ellie's stomach grumbled in fear as she scooted to the edge of her seat.

"How droll," the queen observed dryly. "I remember when I used to be so concerned for Richard's safety. Now if he fell and knocked all his teeth out, I'd laugh and throw a party."

"You would not," Jehanne said, taking the bait.

Ellie was glad for it as the queen turned and bantered with her sister-in-law about the foibles of the king and the flaws of men in general. Ellie tuned them out so she could focus all her energy on Fillip. He looked so young and sure of himself. He tipped his lance at her, to indicate he knew she was watching. Ellie smiled and tried not to worry overmuch. Fillip had had a lot of training—but still, anything could happen.

On the first run, Fillip broke a lance but managed to strike a blow to Edmund. Fillip cantered back, tossing his old lance on the ground and picking up new one from his squire. Ellie had learned that Fillip was a lot like his father in some ways, but thankfully very different in the ways that mattered. Fillip was obviously more sensitive and caring. He listened to people when they spoke, and addressed their concerns with thoughtful intelligence. Ellie thought that had to have been his mother's influence. Despite her caustic bitterness towards the king, she was empathetic and smart.

On the other hand, Fillip had that same desire to impress as the king, that same boyish charm and charisma, the same eagerness to please that could turn ugly in an instant when disappointment was detected. Like most people, she supposed, Fillip didn't like to be in the wrong, and he would try any trick in the book to claw his way out of it. Then after he had said hurtful things and acted like a cad, he would bounce back and want to be perfect friends again, like a dog wagging its tail for treats as though it hadn't just bit your hand.

At least he can apologize, Ellie thought. She hadn't seen the king so much as admit a mistake on his part or even a minor lapse in judgment. Apparently, it wasn't kingly to concede wrongdoing, for it meant that the king's thinking wasn't infallible. King Richard had embraced this attitude so thoroughly that Ellie believed he truly didn't think himself capable of making mistakes or acting wrongfully.

On the second run, Fillip knocked off Edmund's helmet, and Ellie swore under her breath. He was three points ahead, and unless Edmund managed to unhorse him, Fillip would advance. On the third run, Fillip took a nasty hit, but managed to stay on his horse. From across the field, Ellie could see the king's sour frown as his horse whinnied and fidgeted. The wind blew again. Ellie shivered with the cold and the feeling of dread.

"Father against son," Jehanne said, grinning. "Do you think young Fillip will take the fall to spare his father's humiliation?"

"Doubtful," the queen murmured. "Although if he were smarter, he would. Fillip likes to poke a sleeping dragon."

Jehanne giggled. "My brother won't restrain himself," she said. "Ellie, do you have healing skills as well? You might need them. Fillip might have to be dragged off the field."

Ellie gritted her teeth and wished that she could tell Jehanne and the queen to shut up. It might have been funny to them, but it wasn't to her.

"I can stitch wounds and set bones," she answered flatly. "Hopefully he won't be any more damaged than that."

"Can you really?" Jehanne asked. "I was joking when I said that...good lord, where did you come from?"

Ellie ignored Jehanne's pointed gaze and watched as Fillip and the king took their spots across from each other. When the flag was lifted, they both kicked the spurs and raced towards each other. Ellie prepared herself for the moment of impact, blinking and then allowing herself to look.

Both had broken a lance on the other and taken hits. But they were tied with one point each. As they cantered back, Ellie noticed Fillip leaning heavily in his saddle. He was definitely injured, and she wished that she had the power to stop the match. Going on was foolish, but then again, she was dealing with two fools. On the second run, Ellie held her breath at the moment of impact. The results had been the same. One point apiece, a hit and broken lances.

"They're going to tie," Ellie said.

"That will infuriate Richard as much as a loss," the queen said. "If I know my husband, he'll do his best to unhorse him."

"Barbaric," Ellie muttered. "He's already hurt, why doesn't he surrender?"

"And show weakness in front of his father, the king?" Jehanne queried. "Never."

On the third and final run, Ellie stood up from her chair and squeezed the wooden post, not caring if she got splinters. Fillip was struggling to hold his lance steady. She knew that he probably had a wound in his torso, perhaps even a broken rib.

270

With his wobbly lance, he couldn't manage a hit and instead suffered another crushing blow from the king to his mid-left side—the one Ellie suspected was already injured.

As soon as it was over, Ellie rushed down the stairs and ran on the field, watching as Fillip dropped his lance and seemed to hang limply in his saddle. He was breathing heavily when she grabbed the horse's reins and pulled him close.

"Are you all right?" she asked.

Fillip wearily lifted his visor and smiled at her, his face sweaty and blotchy.

"Just winded a bit," he said, wincing as he tried to dismount.

"No, you're bloody hurt," she said, snapping her fingers for some assistance. "You took too many hits to that side. I would bet money that you broke a rib."

"Well, I've had worse," he tried to say bravely, as he slid down the horse with a groan of pain. He attempted to brush the servants away, insisting he could walk, but almost fell after a few steps and Ellie forced him down on the stretcher.

"Not hurt, are you son?" the king called out in mock concern.

"Just a scrape," Fillip replied, settling down.

"I'll have my physician come tend to it," the king promised. "Good form, though. You learned from the best! One day you'll unhorse me, but today's not that day, son!"

He laughed triumphantly with Roland and Edmund. Ellie was annoyed, but at least he wasn't as obnoxious as he usually was. As they were walking off the field, Ellie tried to assess

Fillip's injuries as best as she could by asking him questions. But it was hard for him to answer, and she couldn't see anything through his armor. All in all, she figured that he probably wasn't hurt too badly, and it certainly could have been worse.

She was so fixated on Fillip that she was completely shocked when she felt something heavy and hard hit the back of her head. Lunging forward, Ellie barely broke her fall with her hands as her hearing instantly went out. Still on the ground, Ellie lifted a shaking hand to the back of her head and brought it back, her fingers red with blood.

She could feel her heart pounding slowly and for a long moment, it seemed that was the only thing she could hear. As her ears slowly adjusted and her hearing faded back in, Ellie became aware of raised voices—the loud, booming curses of the king and high-pitched screeching that was vaguely familiar. Where had she heard those voices before?

Ellie turned around and saw two pale, white-faced figures that she thought she'd never again see in her life. Anna and Emma were there on the lawn, clutching rocks in their hands, being forcibly restrained by Lord Roland and Lord Edmund. Emma—always the stronger one—was able to hurl another rock at her. Her reflexes were shaky, but Ellie managed to dodge it.

"YOU KILLED OUR MOTHER!" Anna shrieked. "It's your fault she's DEAD!"

Emma joined in as well. They called her all manner of things. They wished her dead. Ellie knew for as long as she lived that she would never be able to silence their voices in her head. And she would never be able to truly defend herself against such accusations. The king had ordered the prosecution against Frances Hardwick, but what had Ellie done to stop it? She hadn't even protested.

The king was apoplectic with rage, shouting at all the servants, marching back and forth between them and the girls, who were not at all willing to be silenced. But then the king charged at them, like a fighting dog, towering over them with his impressive height, his armor adding to his girth. He must have worn a particularly nasty expression on his face; Ellie could see her stepsister's shrink a bit in fear. She stood up on shaky legs, fearing the worst from her future father-in-law. She could tell by the way that he was instructing the guards that her stepsisters would be taken to the dungeons.

"They were trespassing on royal grounds," he hissed. "How did they get past the guards? This is unacceptable!" he roared at the captain. "I want the names of every guard on the periphery. Dismiss them all, without pay! This is inexcusable!"

In all the chaos, Ellie was vaguely aware that both the queen and Jehanne had come to her side to help her, but she was stumbling towards the king who was still barking orders a mile a minute.

"Take them to the dungeons," he spat. "Make sure they never see the light of day again."

"Please," she sputtered. "Please do not hurt them," she begged. "They...they blame me for th-their mother. This is madness from g-grief, nothing more..."

The king rounded on her, as fierce as a lion, seemingly unconcerned that she was injured.

273

"They have broken the law," he said coldly. "They have assaulted a member of the royal family, which is treason, and they have trespassed on the king's land. They will be charged, prosecuted, and executed."

"No," Ellie said, her heart sinking. She couldn't bear the thought of another execution. "No, please...I don't want them to be hurt. It's up to me...as the injured party...it's up to me."

But the king was steadfast in his determination.

"You are hurt and not thinking clearly," he said, becoming forcefully sensitive as he took her shoulders in a strong grip. "Jehanne, please help the future princess onto a stretcher and make sure all our physicians are called in. Hurry!"

"Please," Ellie begged again.

"I have already ruled on this matter," he stated. "Don't test me."

Ellie opened her mouth again, but Jehanne grabbed her shoulders and steered her away, whispering soothing words in her ear. Ellie was thankful that Jehanne had extricated her before something worse had happened. Ellie should have known by now—the king was not a man to be trifled with. But she still hated the way he made decisions, in the blink of an eye, without a moment's consideration. And the way he viewed her stepsisters' fates—as a foregone conclusion. As noblewomen, they were entitled to a trial, at least as much of one as her stepmother had gotten. And Ellie was sure that the judicial council felt extreme pressure to rule according to the king's pleasure.

With one foolish action, they had sealed their fates.

Chapter Eighteen

Mad as the Mist and Snow

NOVEMBER seemed to pass in the blink of an eye, and quite soon the harbingers of winter began to plague Hartmere, seeming to strike with a particular vengeance. The temperatures plummeted, the sky darkened, and the morning frost killed the grass. Life at Bellbroke Castle continued, changing its routine but a little. There were more masques and plays held in the great hall to compensate for former outdoor activities. Ellie kept to herself and tried not to overstrain her 'nerves', as that had been the physician's advice following her head wound. Fillip, too, was taking it easy as they both convalesced, although his injuries were slightly more serious—he had two broken ribs and a gash that had required twelve stitches.

To Ellie's relief, the king had agreed to postpone the trial of her stepsisters, but he couldn't do so for long, he told her. Word of their attack on the future princess had already spread beyond Hartmere and into the river lands and beyond. According to the king, the commoners were chomping at the bit, demanding the heads of Anna and Emma. Once again, Ellie noticed that his description of their loyalty to her bordered on mania. To Ellie, it seemed that he took far too much pleasure in detailing their glorified and terrifying adoration.

275

But Ellie didn't trouble herself about it. She only cared about making amends. For now, her stepsisters were being held prisoner in the dread fortress of Spindletop, on the mainland, about ten miles downriver from Penchester Palace. Ellie had managed to secure the largest, nicest rooms in the prison and had bribed their guards to keep them well-fed and supplied with books, quills, and parchment for writing. Ellie was determined to do for them what she hadn't done for Frances.

She knew it was a vain attempt to make up for what had happened to their mother. But she had to make it anyway. And she insisted that her involvement be anonymous, so they wouldn't shun the offerings. They may have been horrid to her when they had all lived at Maplecroft Manor. Frances and her daughters had made a point to humiliate and degrade her every chance they got, but that didn't mean that they deserved to rot in a dungeon cell like criminals and have their heads chopped off. The king may have been baffled by Ellie's moral reasoning, but she wasn't willing to adjust it to fit the Crown's idea of justice.

Ellie stared out of her rose-tinted window, down at the view of the lake and the cold, grey clouds that hung above. Now that the days were frigid, she started to view the date of her wedding with anxious anticipation instead of apprehension. She no longer thought of it as a deadline, but rather a date that couldn't come fast enough. Guiltily, she knew it wasn't out of a fervent desire to marry Fillip, but rather out of desperation to feel secure in the castle. Tiresias' warning was never far from her mind and as the temperatures dropped, she couldn't stop replaying that one line in her head: *All I can see is that you'll leave, and it will be cold when you do, so wear furs when you go.*

It was only midwinter and there were still at least three months to go before it started to warm up again. Ellie couldn't think of why she would leave the castle, but his words unnerved her, and the survivalist instincts her father had instilled were beginning to kick in with ferocity. She had pulled out all her warm clothing, putting it in the very front of her bureau for easy access. She had thick woolen stockings, a chemise lined with goose down, coats, sheep wool gloves, and fur scarves all tucked in the very front, in case of an emergency.

She had also taken to locking her bedroom door at night, which was something she had always done at Maplecroft Manor. Her father had told her to, back when she still had a bedroom.

"Even if I'm here, keep the door to your room locked," he had told her. "If someone is trying to break in, they'll have a harder time of it, and hopefully the noise will wake you so you can be prepared."

When Frances had forced her up into the attic, Ellie had dragged a heavy wooden table over the ladder each night, preventing anyone from climbing up without making noise or getting hit with a falling table.

Ellie also started sleeping with a dagger under her pillow. She had never been great at hand-to-hand combat, but she knew the basics. She preferred to be far away, shooting with an arrow from the distance. She could never be sure that her nerves wouldn't fail her in a tense, face-to-face battle. Cornelius had said that had always been her point of weakness—freezing in the moment, fumbling her moves due to anger or fear.

While she was taking all these precautions and convalescing, Ellie also took the opportunity to closely observe everyone around her. If it hadn't been for Tiresias' words of warning, she would have never suspected anyone in the royal family of wanting to hurt her. Now she started to rethink her original assessments of everyone. Queen Adelaide was always kind to her, but still emotionally distant. Ellie had always figured it was to do with her unhappiness with the king. But what if it was more? What if she was reluctant to bond with Ellie for a different reason?

The king was completely volatile and unpredictable. Because of his mercurial nature, he had been the hardest to get a read on. Ellie was sure that he was just a self-centered megalomaniac, but that made him the perfect candidate to launch a conspiracy against her. He had always been nice to her, seemingly caring and fatherly, at least as much as he was to Fillip. There was no marked difference in the way he treated her, no telltale signs of guilt or awkwardness. But Ellie knew that didn't mean anything. The king was always sure in his decisions and never once backed down or felt guilty. He thought his judgment was without flaw and she had observed him to be a man who didn't show or seem to feel remorse.

She remembered a terrible episode that had occurred only a few weeks ago on a rainy day. They had been forced to stay inside with no entertainment save the king's fool and a couple of acrobats. Ellie hadn't even remembered the plot of the play, but she remembered that the fool, in an act, had clutched his heart rather suddenly and play-acted dying. Before his final collapse, he cried out something about a curse, and it being the day before his fifty-second birthday. Almost immediately, everyone laughed and clapped their hands. This must have been an inside joke that Ellie was not yet privy to. But almost as soon as the laughter had picked up, it abruptly died down, and then she saw the flash of recognition in all the courtier's faces as a rippling undercurrent traveled through them, each turning their heads to the king, to gauge his reaction.

Typically, a royal fool was allowed license where others dare not tread. For this reason, the fool had been able to mention the king's various affairs and lampoon them accordingly. He had also been able to criticize the king's infamous temper with impunity and his being a poor loser at games. Oftentimes, the king laughed at himself, if he wasn't in a particularly bad mood. But on this day, the king's face had turned beet red, bordering on purple. He sat hunched over on his throne, his fingers clutching the arms of the chair. Ellie had been reminded of the Westenra symbol of the wyvern. King Richard had appeared to be blowing impotent smoke out of his nostrils, in the same way that the wyvern of his family could not blow fire like a dragon, but could only mimic this action with weak smoke.

Finally, the king had stood up in an explosive show of rage, pointed a dramatic finger at the fool, and addressed his guards.

"GET THAT MAN OUT OF HERE!" he had bellowed. "TAKE HIM OUT OF MY SIGHT!"

Bewildered and suddenly frightened, the fool had fallen to his knees on the floor, prostrating himself before his sovereign.

"Your Majesty, a thousand apologies," he had begged. "I should not have...it was made in poor taste...please forgive me, Your Majesty."

But Richard had turned a cold shoulder on his fool, his once favorite companion. Ellie knew that Richard sometimes called for his fool in the middle of the night and the two could often be seen strolling the gardens, or laughing in corners. Ellie had known that Richard felt he could be himself around the fool. He didn't always have to put on the mask of 'The King'. He didn't always have to be the powerful, authoritarian figure. Ellie knew that whatever the fool had alluded to had been a betrayal of some kind—she just wasn't sure of what.

She had nudged Fillip and leaned close. "What was that about?" she had whispered.

Fillip's lips had tickled her ear. "It was a reference to the Westenra curse," he had said. "When King Henric, the first of the Westenra line, took the throne, he died at the age of fifty-two. And a wise-woman from Wulster proclaimed that none of his heirs would live longer than that, in recompense for having taken the throne in such a bloody and disgraceful way."

Ellie had let these facts register for a moment, watching the king as he paced back and forth in front of his throne, looking more and more like a rage-filled, impotent wyvern. She had noticed that he had been losing weight of late, becoming more scarecrow-like in appearance, scragglier in his limbs, his face gaunt and shadowed. Was it merely the stress of ruling, or was it fear of an age-old curse?

"My father is now fifty," Fillip had explained. "Just two years shy of his predicted death."

"But why should he believe some nonsense curse?" Ellie had asked. "It was made close to a hundred years ago."

"Yes, but since the day it was foretold, it has remained unfailingly true," Fillip had said, with a frown. "Henric's son Willem died at age forty-two. My grandfather, King Alexander, died at age forty-five."

"And yet Tiresias still lives," Ellie had pointed out. "Was he not a son of King Willem? How old is he now? He must be well past fifty-two."

"Oh, he is," Fillip had said. "But most say the curse would not apply to him, since he is not a direct heir of King Henric. He was a second son who did not inherit."

Ellie had pursed her lips, thinking this through, still trying to find a loophole. She didn't believe in such rubbish as curses, but she was beginning to discover that wherever Tiresias was concerned, unexplainable supernatural phenomena seemed to occur.

"Most of the time my father is not bothered by mention of the curse," Fillip had continued. "He's ordered everyone to treat it like a stupid joke, which is why the courtiers initially laughed. They're supposed to treat it like nonsense, to help my father believe that it's nonsense."

"But he doesn't really believe that it's nonsense, does he?" Ellie had asked.

Fillip had shaken his head darkly. "No, he doesn't believe that it's nonsense at all."

Ellie reflected on this particular memory, taking note of the way the king had stalked around his throne irritably. She also remembered the poor fate of the fool. His tongue had been cut out, so that he could no longer make irreverent jokes. The king had admonished him firmly in the throne room, saying sharply that the fool had been lucky to walk away with his life. He was then summarily dismissed and no one had seen nor heard from him again. The king was certainly on edge; plagued by an ancient curse that he was afraid would come true. Ellie could see how that could push a man to commit terrible acts, but she couldn't make the connection between that and herself. Why should *she* be a threat to the king's fear of mortality?

As for the king's brother and cousin, well they were cut of the same cloth. Edmund and Roland were like two thick tree stumps—quiet for the most part, always grunting in agreement with the king. They were like blunt instruments, and Ellie began to study them for signs of weakness or a slip-up. Neither seemed very sharp and she knew that time was usually the best stumbling block for slow people. Intrigue was a game that only the smartest could play for very long. But perhaps they weren't in on the plan—if there was one—precisely *because* they were too dull and sluggish.

Jehanne was cleverer and subtler than Roland and Edmund. Ellie got the impression that Jehanne knew about everything that was happening in the castle. She gave off that aura of being 'in the know'. Ellie was sure that Jehanne could tell her things that would make her hair curl—things both past and present. And while this unnerved Ellie, she didn't feel threatened by Jehanne. Ellie had already proven that she was more skilled in terms of fighting and surviving than the king's wily sister.

All the same, she didn't trust her as far as she could throw her. She didn't avoid Jehanne, but she also didn't make any attempt to get closer, or to foolishly attempt to wheedle secrets out of her. Jehanne would sniff her out in an instant, and that would put Ellie at an even greater risk. No, she didn't want to tip anyone off. She wanted to stay right where they thought she was—in blissful ignorance. And so she tried to be as cuddly and adorable with Fillip as she could, to give the impression of being an eager bride, ready to settle down into married life.

While her public persona had been a superficial act, Ellie hadn't realized how well it was working on Fillip until very recently. He had always been doting and clearly into her from the night of the ball, but Ellie started to notice signs of growing affection. He was becoming besotted.

"I want to do something special with you tomorrow night," Fillip had said. "Be ready at eight 'o' clock."

Ellie wasn't sure what he had in mind—it was a surprise. She continued looking out onto the lake and the snow that was falling quietly, but rapidly. The snow always amazed her. It was so beautiful when it fell, but it wreaked so much havoc once on the ground, like nature's silent vengeance. The ice was worse, but Ellie could remember years when the snow had fallen so quickly and quietly, it had dropped eight feet in sixteen hours—an astonishing six inches per hour!

People had died in snows like that. Some people had died of heart attacks trying to shovel the snow and others had died from being trapped inside their homes, unable to dig their way out. That mostly happened in very rural areas. There was a good sense of community in Hartmere, and royal officials were almost always dispatched to help with snow removal. Still though, Ellie was always wary when it snowed. The results were unpredictable and she hated the idea of being backed into a corner with no way out.

WHEN Fillip knocked on her door at eight 'o' clock sharp, he presented her with a bouquet of red roses. Ellie couldn't help but feel discomfited by the symbolism, and wondered where he had gotten them.

"They're made of silk," he had explained.

"Oh my," Ellie said, admiring the craftsmanship. "They're beautiful."

"Not nearly as lovely as you are," he replied. "Look, they have diamonds sewn in the middle. I thought they would add a nice touch."

"Very," she agreed. "So where are we going? It's already dark and we've had dinner."

Fillip scoffed. "As if all we can do is have dinner together," he said. "Honestly, Ellie Kate, you are silly sometimes."

He winked at her and she knew that he was being facetious. They usually did only have dinner together, especially since they had both been injured. There simply wasn't much else to do. Dancing was out of the question considering Fillip's ribs, and Ellie had never been much of a chess player. They had attended masques and balls, but there wasn't anything like that going on tonight.

As Fillip continued to lead the way, Ellie began to suspect that he was taking her somewhere outside, and that made her a bit nervous considering that it was still snowing. When they reached the doors, Ellie took a great big gulp of warm air before being hit with the frigid winds.

"What are we doing?" she shouted, as he wrapped his arms around her.

"Going to the garden," he explained, shielding her from the worst of the wind. "Don't worry—we're almost there."

Ellie tucked her head closer to her chest and leaned against Fillip for warmth as they walked. Snow was blowing wildly, and the night sky was strangely lit with an eerie reddish orange glow. She had never seen anything like it before. When she looked up, through a patch in the clouds, she saw stars alight in all their glory, with green, nebulous streaks in the sky, like a celestial paintbrush had made its mark on the night.

When they reached the garden, Ellie sighed in relief as she realized that some sort of clear tent had been built up around it, creating a protective sphere. As soon as Fillip opened the door, the sharp whistling of the wind abated and they were left inside the magical glow of the garden. Looking around her, Ellie couldn't help but be awed.

There were heat lamps scattered throughout the hanging garden, on every tier, and their effect was palpable. Ellie actually felt warm inside this tent. There were also multi-colored ornamental lamps hanging from wires that had been strung across the ceiling. As on the night of the ball, votive candles had been interspersed throughout as well. And at the very far end of the garden, on the balcony where Fillip had taken her on her first night at Bellbroke, a large blanket had been laid out with pillows and a table. Ellie could see the sparkling champagne and baskets of chocolate and imported fruit.

"It's the first snow of the year," Fillip said, grabbing her hand. "I've always loved seeing the first snow, but I've never liked how cold it has to be," he said, laughing. "So I've arranged for us to watch it in comfort and warmth. Tonight is supposed to be especially incredible—it's a rare thundersnow."

"Thundersnow?" she said. "Is that why the sky is so strange looking?"

"Yes," he answered. "You've never seen thundersnow before? I know it's more prevalent on the lake...you must have been too far away at Maplecroft Manor."

"I guess so," she said, taking a seat on the cushions and pillows. "I've never seen anything like this."

"Beautiful, isn't it?" Fillip asked, looking out on the lake. The horizon was almost completely obscured by the swirls of mist and fog that were forming on the surface of the water. The sky was still eerily aglow and Ellie might have described the scene as more frightening than beautiful, but she supposed that it was beautiful in a dangerous sort of way.

"I had a tutor once," he said. "Crazy old man by the name of Yeats. Whenever there was a storm, he would run frantically to the windows, making sure to bolt and bar them. Sometimes he would even do it on a sunny day. Mother said he was a man who was afraid of his own shadow, and saw conspiracy around every corner. He used to say that everyone was as 'mad as the mist and snow', and one time he even bemoaned that his long dead idols, the ghosts of men in the ancient past, philosophers and writers that he greatly admired were mad as the mist and snow.

"I always thought it was an odd phrase of his, but I liked it," Fillip continued. "*As mad as the mist and snow.* I confess, I didn't know exactly what it meant…at least not until tonight."

He turned to look at her pointedly and his eyes seemed so heavy and blue in that moment, Ellie thought she might drown in them.

"Just look out there and you'll see what Yeats was talking about," he said. "Mad as the mist and snow. I've never felt that way, until now. Just look at it," he urged, gesturing out to the panorama of swirling snow in an orange and purple sky. "Do you see all of that? It's the same inside me…in here," he took her hand and placed it on his chest, above his heart. "When I look at you, my heart beats a thousand times a minute and I feel as mad as the mist and snow."

Almost as if on cue, a bolt of thunder struck and made Ellie jump a bit in fright. The snow kept falling furiously, as if determined to prove the ardor of Fillip's feelings. He took her hand in his.

"I love you, Ellie Kate," he said, very seriously. "I knew I liked you at the ball, but I wasn't sure how things would work out between us. I hoped for this, obviously, but my father was pressuring me to choose someone. I had no idea that it would have ever turned out this good."

He had a way of speaking that made Ellie believe him, that was believable in and of itself. There was no guile or falseness in his words. As she looked in his eyes and listened to the words coming out of his mouth, she knew that she could count upon them. She knew that in the world of uncertainty that was Bellbroke Castle, at least she knew that Fillip wasn't deceiving her. Everything about Fillip rang true.

"I...I don't know what to say," she confessed.

"You don't have to say anything," Fillip assured her. "I don't want you to say something if you don't mean it. I just wanted you to know how I feel. I love you, and I cannot wait until we are married and I can express that love to you in every way."

Ellie smiled, still a bit nervous at that bit of the wedding. She had heard bawdy stories from Jehanne about the bedding down ceremony, and she still wasn't entirely sure of everything that would happen or that was expected of her. But she trusted Fillip, and he cared for her, and that was all that mattered.

As she moved over to sit closer next to him on the cushions, Ellie tried to assess her own feelings, but they were strangely harder to gauge than Fillip's. His feelings were almost tangible. It was in the way he touched her skin, the way his fingers laced through hers, the way he held her close, his hand

288

settling on her waist. Ellie certainly felt physically attracted to Fillip, and there was a closeness, a bond that had been forged with every touch, every kiss, and every conversation. But the troubling part was that Ellie wasn't entirely sure that what she felt was love. How would she know what that felt like, or looked like?

She didn't know that she had ever seen two people in love. Certainly, not her father and Frances, and she had never witnessed the love between her mother and father. Mr. and Mrs. Tuttle loved each other, there was no doubt, but the ardor of their youth had worn off considerably, and Ellie wasn't ever sure that they had loved each other with a burning passion—not the kind one read about in novels, at any rate. When Mrs. Tuttle had spoken of her past with Mr. Tuttle, Ellie couldn't help but imagine the mild pairing of a dog and goose in the idylls of summer. They were companions more than they were lovers. Ellie knew enough to perceive the difference.

Despite all of this, Ellie knew that she had to reciprocate Fillip's feelings at least verbally. She would have been foolish not to, from a practical perspective, and besides that, it was the sensitive thing to do. So she affirmed that she loved him too, and when she spoke the words aloud, they didn't feel like a lie. Not with his arms wrapped around her, the sky a milky painting above them, the lake a swirling madness of mist and snow before them.

Chapter Nineteen

Midnight Sortie

THE thundersnow had laid down an impressive amount of snow. There were drifts as high as six feet in parts of Hartmere. The snowfall at Bellbroke wasn't too extreme—the ground was thoroughly covered, but they didn't have to trudge through several feet. Ellie thought that the wind had probably blown it more onto Hartmere and spared the lake. Temperatures were still well below freezing, and the snow didn't melt for several weeks.

By the middle of January, the lake was completely frozen over, and winter had officially settled in. But instead of feeling despaired by this, Ellie began to feel more and more positively. Not only had Fillip declared his feelings of love for her, but things had begun to look up at the castle as well. Shortly after their thundersnow outing, the court celebrated its midwinter feast, complete with twelve days of revelry and merrymaking. There was dancing every night, grand parties, and the richest, finest food. Even Queen Adelaide seemed cheered by the festivities.

"This is my favorite time of year," she had confessed to Ellie. "Everything seems so magical, as if the whole world could change, as if time could be wound back and start all over again."

Indeed, it did feel that way, even to Ellie. And as they rang in the New Year with actual bells, Ellie felt as though she could turn over a new leaf in Bellbroke Castle. Perhaps she could have a fresh start without all the worry and the fear of conspiracy. She had heard Fillip's story about his tutor, Yeats, who saw enemies in every shadow and told herself that that wasn't how she wanted to live.

Ellie eased up a bit on her protective measures. She tucked the dagger back in her dresser drawer instead of keeping it under her pillow and she didn't lock the door at night. Both the king and queen kept referring to Ellie's wedding day, making specific remarks and plans, and that was comforting. The queen wouldn't have her choose fabrics and colors if there weren't definite plans. Moreover, Ellie saw the cook baking a practice cake for the big day, trying to get a design finalized with the right kind of frosting.

Everything seemed to be moving along nicely. But Ellie should have known that good things never lasted very long. At breakfast one morning, Ellie knew from the minute she walked in that the king was in a very bad mood. He sat sulkily through the meal, staring off into the distance, flexing and un-flexing his fist while Jehanne prattled on about something. Ellie wasn't listening. She was trying to eat her eggs and toast while paying close attention to the king.

At some point the king had had enough of his sister's chattering. He banged his fist on the table and glared at her.

"Damn it!" he roared. "Can we never have peace and quiet around here?"

Storming off, he left everyone to sit silently in the wake of his explosion, waiting for the explanation to fall or for someone else to take up the mantle of conversation. Jehanne supplied the answer they were all looking for.

"The council denied his request for war again," she murmured, her eyes twinkling. "He presented evidence that Grunwald was planning an attack, and the council promised to review his evidence. But they came back two days ago and said it wasn't enough to warrant a full-scale war. Instead, they said they would send their operatives to thwart any plots overseas."

Queen Adelaide shook her head. "I'm afraid my husband's lust for war will never be sated until Grunwaldian blood is spilt on his sword."

"I'm afraid you're right," Jehanne agreed. "But I think we should go to war. Richard is a strong king and a good general. He was meant for the battlefield, not to sit in a chamber all day listening to people's petty complaints."

"Yes, but kingship isn't just about war and glory," Queen Adelaide countered. "A king should only go to war when necessary. I agree with the council. I don't think he has sufficient grounds to declare war on Grunwald, or any other nation for that matter."

"Luckily what you think doesn't matter," Jehanne said, rather rudely. "And maybe that's all the lazy kings of Kronstadt did—deliberate with useless councils of men and listen to dirty peasants read off their list of endless complaints. But that's not what the kings of Trenway do, and especially not the Westenra kings."

Queen Adelaide rolled her eyes and took a sip of her juice, deciding to let it go. Ellie noticed that Fillip's opinion on
292

the matter was conspicuously absent. He hadn't said a word, but continued to eat ravenously as though he had skipped three meals and was trying to make up for it.

"What do you think, Ellie?" Jehanne asked, turning those hawk-like eyes onto her. "Do you think the king should go to war with Grunwald?"

As Jehanne popped a nut in her mouth, Ellie couldn't help but feel overly scrutinized. She had to weigh her words carefully. She knew her true position—war was never a prudent choice, not fiscally or morally. But Jehanne was her brother's best spy, and Ellie knew that anything she said would be reported back to the king. At the very least, she had to treat it that way.

"I wouldn't presume to know more than the king on matters such as war," she answered evenly. "If he thinks we should go to war with Grunwald, then I believe that is the wisest course of action."

Jehanne continued to stare at her as if she was a field mouse, and then her eyes narrowed further into the tiniest of slits as she popped another cashew into her mouth.

"Good girl," she said condescendingly. "For a moment, I thought you were going to spout some moral platitude you picked up from that sainted father of yours."

Jehanne snorted as she stood up and left the room. Ellie suffered a sudden wave of nausea and dizziness, as if the world around her was blurry and out of focus. She couldn't believe what Jehanne had said. It took her aback, the rudeness of it, and the acerbity of her response. It was as if Jehanne hated her, and Ellie hadn't ever had that perception of their relationship before. The queen seemed to sense her surprise.

"Don't worry, dear," she said. "Jehanne is infrequently cruel like that. It's a phase and it shall pass."

Fillip finally seemed to wake up from his food-induced stupor to chime in on the matter, but he merely smiled at Ellie pleasantly. His face was wan, and his smile seemed pinched.

"She shouldn't talk to you like that," he said. "I'll speak with her in private. It's unacceptable."

After that, no one left at the table had felt like eating another bite, and they all went their separate ways. Fillip had a busy schedule of meetings and appointments ahead of him, all taking place at Penchester Palace. The queen, similarly, had public appearances and engagements to attend. That left Ellie alone for the afternoon. Had she known that it was to be her last full day at Bellbroke Castle, she might have made more of it. As it was, she simply settled down in the library to read until luncheon, and then spent the afternoon working in the apothecary with Hazel.

Dinner was a quiet, muted affair. Still angry with Jehanne, Ellie had been determined not to make eye contact or speak to her at all unless asked a direct question. But Jehanne ignored her too, and Fillip behaved the same way at dinner as he had at breakfast. It was all very bizarre, almost surreal in a way. Ellie had intended to ask the king about his decision regarding her stepsisters, but given his strange, detached behavior, she didn't feel comfortable doing so.

By the time she went up to her room for the night, Ellie suffered the same lurching feeling in her stomach that had gone away in the three weeks since the thundersnow. Within a matter of hours, she was back to seeing enemies in the shadows, back to feeling worried and unsafe. Just before she climbed in bed, she turned the lock on her door, and pushed a table up against it, to be safe.

She was shaking as she pulled the covers up over her shoulders. The crippling fear had returned with full intensity, and she knew that there would be many sleepless nights ahead, if she was granted any. She couldn't stop hearing Tiresias' voice in her head: *All I can see is that you'll leave, and it will be cold when you do, so wear furs when you go.*

Ellie tried to resist the weak pull of tears that tugged at her eyelids. She had become accustomed to her cozy life at the castle, not only that, but she had grown fond of it. The thought of having to leave, especially under threat of danger, was not only terrifying but sad as well. Ellie tried to calm her breathing, tried to rationalize so that she could get some peace of mind. She told herself that the king was just in a bad mood about the war, and that had nothing to do with her, and that Jehanne was infrequently cruel, as the queen had said.

Nothing to worry about. She was safe and sound. Safe and sound. Repeating it under her breath like a mantra, Ellie eventually fell into an un-restful sleep.

ELLIE had never been a light sleeper, but quiet, repetitive noises had always tended to wake her up. Birds chirping obnoxiously, the sound of water dripping, the ticking of the clock...noises like that disrupted Ellie's sleep and would wake her every time without fail. On this particular night, it was the sound of scraping and the jiggling of metal, like someone trying to break through a lock.

And when Ellie finally opened her eyes and focused in on her door handle, she realized that that was exactly the noise she was hearing. She had less than a second to panic as every single muscle in her body froze. As her mind raced frantically, she seemed incapable of motion. Paralyzed with fear, she watched as the door handle moved back and forth, the person on the other side insistent upon breaking in.

There could have been a legitimate reason for someone to sneak into her room in the middle of the night, but the odds of that were extremely slim—ninety to ten at the most optimistic rate. Ellie knew that those weren't odds to live by, so she willed herself out of paralysis and slid quietly out of her bed. She knew it was probably the most obvious place to hide, but she dropped to the floor and went directly underneath. She didn't know how long her intruder had been fiddling with the door, but she could tell that he was close to opening it.

Ellie cursed under her breath. She should have been more prepared for this. But for what? She still wasn't sure what was happening; only that it couldn't be good. *Think, think, think!* She urged herself to think of something. Anything. What could she do? Where was the most accessible weapon? *Why* had she stopped sleeping with the dagger under her pillow?

She heard the unmistakable click of the lock sliding into place and knew that her intruder had succeeded. Her heart was pounding so loudly she thought that it would give her away. Squinting out from under the bed, she saw a pair of boots enter the room with an ominous thud. He stopped near the bed, and Ellie prayed fervently that he wouldn't squat down and immediately find her.

After a moment's hesitation, the boots thudded away, around the bed and towards the fireplace and her bureau. Ellie urged herself to think once more. She had caught a lucky break and now she had to use it to her advantage. *Yes!* Foolishly, she had left her bed warming pan under the covers. Since he was on the other side of the bed, Ellie was relatively confident that she could reach up and grab it without alerting him to her presence.

Crawling ever so carefully, Ellie reached her arm out and brought it up to the far end of the bed, groping blindly for the handle. When she found it, her fingers grasped the wood firmly and eased it out. Ellie placed it gently on the floor and crawled out from under the bed, her heart still pounding furiously. The suspense was the worst of it. She knew that once she sprang into action, it would be easier, but sneaking around in imminent danger was the worst.

Just as she had crawled out from under the bed, she heard the sound of glass shattering. One by one, all four outer windows in her room exploded one after the other. Ellie thought at first that maybe the man with the boots had done it, but when she peeked up over the bed, she saw the last two windows spontaneously shatter. The man with the boots was watching too, standing next to her bureau with his back turned to her. Ellie saw that he had a dagger in his hand. It was all the proof she needed. He was there to harm her.

Ellie knew she couldn't waste the opportunity. The shattering of the glass had given her the element of surprise. Grabbing the bed warming pan, Ellie strode across the room as quickly as she could, building up momentum, and at the last second, she pulled the bed warming pan back past her shoulder and swung it down as hard as she could. As it whizzed by her ears, she heard the *whoosh* of the great force and watched as it struck the intended target—the back of the man's head.

Being a large man, he was not instantly brought down, but he staggered forward with a great roar, and when he turned around, Ellie had dropped the bed warming pan and stepped backward ready to pick up her next weapon. By the fireplace now, she quickly grabbed the sharpest tong and ran forward with it, taking advantage of her opponent's momentary stumbling. Ellie gritted her teeth and drove it straight into his belly, hearing the sickening squelch of impalement. Her father had trained her for such skirmishes, but she had never had to kill a man before. Not entirely prepared for the intensity of it, Ellie forced her mind to think of him as something else—a bear, perhaps.

The bear stood in shock as he looked down at the fire tong sticking out of his stomach. His hands hovered shakily around it as blood began to drip from his mouth. Ellie backed away, trying not to look at his shiny eyes that were peering
298

through his great shaggy mane of hair. With another roar, he lunged forward at her, groping and grabbing with his hands, but Ellie moved much faster. The name of the game now would be speed and agility. If she could avoid him for long enough and continue to injure him, she could eventually bring him down. Her father had taken her to enough horrific bear-baiting rings to know. The principle that the dogs operated on was the same, and they usually won.

Of course, Ellie was evenly matched one-to-one with her attacker, unlike the dogs who worked in teams. Regardless, Ellie plucked another fire tong as she continued to dodge his fumbling swipes. The man had pulled out his dagger now and was trying to slash her, but Ellie was still faster—running around the room, jumping up and darting across the bed. She had done several laps, slashing at him wildly with her fire tong, but not making much contact. She was still afraid of getting too close.

After running a third lap around the room, Ellie thought of a plan. But she would have to act fast and the angle would have to be just right. Leaping on top of the bed, Ellie caught him at a sideways slant and plunged the fire tong into his shoulder, at the critical point just between the neck and the top of the arm bone. It was a hard strike to make, pushing through all that bone and tissue, but Ellie had the right vantage point from up above to help with it.

At this, the man let out an almost inhuman-sounding scream that so unnerved Ellie it made her skin turn to goose flesh. He collapsed to his knees, and she heard his dagger drop to the floor with a resounding thud. He was bleeding profusely and as

299

Ellie jumped off the bed and came around to face him, she saw that his eyes were beginning to go glassy. Once again, he reached a shaky arm to his shoulder as if to try and pull the fire tong out.

"Who are you?" Ellie demanded. "Who sent you?"

The man didn't answer, but managed a rueful smile even in his death throes.

"B-bested by a girl," he gurgled. "D-damn Fiordiligi..."

Ellie repeated her question, but the man wouldn't answer, he just kept staring at her with that deranged glassy-eyed look, a mocking smile plastered on his face. Picking up the dagger beside him, Ellie decided to end his misery. She drew it across his throat, stepping back to avoid the spray of blood. Choking, the man reached instinctively to his neck, but she knew he would never stop the bleeding. He would die in three minutes or less. As he fell to his back on the floor, Ellie wiped the blade of the dagger on a nearby rug and then closed the door to her bedroom, locking it again.

She pulled a heavy table in front of the door to deter any other assassins that might try to come through. She knew that when this one didn't return for a while whoever had sent him would come looking. Striding over to her bureau, Ellie flung the doors open and started dressing for the cold.

Her hands were shaking as she thought of Tiresias' words. She never truly thought she would actually be in this moment—fighting for her life, preparing to flee the castle. It had been one of those shadow ideas, floating around in the back of her mind, but since she'd had no tangible evidence, and no significant clues of it coming, she had honestly just thought of her

300

precautions as the product of a paranoid mindset. Like a game, she had been playing detective, assessing the royal family, investigating the castle, and deciphering the invisible ink.

But as Ellie pulled on her thick woolen stockings, she realized that this wasn't a game any longer. It was as real as real could be. The dead man lying not five feet from her attested to that. Tying a sheath around her thigh, she slid the dagger there for easy access, and put on as many layers of clothes as she could, finally easing into her biggest pair of fur-lined boots. The one nice thing about the castle was that she was well equipped for an escape such as this.

Ellie also grabbed a small rucksack bag and packed up all the books she'd pilfered from the library. She didn't know when they might be handy. She also rifled through the drawers of her tables for any small bags of coins that she could find. Fillip had given her an allowance each month and she'd hardly ever spent it, so she knew she would have a good amount to live on once she was out there...Ellie suffered another momentary spell of fear and insecurity. Out there in the wilderness. What would she do? Who would help her? How far would she get before someone caught up to her?

Ellie pushed these thoughts back as well. There was no use in even thinking them. She had to live in the moment. She had to do as her father had taught her—think only one, maybe two steps ahead, but don't think big picture. *To survive, you've got to stay firmly rooted in the here and now,* he would say, *don't think more than fifteen minutes ahead.*

Turning her attention back to the assassin, who was now definitely dead, Ellie thought it might be wise to hide him. She would want everything to look as normal as possible—as if the plan had worked and he had just gone rogue or something. She dragged him under the bed, heaving and struggling to move his girth. Using her legs, she kicked him the rest of the way under the bed and then pulled one of the rugs in the far corner to the middle to cover the large bloodstains.

Standing in the room, Ellie lifted her hands shakily and stared at them as if they were no longer part of her body. They felt dirty and cursed, in some way, having not only killed the man, but defiled by contact with his dead body as well.

Push it back, she counseled herself, *you don't have time for this.* Ellie knew that if she ever did have the luxury of time again, this would all come back to hit her with the blunt force of the bed warming pan she'd whacked him with. How to process such a thing? How to cope with the sudden and dramatic change of events? *We all live on the wheel of fortune,* Mrs. Tuttle had often told her, *and it turns us topsy-turvy 'til we can't see straight. One day we're on top, the next we've spun and sunk to the bottom.*

Ellie was too familiar with the wheel of fortune for her liking. She had been pinned to it all her life, riding it up and down, and she was upset that it had swung so low after having lifted her so high. *Push it back,* she told herself, more insistently.

The cold wind blew against her back from the broken windows. *Fiordiligi.* Ellie pulled out the book of architecture, remembering that there was a small entry point in her room to a secret passageway. Sparing a moment to think about the

302

windows, she was shocked that they had shattered like that after having been so recently replaced. It wasn't Fiordiligi's glass anymore. And that was when Ellie began to wonder if the glazier's curse had been real, all those years ago.

She remembered when she first arrived at Bellbroke Castle and Fillip had told her of the phenomenon—*but haven't they replaced all the faulty glass by now,* she had asked. Only in this moment did she consider that it wasn't the glass that was faulty, but the castle. The frames the glass was set in. Fiordiligi had cursed the king and the castle, and his glass was only a small part of it. She also couldn't help but be thankful for it, considering that the shattering of the glass had given her the perfect opportunity to save her own life.

Thumbing to the right page in the book, Ellie pinpointed the location of the secret passageway and headed to the back corner of her room, sparing no backward glance for the dead assassin under her bed or the lavish life she was suddenly and forcibly leaving behind.

Chapter Twenty

Seven-Mile Trudge

THE one flaw in Ellie's escape plan was light. She hadn't accounted for how dark the secret passageways would be and she hadn't thought to bring a candle. Torches lit the main corridors of the castle; hanging ominously on the wall, casting eerie shadows and blackening the stone ceiling with soot. But the secret passageways were as black as night—blacker, even, for there was no light from the moon or the stars. The air was cold and damp in the passageway as well, and Ellie could hear the sound of her own ragged breathing as she kept one hand on the damp stone wall, the other out in front of her to sense any obstructions.

Of course, she had a map to the secret passageways in her rucksack, but without any light, the pages didn't do her any good. She would have to wait until the passageway led to a source of light…if it ever did. Racking her brain, she tried to recall the images on the pages of the book. What had the passageways looked like? Could she remember the snaking, serpentine paths? She remembered that all the secret passageways were linked, meaning that you could travel throughout the whole of the castle.

The passageways looped around the whole of the castle like many circles layered on top of each other, and thus, through roundabout means, you could go from the southern half to the northern half and back. Ellie had learned that there was an outer layer of wall, and an inner layer—the secret passageways were sandwiched in between. The passageways had been designed to add a level of insulation and protection from the outside elements. There had been a practical, architectural purpose in their construction.

This explained why it was much colder in the passageway—Ellie could hear the howling of the winter winds outside—she was only one wall away from the outside, whereas before she had had the inner wall, the air of the passageway, and an outer wall as a buffer. As she was walking, she knew that she would have to use this time to think of a plan. Doubtless her enemy would know of the secret passageways and it would be the first place they would come to look when they realized their assassin had failed.

One thing was certain: Ellie could not stay at Bellbroke Castle. The risk was too great. Part of her had known it as soon as the assassin had come through her door. As much as she wanted to, she couldn't turn to Fillip for protection. She couldn't trust anyone in the royal family. Now that she knew she was in danger, she needed to get as far away as she could. The realization was heartbreaking and at the same time terrifying. What would she do? Where would she go? How long could she make it on her own?

Her father, being the self-proclaimed survivalist that he was, had certainly imparted much of his wisdom and knowledge regarding survival. But Cornelius Marchand wasn't here to help her, and she very much doubted that his advice would apply where the Crown was concerned. They had infinite resources at their disposal to hunt her down and kill her. With money and power, they could easily burst through any obstacles or barriers she might try to throw in their path. The only thing she could rely upon was her own wit and a measure of luck. She had to be constantly vigilant. She couldn't allow herself a moment to slow down or look back, or really to think at all. She had to react to her environment as if she were a fox. Animals didn't sniff around, linger, and try to figure things out. They ran. They ran as fast as they could without a backward glance. They hid, they defended themselves, and they fought. And in some cases, Ellie knew that even the underdogs could win.

HER eyes became aware of a perceptible difference long before her mind processed it. As she came closer and closer, she suddenly began to see flickering shadows on the stone walls, the dreary gray that sometimes dripped green with moss from the spray of the lake. Light was coming from somewhere and it was only a matter of seconds before Ellie found out from where.

She heard the sound of muted voices and then saw a flashing glint before she ducked down quickly, hoping that no one had seen her. She had come upon a glass window that looked in on one of the inner rooms. It was an example of just how absurd some things were in the castle, these windows that had been placed where no light could come in, a window that looked out upon what was supposed to be a secret passageway. But then she remembered Tiresias' story—it was exactly why King

Frederick had put the windows in odd places—to see the nooks and crannies where his young wife might have been with someone else.

Ellie's ears perked up at the sounds of the voices in the room, trying to ascertain if anyone had seen her. But the droning sounds of dull conversation continued, and Ellie breathed a sigh of relief. Pulling out her rucksack, she rummaged through it to find the book on the castle's architecture. Lifting it slightly, she began to look at the pages carefully, flipping to the section on the secret passageways, studying them intently.

She had finally found the passageway that emptied into her room and was following her finger along the winding trail when the voices in the room picked up in tenor. The door of the inner room slammed open on its hinges and a new voice joined the others—an angry, insistent voice that Ellie knew all too well. It was the king.

Straining her ears, Ellie tried to hear what he was saying, but for once his voice was muffled, his words indistinct. It was like he was growling. But Ellie could tell that he was angry, especially when she heard him abruptly bang his fist on the table. She was desperately curious as to the root of his anger—was he mad because she had escaped, or because someone had tried to harm her? Or was he angry about something else entirely? The possibilities were endless. Until she heard him bellow one line:

"Now the war is compromised!"

He banged his fist one more time for effect, but at the same time the glass from the inner wall shattered unexpectedly, raining shards down upon Ellie's head. Once again, she was thankful for the fact that she did not scare easily and that she hadn't screamed and given herself away.

"Damn Fiordiligi!" she heard the king roar. "Something is wrong…"

Ellie heard footsteps approaching the shattered window, and that was her cue to move as quickly as she could. She darted forward in a violent burst of motion that sent her nearly falling to her knees. But she ran as quickly as she could, rounding the corner of the passageway. Despite the darkness and the uncertainty of the path, Ellie did not stop running until she approached another source of light in a place she never expected to find.

HARTMERE, being the capitol city of the country, boasted several dungeons and fortresses for the purpose of keeping prisoners. There was a distinction between prisoners, not only to do with social class, but also based upon the type and severity of crime. Spindletop was the royal prison of choice for traitors and nobles who had committed acts of fraud, deception, or even murder. Ellie had assumed that all criminals in Hartmere were accounted for in Spindletop or the other prisons of Hartmere. She never imagined that there was a dungeon in Bellbroke Castle, for instance, and that it housed criminals of a much different nature.

But this she discovered upon coming to the end of the secret passageway. It emptied into a circular chamber that resembled a pit. The room was dirty and filthy and the stench was awful. Ellie immediately covered her nose and stepped forward tentatively, not sure what she had stumbled into. It soon became very clear.

Directly ahead was a row of cells with thick iron bars and straw sticking out at the bottom. In between her and this row of cells were multiple rows of actual pits that had been dug into the foundation of the castle, much as it was. Ellie could see down into these pits, for they were very shallow. But the disturbing part about some of them was that they extended into the lake.

Prisoners had been put in iron cages or chained and lowered into the pits. Now that the lake was frozen, when Ellie peered into the depths of these *oubliettes*, she saw the frozen surface of the water, and in some cases, she saw the tips of frosted fingers sticking out. In one particularly gruesome pit, she saw half of a body sticking out, slumped over, the poor creature having obviously died from exposure, stuck to his waist in freezing, now frozen water.

Horrified by the brutality of what she saw, Ellie was surprised to see anyone *alive* in this chamber of torture and death. When she heard a man's voice, she practically jumped out of her skin, but still did not shout out in fear. With trepidation, she approached one of the dark cells in the corner, finally making out a shaggy mane of hair and the figure of an emaciated man.

"Spare a crumb?" he asked, coughing pathetically. Ellie realized he was asking for food and she answered that she did not have any.

When he heard her voice, the man's head bobbed up and as his eyes caught the light, suddenly a leering smile lit up his face as he wheezed with laughter.

"P-princess Eleanor," he said, mock-bowing. "How nice to finally meet you, at last."

"What are you talking about?" she demanded. "Who are you?"

"Why, haven't you figured that out yet?" he asked. "I'm the man who's here to kill you. I'm your murderer."

Ellie took a step backward. "What?" she said again. "Explain yourself."

His eyes slanted downward at her, a frown tugging at his lips.

"No, this can't be," he murmured. "The girl whose head a pound of gold knows surely she has far to go..."

"Stop speaking in riddles!" she commanded, pulling out her dagger. "Tell me how you think to kill me, trapped in this cell."

He laughed again, wheezing so heavily that he nearly collapsed in a fit of coughing.

"I don't mean to kill you, girl," he spat. "That's the whole point. But I'm the one they'll blame. I'm the one meant to take the fall."

"Why?" she demanded. "Who's they? Who orchestrated this?"

"Who do you think?" he sneered. "Here...I'll give you a hint. I am from Grunwald. I was kidnapped and forcibly taken here. We've known what they've been up to for years. When your name was mentioned, it wasn't hard to put together."

"You're from Grunwald," she repeated. "And they brought you here to kill me. Well...to take the blame for killing me."

"Yes," he said, waving his hands dramatically. "Do you understand yet, slow girl? Forgive my insolence, a dead man cares not to whom he speaks nor how."

Ellie grimaced, realizing the plan, chastising herself for being so dull and oblivious to it. All the pieces had been there— *why* hadn't she put them together?

"My death will spur the country to war with Grunwald," she declared. "The king will get what he wants in the end...it's as he's said, the people love me."

"Yes, they love you and they'll be riled by your death. There will be shouting and rioting in the streets. There will be calls for blood and with the whole country itching for war, the council will have no choice but to proceed."

Ellie closed her eyes thinking of the people rioting in the streets, imagining the people who had rioted at her stepmother's execution. The king had certainly painted that picture for her, hadn't he? She could see them in her mind's eye—shouting, cursing, and calling out for her death as soon as Frances had spoken a word against her. She was the people's beloved princess, even though she technically wasn't a princess yet. But still—she was the key to King Richard's war. She was the checkmate to his councilors in a long game they had played, one in which Richard would finally get his way. His road to glory would be paved with her bones.

Her eyes flashed open with hatred as one thought crossed her mind—*the hell it would.* She wasn't going to let that happen for as long as she could help it. If King Richard was determined to get rid of her, then he would have to bring his all, because she was going to give hers. She hadn't made it easy already, but now she was determined to make it a hell of a lot harder. If he wanted a war, then he would get one—just not where he expected it.

Ellie gritted her teeth and glared at the Grunwaldian prisoner who was smiling at her in satisfaction. She didn't know what he could possibly be happy or gloating about. No matter which way one looked at it, he was a dead man. Perhaps he was getting his final amusement where he could, but it was irritating to her.

"So, you see now," he said. "You see now why you have to die. It's only a matter of time."

"I don't see it that way at all," she replied evenly.

The man snorted. "You may have fought off one assassin, but don't fool yourself—he'll send more."

"Oh, to be sure," she answered, flipping through her book again, quickly trying to locate the end of the secret passageway. She needed to figure out where she was in relation to the inside of the castle.

"He'll send dozens, he'll send scores!" the man exclaimed. "There's no way you can avoid this. Death is coming for you as surely as it is coming for me!"

Having figured out her location, Ellie shoved her book back in her rucksack and addressed the Grunwaldian.

"Death will have a long road to travel if it wants me," she said. "I'm not going down without a fight."

Turning her back on the Grunwaldian, Ellie ran past all the shallow pits and back into the dark of the secret passageway. There had been a turn that she had missed, a turn that would bring her out into the main part of the castle, to a room filled with musical instruments.

As she made her way back through the secret passageway, Ellie realized with a jolt of fright just how close she had come to murdering the Grunwaldian in the dungeon. The thought had fleetingly crossed her mind before she had quickly worked out the ramifications, not to mention the guilt that would plague her. On the one hand, she was afraid that the Grunwaldian would tell the king and his officials that she had been down in the dungeon, and she didn't want them to have more of an advantage than they already did. But on the other hand, throwing a dagger in his throat wouldn't have solved that problem. By seeing him in that state, they would have deduced her presence there immediately.

No, there was no way to keep them from knowing that she had made her way down to the dungeons. Perhaps the Grunwaldian wouldn't squeal—it was hard to know, and moreover, it didn't really matter. What did matter was that Ellie escape the castle as quickly as possible and put as many miles between her and Bellbroke Castle as she could.

In that regard, she knew exactly how she wanted to exit. She remembered when she had first explored the castle, she had found a music room with an odd hallway in the back, shrouded in darkness, concealing a staircase that led to a door which opened to nowhere—just the open air and a twenty-foot fall to the lake below.

Ellie knew there was inherent risk involved in this scheme, but in her mind, there was no better way to leave. All the doors would be guarded and all other exits flanked with heavy surveillance. Trying to rappel down from a tower window would be far too risky—there was a greater chance of being seen and an equally greater chance of slipping and falling to her death. No, the strange door that had no porch, no deck, nothing of any kind around it for guards to stand on—that was her best bet. Her biggest fear was the jump and the landing.

She would have to be prepared to roll out of the fall, and she would also have to hope that the ice was thick enough not to crack upon impact. She shuddered to think at what would happen if it broke and she was sucked through to the frigid water beneath. Unbidden, the images from the dungeon flooded her mind, all those prisoners trapped in the *oubliettes*, condemned to a slow and terrifying death.

Ellie would have laughed were she not afraid of throwing up if she opened her mouth. That her best bet could lead to her worst nightmare was an irony not lost on her. But she knew that there was no other choice and there could be no looking back. As
314

she walked, she thought ruefully of Fillip. She hated to think that he could have been involved in any of this. *No,* she said, shaking her head, *Fillip couldn't have known.* She prided herself on being a good judge of character. Fillip had that air of authenticity about him—he was genuine when he said he loved her. He would never have deliberately put her in danger or been involved in a conspiracy such as this. It was his father who wanted to go to war, not him.

At the same time, Ellie knew that she couldn't trust Fillip to help her in this situation. As much as she wanted to run to him, to unburden herself in his arms, she knew that such a weak option would be suicide. Fillip was only a prince. He didn't command the power that his father did—his protection could only extend so far. No, Ellie knew that the longer she stayed in this castle, the sooner she would die. All the same, she mourned the loss of her relationship with Fillip. She felt her heart shatter and break like the cursed glass of Fiordiligi. She would probably never see Fillip again, would never feel his arms wrapped around hers, would never hear his voice, his sweet breath tickling her ear as he whispered words of love.

Tears formed in the corners of her eyes, blurring her view of the music room in front of her. Ellie wiped them away impatiently. *Push it back,* she told herself, more urgently. Almost stumbling into a standing harp, Ellie ran towards the shadowed corner in the back, feeling a bit of relief as she began to climb the steep stairs. When she reached the top, Ellie wrapped her fur scarves and coat tightly around her. She wound one of the scarves over her mouth and nose, leaving a small gap for her eyes, but continuing up around her head. In cold such as this, she couldn't afford to leave much of her skin exposed.

Opening the door, Ellie felt the cold hit her like a knife to the chest. Taking a deep breath, Ellie stepped a bit further out, closing the door behind her and then without another thought, she let herself fall, remembering to tuck up her knees.

With a hard thud, she landed on the ice and rolled out of the fall as best as she could. Standing up, she brushed the snow from her clothes and took another steadying breath. That hadn't been so bad. The ice hadn't broken and she would walk away with only a few bruises.

Being on the frozen surface of the lake was surreal to her, as she took her first tentative steps out into the open. It was a dark, gray, cloudy night as quiet snowflakes swirled around her. *Mad as the mist and snow,* Ellie thought, hugging herself tightly. All she could think as she made her way out onto the lake was that she was venturing out into the madness of the mist and snow.

THE walk was long and cold: an arduous trudge through a thin layer of snow in the freezing cold atop a sheet of ice that Ellie knew could crack any minute. It seemed thick enough beneath her feet, but with ice there was no way to be sure. At a certain point, she felt her extremities begin to go numb until she couldn't feel her toes or fingers. She didn't know how she kept her legs moving, she only knew that there was a determined intensity burning in her core. Perhaps that was what powered her to keep moving.

She also remembered Tiresias' words—*there's a cottage in the woods by Aschenputtel. Go there when you must.* The name had been familiar to her, even when Tiresias had said it, and then she'd remembered. Fillip had mentioned Aschenputtel on her first night at Bellbroke Castle after having been rescued from Maplecroft Manor. He had told her that the lake continued for miles yet, but seven miles south it took a turn at Aschenputtel. Tiresias had told her of a cottage near Aschenputtel, on the edge of the woods. Presumably she would be safe there. At this junction, she didn't have any other option.

This also pushed her forward—the fact that she only had seven miles to go. Seven miles did not seem so far in her head, but as she kept trudging forward, it soon became an impossible distance. The bitter winds raged on, and while Ellie was thankful for the combination of clouds and snow that cloaked her in near invisibility, she also began to worry that she had been wrong in her boast to the Grunwaldian, that Death need only go seven miles on its journey to claim her.

BY the time she reached her destination, Ellie wasn't sure if she was hallucinating or if she had already died, imagining the cottage before her while really lying belly up out on the ice somewhere. Every part of her body felt numb and she was sure that even her eyelashes were frozen. Through her blurred vision, she saw her hand reach out and knock on the door, but she couldn't feel it at all. It was very surreal—far more surreal than it had been first stepping out onto the ice. Ellie felt as if she was out of her body, as if she didn't have a body anymore. She was just a formless mind, floating around in a dizzy vacuum, able to see but unable to perceive anything beyond dim sight.

She could remember the endless walk on the ice. Somewhere on that perilous trek Ellie had begun to lose sight of herself. She had become so cold that certain faculties started to fade in order to put energy towards merely staying alive, towards putting one foot in front of the other. But at some point, she did remember seeing a change in the landscape in front of her. She remembered seeing the trees looming closer and closer until they were upon her. Until she was falling onto a frosty shore, her boots crunching on hard soil, her feet unused to anything but solid ice.

Stumbling and crawling, she had made her way up a hill, her mind almost completely gone. She knew she had forgotten everything—where she was going, why, and everything that had happened in the last several hours. She could only think of one thing: getting warm. Which was why she put every last bit of energy she had into knocking on the door. Swirls of smoke drifted peacefully out of the chimney, and Ellie felt slightly warmed just by the sight of it.

Knocking again, this time more insistently, Ellie felt a wave of dizziness descend upon her and she could feel her knees buckling underneath her weight. She was going to fall. She was going to collapse and fall and die here on the threshold of someone's cottage. Catching herself against the doorframe, Ellie felt the weight give way and realized that someone was looking at her with a bewildered expression.

She tried to open her mouth to say something but the words were trapped. At the sight of the roaring fire behind the man who had opened the door, Ellie felt the wave of heat hit her face and it completely overwhelmed her. She fell forward as her vision faded to black.

Made in the USA
Columbia, SC
19 August 2017